SPARK

The Firebrand Chronicles Book 1

SPARK

The Firebrand Chronicles Book 1

J.M. Hackman

ISBN: 979-8-9921251-1-5

Cover by C.S. Hackman

Second edition printing November 2025

This book is dedicated to the Most High King.

There are no ordinary people.
~C.S. Lewis ("The Weight of Glory")

JASPER TERRITORY

Author's Note

Brenna James is your typical teen. She likes to hang out with friends, enjoys time off from her studies, and dreams of acing her history exam. But she struggles with impulsivity, time management, and poor choices. Why does she do the things she does? When is she going to "grow up?" Welcome to ADHD, Attention Deficit Hyperactivity Disorder.

ADHD is usually recognized as the child running around the classroom, yelling out answers without raising their hand, or incessantly picking on the classmate in front of them. But it's also the quiet, withdrawn kid in the back row, distracted and unable to focus on their classwork. It's called ADHD, Predominantly Inattentive (It's a sibling to the better-known ADHD, Combined—which includes a hefty dose of hyperactivity—and the lesser known ADHD, Unspecified). ADHD, Predominantly Inattentive affects girls more often than boys. In all three types, there's a lot of "noise" or extra information in their head, so that concentration becomes impossible. They have trouble focusing on tasks, tracking or managing time, and making (and keeping) friends.

But this condition is real—it's not an excuse for laziness or bad behavior, or something kids can control or grow out of. (ADHD children grow into ADHD adults who use techniques, coping mechanisms, exercise, and/or medication to help them focus.) These children are also bright, creative, and determined. They're not broken—they just learn and process the world around them differently.

If you'd like to learn more about ADHD, check out www.a ttitudemag.com or https://www.chadd.org.

CHAPTER ONE

TINY FLASHES SPARKED FROM my fingertips. I yanked on my locker, and the door crashed open. Thrusting my shaking hands into the murky interior among the books and papers, I waited. It'd happened again. The magnetic mirror on the inside of the door reflected my pale face, my gray-blue eyes too wide. My heart pounded, making my head throb with a dull *thud-thud*. One by one, the flashes winked out. Releasing a breath, I sagged against the bank of metal lockers. All day long, whenever the flickering lights sparked and flashed, I hid my fisted hands in my hoodie pockets. Dry, fall air created static. That must be it. *Don't freak out.*

Right.

Closing the locker, my hands tingled a warning. Warmth spread over my palms, making them sweat. Maybe I carried a bizarre incurable disease. Didn't strange stuff like this happen before a diagnosis on those cheesy television movies? Nausea swirled through my stomach, flipping my lunch like pizza dough. Closing my eyes, I leaned against the wall. Scents—floor polish and chicken noodle soup from lunch—mingled in the hallway. I hated chicken noodle soup.

At mid-period, only a couple of kids roamed the blue-tiled hallway. Tiny, my best friend, would be here any moment. She'd borrowed my American history notes, and we'd planned to meet here so I could get them back. I checked my watch. The pass from the study hall teacher was only good for a few more minutes. Where was she? I needed every available minute to cram for the test. Tomorrow morning. In first period.

Despite my good intentions, I'd spent last night watching the new reality show on television. Thank you, ADHD.

"Hi, Brenna."

I started.

Tiny appeared at my side, her blue eyes laughing. "Jumpy much?" Her long, platinum-blonde hair hung straight down her back, emphasizing her petite five-foot frame. Even in a baggy hoodie, gauzy skirt, and boots, she didn't weigh more than eighty pounds after a Dunkin' Donuts binge.

Buried in the pockets of her hoodie, her hands were shapeless lumps. She pulled them out, and I stared. Her empty hands.

"Do you have my notes?"

Dumb question. Of course she did. Dependable Tiny—one of the few people who didn't get annoyed when I zoned out or hyperfocused. We'd been inseparable since I moved here.

"Um, funny thing about those notes..."

My heart sank. "Yeah?" Why oh why had I watched that stupid reality show?

"They're kinda, um, lost." She offered me a guilty smile.

"What?" My voice was loud in the empty hallway.

"I'm sure I'll find them."

"Tiny, I need them for the test tomorrow morning!"

"Look, they'll turn up. Or I'll find them. Okay?"

Without those notes, my exam would receive a big, fat, red F scrawled on top. Definitely not okay.

Behind her, next to a glass trophy case, hung the school spirit display. Red and white glittery pom-poms surrounded a sign reading *Go Cloverdale Lions!* I bit back my rising anger and focused on the red block letters until my eyes crossed. *Breathe deeply. Inhale, exhale.* Not helping. *One, two, three...*

Her voice interrupted my efforts. "Maybe if you would've studied more, the notes wouldn't be so important."

My temper exploded. "Thanks a lot! It wouldn't matter if you hadn't lost them!" I pointed a finger. A narrow yellow flame burst from my fingertips, shooting over her shoulder.

The fire didn't fizzle into a shower of sparks like embers from an arc welder. Don't know why I expected that. Instead, the flame arrowed straight into a red pom-pom, melting a hole and shriveling the glittery plastic strands. With a quiet hiss, it devoured all the other pom-poms arranged in the display. In seconds, the blaze engulfed the pep-rally poster.

"Whoa," Tiny said, her eyes going wide.

I couldn't move. Racing along the poster's edges, the greedy flames crackled. The fire alarm began to shriek.

She tugged my arm. "Come on."

We turned to leave, and the sprinkler system in the hallway kicked on. Great. Just great. I hunched my shoulders against the cold spray. Exactly what I needed to make this day perfect.

Outside, the vivid landscape of reds, golds, and browns barely registered. A flame had burst *from my hands.* The faint scent of smoke clung to my fingers. But no pain. What was going on? Shouldn't my skin be red or blistered? Flexing my fingers, miniature yellow flames flared. A cold sweat broke out under my arms. I didn't want to see that again, and I didn't want anyone else to see it either. Hiding the evidence, I pressed my fisted hands together and joined my class lining up on the football field. Mr. Lynn, the study hall teacher, began counting students.

A fire truck siren pierced the air, growing in intensity.

Tiny stood in line, flirting with a cute guy from our Geometry class.

"Hey." I nudged her. "Why aren't you freaking out?"

"Stuff happens."

"Like fire?" My voice cracked. "That doesn't just happen."

A fire truck pulled into the school parking lot, spilling its firefighters into Cloverdale High like an invasion of yellow jackets.

"You'd be surprised." She pulled out her cell phone. "I'm gonna text my mom and tell her I'm okay."

My mind raced while the teachers accounted for all the students and the firefighters determined the school safe to reenter. A wave of homesickness flooded me, and I closed my eyes. Mom had been gone awhile, but today I really needed her. Blinking fast, I shut down the tears pricking my eyes. Maybe she'd know why I was firestarting on my sixteenth birthday. Even if she didn't, I would've felt better after talking with her. I couldn't talk to my dad. He didn't do the up-close-and-personal thing, at least not lately. And I wasn't sure what to make of Grandma Helen—somewhat spacey, nervous, maybe a few cornflakes short of a full bowl.

After an hour on the field, Mr. Lynn herded the class together. "Due to the fire," he said, "when you go back in, enter through the art room hallway. We'll be monitoring the halls. Proceed to your locker, gather your belongings, and head for your bus."

The first yellow school bus pulled up, its motor rumbling. We headed inside.

On the way to my locker, I walked past the cordoned-off hallway where the fire began. The sharp smell of burnt plastic lingered in the corridor. Black charred edges rimmed the sodden pep-rally sign. It now read *Go—ions*! My fault. The melted pom-poms, greasy soot, and smudged trophy case—all because of me.

Tiny, my silent shadow, followed me while I threaded through the halls on autopilot. Maybe she was worried I would spontaneously explode. I ran my fingers along my palms—everything felt normal, even if it wasn't working the way it should. Near my locker, two guys debated the cause of the fire, their voices loud and obnoxious. One of them mentioned a smuggled cigarette. It made a lot more sense than the truth. The air pressed in, smothering like a wool blanket. Every lungful held a harsh, scorched odor. Shouldering my bag, I waved goodbye to Tiny and hurried toward the double glass doors of the building.

Past the entrance, a group of kids shuffled toward one of the waiting buses. Fluffy clouds scudded across the hard-blue sky, obscuring the sun. I trudged across the street to the wooded trail leading to our house.

Dad and I had left Vermont and moved in with Grandma Helen at the beginning of June, so we called this place home, at least for now. The house sat about a quarter of a mile away. Pennsylvania wasn't that different from Vermont—smaller mountains, warmer weather.

While I walked, I replayed the start of the fire, my memories looping like a broken movie reel. Me, furious, pointing at Tiny, the bright flame arrowing from my fingertip—

"Brenna!"

Tiny caught up to me and handed me a notebook. "Your notes. In the bottom of my locker. I'm sorry." She furrowed her brow, her blue eyes serious.

"'S okay. Quit looking at me like that."

"Sorry. Again. Relax, okay? It's not your fault."

"Not my fault? Are you kidding? I started *a fire*. With flames and smoke and—" There were no words for the horror story I was now living.

"Why don't you talk to your dad? You could, um, tell him what happened, and—"

"That's so not happening. How would that go? 'Hey, Dad, guess what I learned today?'"

"I think he might surprise you." She gave me a small smile and handed me a card. "Happy birthday."

Of all the people in my life, she remembered my sixteenth birthday first. Of course.

The simple act sprang a couple of tears from the corners of my eyes, but I wiped them away. "Thanks."

"Brenna!" Ahead on the path, my dad walked toward us, still wearing his typical work uniform of nice jeans and a blazer.

"Hi, Mr. J," Tiny said, sing-songing like a preschooler.

"What're you doing here?" Most days he waited at home for me to show up.

"I texted him when we were outside. You were out of it," she said.

His concerned eyes inspected me for singe marks. "Are you okay? Tiny said no one was hurt."

What else she had told him? "I'm good."

He smiled, a fake one that never reached his eyes. I hadn't seen his real smile for weeks. "How did a fire get started in the hallway?"

"Someone said a smuggled cigarette." I adjusted my backpack.

When we came to a fork in the path, Tiny waved. "This is where I get off. See ya tomorrow, Brenna." She walked toward her house.

"Maybe they'll cancel school for a few days—for renovations," Dad said.

If I could only be so lucky.

"Anyway, it's a moot point. We need to head out of town."

Thunder growled out of the north and bounced off the mountains. Low clouds shifted, the sun breaking through before another bank of clouds hid it from view.

A trip sounded promising. "To where?"

"Consider it a birthday gift."

A bright flash followed by a clap of thunder split the air. The sharp zing of ozone laced the breeze. "We should hurry home. It smells like rain."

Checking the sky, he shook his head. "Grandma Helen's supposed to meet us at Big Rock with a birthday picnic for you."

I winced. Her best work wasn't done in the kitchen.

He noticed my expression. "Be nice."

Despite the weather's threat, we left the well-worn path for a smaller one that curved through the woods. About two hundred yards from Grandma's house, Big Rock stood sentinel. The oversized rocky outcropping rested on a rise that included a view of Tiny's house, Grandma Helen's house, and the old Cloverdale reservoir. The now-abandoned reservoir came complete with a fieldstone wall and a cobblestone spillway.

We climbed the mound, Big Rock jutting out of the soil like a colossal sleeping giant. No sign of Grandma Helen.

"Mom?" Dad rounded the backside of Big Rock.

"Be quiet," she hissed, her voice muffled.

I walked around Big Rock, avoiding gnarled tree roots. Both of them crouched behind a smaller cracked boulder. Steam radiated from the fissure, marring its rough surface.

"Get down, Brenna." She yanked my arm, bringing me to ground level. "And keep away from that rock—it's still hot from my lightning. The enemy's here, and there's no sense in making yourself an easy target." Her usually braided, white hair hung frizzy and loose, and purplish shadows ringed her eyes. The inch-wide strip of dyed crimson hair near her temple fluttered like a red warning flag. "I've eliminated two, but there are more. They're guarding the portal. But remember, you must get through, no matter what." With that announcement, her eyes rolled back in her head, and she fainted with a soft *thud*.

"Gram?" My breath snagged, wedged in my too-tight throat. "Is she okay? What's going on?"

After checking her pulse, Dad glanced toward the reservoir. "She's okay. In a minute, she'll come around."

"Why'd she pass out?"

"She overdid it. Let's wait for her to wake up. We have something to tell you, and I'd like her to be awake for it."

I leaned against Big Rock, keeping a close eye on Grandma Helen's still form and staying away from the scorched rock.

"By the way, happy birthday." He gave me a one-armed hug. "It's hard to believe my little girl's growing up."

"Yuck, Dad." I grinned. "Don't get all sappy on me, okay?"

"Too sappy," Grandma said, rousing with a cough.

"You're back." He gave her an encouraging smile.

She glared, and he helped her sit up.

"We have a birthday present for you." He pulled a box from his inner blazer pocket.

"A gift you should've had several years ago." She struggled to her feet and peered over the edge of the boulder. "No change. We're safe for now."

My dad had dragged me into a forest meeting with Grandma who'd ranted about an enemy, then fainted. Fun stuff. "Couldn't we have gone to a nice restaurant instead of meeting here?"

She pulled her eyes away from the reservoir for a second to stare at Dad. "You still haven't told her?"

He handed me the wooden box, about three inches across, with a strange seal carved on the front. The engraving covered the lid, ivy circling an elaborate eight-pointed star in the center of the design.

Inside, the red velvet lining cradled a glistening chain with a faceted stone set in an elegant silver setting. The gem glowed with a red fire, glimmering with a mystical luminescence.

"It's so pretty. Where'd you get it?"

"This might sound a little weird, Brenna. Your mom was supposed to tell you all this stuff. But now you need to know..."

"What?"

"Spit it out, Harrison. Heaven knows why you two didn't tell her sooner." Grandma still gazed toward the reservoir.

He glared at her. "Sarah wanted to wait until signs of a talent appeared."

She pursed her lips but said nothing more.

Dad turned back to me. "That pendant is a Mivrah Jasper from Linneah. It signifies Elyon, the Most High King, has blessed you."

Grimacing, I traced the glowing stone. Geography and I weren't close friends. "Is that one of those little countries next to Russia?"

"No. Grandma Helen is from Linneah. It's a parallel reality, called an alternity. Another world, like Earth, but not." His shoulders slumped. "I'm doing a lousy job of this."

"You certainly are," she said.

"Ha. Funny." Opening my backpack, I pushed aside my History notes and my Art Club binder. If I moved the jumble of pens and an old Snickers wrapper, the box would just fit in the corner at the bottom. "I've sat in on some of your classes, so I'm not falling for that one." Dad taught quantum physics at the local college.

"Forget my classes. There are parallel alternities, and Linneah is one of them. Your mom planned to take you for a visit at the beginning of the summer, but then she was called away on that business trip. And now time is something we don't have. All Linneans must cross the portal by their sixteenth birthday. Today." He sighed. "I kept waiting, hoping your mom would come home. She really wanted to share the trip to Linneah with you."

"For some reason, someone sent deterrents to make our journey more difficult," Grandma said. "Not impossible, but a wrench we hadn't planned on."

Alternities, portals, Linneans. My mind spun, the words making no sense. I shook my head to clear it. "Why do I have to go at all?"

"You have a special talent you'll grow into during your teens. All Linneans go through this. They can help you learn how to use it," she said.

Buried in my bag, my hand froze. "What kind of talent?" Did pyromania count?

Dad gave a small shrug. "Whatever it is you've been blessed with. Each child's different."

Different. I knew all about that. Having ADHD automatically set you apart from everyone else. I knew the names, too: space cadet, stupid, airhead, ditz, among others.

"Can't you help me instead?" I zipped my backpack.

"Sorry, that's not my department. Mom and Grandma Helen are Linneans but not instructors. You have to go, Brenna."

"Alone?"

"Relax," Grandma said. "I can guide you both through."

Dad's brow furrowed. "The portal's dangerous to foreigners. But with Grandma, you should be okay."

"What about you?"

"I've been there. Once," he muttered with a sheepish smile.

"Okay." But it wasn't. Nothing about this was okay.

"There's another plus about this trip." Grandma Helen brushed off her pants.

"What's that?" I slipped the backpack on my shoulders.

"Your mother's in Linneah."

I glared at Dad. "You said she left on a business trip."

"Yes, in Linneah. We expected her to finish in a few days. Although that didn't happen, every week we received an update from Mom. Those stopped a month ago. I'm sure she's fine," he said. But he didn't sound confident. "When we get to Linneah, we'll ask around."

"We have a problem." Grandma scowled at the reservoir. "Or rather, four problems."

I glanced behind me. Taking a step backward, my stomach went hollow. Aliens. We'd been invaded. Four green creatures waited near the stone wall. Each was a clone of the next—four flexed, skinny legs, two muscular arms the same length, triangular heads, long necks, and big abdomens. They stood tall and rigid in green skirts. When the skirt flapped wide on either side, it morphed into a set of powerful wings. My knees turned to water.

Leaning against Big Rock's bulk, I let it take my weight. "They look like insects." But that couldn't be right. Bugs weren't five feet tall.

She shared a look with Dad. "Largamants, sent through the portal to stop us. Someone knows it's your birthday."

"What are they?"

She cocked her head. "They're kind of like giant praying mantises, only vicious and a lot smarter."

Cold sweat slicked my palms. A bad experience with biting ants had soured me on all bugs, small or giant.

"Here." Dad handed me an old pocketknife. "This is the best I can do for protection. Use it if you have to."

"She's not going to need it, Harrison."

I tucked it in my palm, closing my fingers around the red, plastic handle. Oh, yeah. Huge help against five-foot bugs.

"Here's the plan—we use the available camouflage." She pointed to a stand of trees and tall bushes scattered throughout the forest. "When we get to that last cluster of trees, the maple with the double trunk? We gather there, then run. Jump the stone wall and head for the spillway. I'll protect you."

"Sounds scary," I said. And insane, and suicidal, and...

"It is. Does anyone have a better idea?"

"No. I wish I did." Dad paused for a moment. "Okay."

Okay?

CHAPTER TWO

I HAD NO TIME to offer an excuse for why we shouldn't be doing this. Grandma Helen pointed to her eyes with her first two fingers. "Largamants have two compound eyes with three simple eyes between them. Do not let them see you."

Right. Four creatures. Five eyes each. No problem.

"That's our first stop." She gestured to the closest cluster of trees and gave me a nudge. "Go."

With one last glance for the insects hanging out at the old reservoir, I dashed for cover. The wind kicked up dead leaves, covering exposed tree roots. Grandma Helen and Dad followed, their feet crunching autumn foliage on the forest floor.

For the next ten minutes, we followed the same routine. Grandma directed us to our next destination, I checked for beady insect eyes, and everyone scurried for cover. As we drew closer to the reservoir, the insects came into terrifying focus. Thick, sharp spines decorated their bent legs and arms. Knife-like pincers protruded from their mouths. Their heads turned almost one hundred and eighty degrees as they scanned the area. In other words, terrifying.

Within forty feet of the spillway, Grandma Helen laid a firm hand on my forearm.

All four Largamants remained motionless, their forearms raised, looking in our direction.

Her lips didn't move. "When I say 'now,' both of you sprint for the spillway. Don't wait for me. I'll distract them, then I'll catch up with you."

I nearly groaned. Unless she had an industrial can of insect repellant in her pocket, she wouldn't be much help.

A solitary breeze whistled through the branches, then died out. Birds stopped singing. The silence stretched, becoming gossamer thin until my breath caught in my throat.

In that hush, she said, "Now."

And I ran, Dad behind me, his hand pushing my shoulder, urging me to go faster, keep moving, don't slow down, focus on the spillway, run, run, run. Glancing over my shoulder, I stumbled. Grandma knelt on the ground, her arms extended high above her head, offering herself as a living, breathing snack.

"Grandma?"

"Go!" He gave me another push.

"But look!" A gust of wind slapped my face. Two insects stalked her, coming within mere feet. Spreading her hands, a whirling gray funnel grew, widening and stretching until it spun into a vortex of wind, leaves, and light. My mouth dropped open.

The insects never stood a chance. With a ripping sound, the tornado dashed them into bug confetti.

"Go! The spillway." He shoved me over the stone wall.

Strange buzzing filled the air like the drone of a motor. I glanced up. High above, two more insects gained on us. "Dad, run!"

At the spillway, I slipped and landed on my knees in several inches of freezing water. He tripped next to me, crying out. Thrusting him toward the other end of the spillway, my hand came away red and sticky. A sizzling *snap* split the air. My head jerked toward the sound, my heart skipping a beat. Grandma gripped two shafts, crackling rays of sparkling light. I blinked several times, but the view didn't change. Tracking the insects to the spillway, she tossed both rods like javelins. The insects whirred and dodged, the poles missing them by inches. Scents of a coming summer storm, ozone, and humidity filled the air.

I had to be dreaming.

But the frigid water seeping through my sneakers? Totally real. Looking behind me, shock seized my heart in its tight fist. Dad faded, then disappeared. Grandma dissipated, leaving the spillway empty. I stopped, alone.

My vision fogged like looking through a grimy window. Before I could take another breath, a wave of heat slammed into me, followed by the sting of cold. Squeezing my eyes shut, another surge of heat hit. I was going to be sick. The air turned thick and heavy. When the freezing water of the spillway vanished, the earth fell away.

"Dad?" Sandpaper grittiness coated my throat. Alternating waves of scorching heat and arctic cold battered me, and I puked. The reassuring touch of a warm hand on my forehead relaxed me, but it faded too soon. Another surge of heat seared me. Bile rose again, my stomach heaving.

Time ceased to exist in that no-man's-land of heat, cold, and vertigo. When I finally opened my eyes, I rested on a ten-foot wide cobblestone disk, ringed with a spraying fountain of water. The droplets created a sparkling transparent curtain, about five feet high, catching the sunlight. It was beautiful, but I had no time to appreciate it.

Two downed insects stumbled toward me with an ominous buzzing. I couldn't move, my muscles like jelly. A man rushed toward the fountain, waved his hand to cut off a large section of the spray, and attacked the insects with a sword. With wide, efficient swings, he sliced the heads off both. My already-shaky stomach plunged again.

He wiped his sword on his brown pants then sheathed it, his keen hazel eyes studying me. In his mid-twenties, he wore an embroidered forest-green shirt and pants tucked into brown boots. Despite his casual outfit, he remained in full control and would have no problem dispensing with a terrified teen.

"What is your name?"

I resisted the urge to salute. "B-Brenna."

"Stand up." He grabbed my arm, his grip just this side of painful.

People in the area stopped and peeked into the fountain's center, their expressions guarded. My face heated.

Letting go of my arm, he relaxed. "You are unarmed."

"Yeah." Did my dad's dull pocketknife count? Maybe I'd need it before this was over. I could bruise him to death.

"My name is Erhardt. Are you hurt?"

"No, but my dad and grandmother—" I spotted them behind me. Their bodies lay still and pale, crumpled next to each other. Hurrying over, I crouched down and shook my father's arm. "Dad?" He didn't move. Dread coiled low in my gut.

Erhardt knelt next to me, his blond hair shining in the bright afternoon sunlight. Although most of the people had resumed their business, some still looked my way before averting their gaze, unwilling to meet my eyes. I touched my dad's neck, his warm skin rough with whiskers. The light thrum against my fingers felt fragile and unsteady.

He rolled my dad onto his side away from Grandma Helen, careful not to touch the bleeding wound on his back. "How did your father become injured?"

"One of those things stabbed him." I indicated the beheaded insects lying behind me. Their blood oozed along the cobblestones near their bodies. "My grandmother seemed okay before we came through the portal."

"Although your grandmother is recovering, your father needs medical attention." His words and pronunciation were crisp and clear. And annoying. He talked like a robot, in precise formal speech, without a contraction to be found anywhere.

When he stood, the sun highlighted a stripe of emerald hair near his temple. "Your hair!"

His fine features hardened. "Yes, all Linneans have this. Please wait here while I find assistance."

I nodded absently, my mind still on that crazy hair of his. My mother and my grandmother both had a similar ruby streak in their hair. Maybe this whole alternity thing really was true...you know. If the portal and the Largamants and the lightning bolts hadn't already convinced me.

After the portal experience, the refreshing mist from the fountain cooled my overheated skin. The clear opening in the glittering spray allowed me a small view of the town and the surrounding central court area in this strange new place.

Sprawling, sturdy buildings of gray cobblestone and wood faced the courtyard. A bigger building stood among them, towering over the rest with a spacious set of steps leading to ornate, carved double doors. Erhardt had disappeared through them a few minutes ago to "find assistance." Kelly-green grass, thick as a plush carpet, bordered the buildings. Beyond the low wall surrounding the complex, the sea glimmered, an endless ribbon of blue silver.

A light breeze played with my hair, flinging water drops from the fountain onto my forehead. Wood smoke and the briny scent of the sea perfumed the air. I breathed deep of the surrounding peace.

My dad's breathing shifted to a gasping wheeze. My attention jerked back to him. *Don't think about being alone, an orphan, one parent missing and the other*—no. He'd get better. All he needed was a doctor. They had those here, didn't they? Swallowing hard against the thick lump lurking in my throat, I checked Grandma.

Her chest rose and fell, her breathing easy. A light flush colored her cheeks.

When Erhardt descended the stairs, several people trailed him. Two of them separated from the group and carted away the dead bodies of the insects. The other four stopped in front of me.

"Welcome to Linneah. As I mentioned, I am Erhardt, son and advisor to the king. This is Rosamunde, secondary advisor to the king"—he gestured to the woman on his right, then to the men on his left—"our physician Renke, and his assistant Dirk."

"Welcome," Rosamunde said with a kind smile. Her wavy chestnut hair glistened, a wide golden-blonde stripe near her temple.

All the people wore clothes similar to Erhardt's outfit. Tunics in rich jewel tones of wine, indigo, and plum skimmed brown or black pants. Black embroidery, like tattoos, scrolled across the sleeves and back of the shirts.

The white-haired doctor knelt next to my dad. His brown eyes missed nothing, his wrinkled hands gentle.

"Can you help him?"

The assistant hovered near the old doctor's shoulder. "Do we need to operate? I sharpened the tools yesterday."

"Operate?" Maybe I should take Dad to a hospital at home.

"Calm yourself, Dirk. He needs rest. Only rest. The wound must be cleaned and bandaged." Renke's black hairstreak slipped forward. He peeled back my dad's bloodstained shirt and winced, then glanced at Erhardt. "Help me lift them both."

The three men carried my father and grandmother toward the large building with the double doors. Rosamunde offered me a hand up.

"Can I go with them?" My throat tightened against the question.

She shook her head. "We will give your family the best treatment we have at our disposal in the infirmary. You may stay in the castle as a guest and visit your family members when they improve."

She gave my shoulder an encouraging squeeze, then turned to the fountain and waved a hand. The opening in the watery curtain filled with a gentle *swish*.

"I don't think they should operate," I said, walking toward the enormous stone building.

"Renke would discuss something that important with you. Do not worry. Rest and eat. Then you can tell us how you came to be in Linneah."

She talked in the same formal way Erhardt did, no contractions or slang. Coming from her, though, it wasn't irritating. Instead, with her friendly voice and comforting smile, I could almost pretend I was a privileged guest visiting royalty.

We climbed the steps. At the top, a muscular guard stood, his meaty hands holding open one of the large wooden doors. His dark eyes studied me, and I hurried ahead.

Rosamunde joined me and smiled. "Welcome to Linneah Castle. I will show you your room."

Beyond the double doors, high ceilings soared thirty feet high. Gray cobblestone floors and walls merged with weathered wooden beams and doors. Scrolled black iron sconces filled the wide stone hallways with a golden glow.

The men took my father and grandmother down a different hallway. I had no choice but to follow Rosamunde. She kept up a pleasant running commentary, but the words ran together, meaningless noise in my head. The last few hours blurred into a confusing mix of chaos and plain weirdness.

After leading me to a room on the third floor, she opened the rough-hewn door to a bedroom built in gray stone. Windows paned in thick, wavy glass framed the sleeping area. Long embroidered tapestries depicting coastlines in shades of green, blue, and purple hung on the wall. She pulled the wall-hangings closed to block the sunlight.

"Your private bathroom is over here, hidden in this alcove, should you need it. For now, you may rest. Someone will come for you when the evening meal is ready."

Murmuring my thanks as the door closed, I dropped my backpack in a corner. I kicked off my Converse, stumbling on the fringe of the rug near the bed. The edge of the mattress gave when I sank onto it. My fingers curled into the fuzzy blanket folded and placed at the end of the bed. The dark room, plush mattress, and warm blanket—a perfect invitation. Pulling the blanket around me, I lay down and fell asleep within seconds.

CHAPTER THREE

A surge of cold, followed by a rush of heat, assaulted me. Sweat dripped down my back, then froze, the whipping cold slicing through my bones. I relaxed into the brush of a protective, gentle hand on my forehead. The brilliant creature gleamed a blinding topaz in the center of the portal.

"Brenna, you must not be afraid. Things are about to change for you."

Stretching out her arms, the towering six-foot figure created a huge, lighted sphere. It slipped down and enveloped us in a perfect golden bubble. Cold and heat faded away. Lit by her presence, the portal remained quiet.

"Who are you?"

"I am one of the Sahale, the Lighted Ones, here to help you on your journey."

"I could've used a little more help last time."

"Did you not feel me touch your forehead? Without it, your experience would have been horrific. You survived, which means you are strong, stronger than you think. Do not shy away from what is set before you. Great courage and skill is required to fulfill the First Prophecy of Linneah."

"What?" I bolted up in bed, my long hair in my face. No portal, no glowing being. A wall sconce flickered high on the wall, casting cozy shadows on gray stone.

The traumatic portal incident had messed with my head. Still, the golden glow persisted, filling me with a sense of...happiness.

Pushing my straight, black hair away from my face, I slid out of bed. My stocking feet warmed on the small rug near the bed. Heat radiated from a clear tube running the perimeter of the room, filled with a green luminescent liquid. Two fish raced the length of the tube before vanishing into the wall, their gold scales flashing. I blinked. Fish?

After a tentative knock at the door, a young girl edged into the room. "Hello, I am Dabeer. A meal is being served. Are you hungry?"

My stomach growled, a reminder of my missed supper. "Yes, I am. Thanks."

"Please follow me."

"Excuse me, but what's this?" I pointed to the tube.

"It is the castle's heating system."

I raised an eyebrow. "Are there fish in there?"

"Yes, the glowfish. They heat the liquid from the spring. If you will follow me?"

The girl led me down the sprawling staircase to the first floor before ushering me into a gigantic dining room. Rows of wide tables and groupings of smaller square tables filled the room. Exposed wooden beams studded the high ceiling at regular intervals. Three massive windows offered an expanded view of the ocean, disappearing in the falling darkness. My mouth watered at the mingling aromas of roasted meat and fresh-baked bread. One of the square tables near the windows glinted with beautiful china and silverware. Rosamunde and Erhardt stood nearby, talking with an older man.

Rosamunde sat at the table and motioned for me to join them. Erhardt and the older man took their seats. A faun wearing only pants and an embroidered vest trotted to the windows and pulled the intricate hanging tapestries across the windows to block the encroaching night. Linneans identified by their hairstreaks, thin people whose torso and hips faded into glowing misty contours, and bald, broad-shouldered people brought steaming bowls of food to the table. A dark-skinned girl with sculpted angular features and double-lidded eyes lit two tapered candles on our table before heading back to the kitchen.

The older man caught sight of my approach. "Ah, one of our unexpected visitors. Come eat with us." A welcoming smile lit his face, a charming dimple winking in one cheek. His white hair and teal hairstreak contrasted with a strong set of dark brows. An aristocratic nose completed his face. He exuded charisma and importance. I liked him immediately. "Brenna, it is a pleasure to have you at our table. I am King Donalt of Linneah."

Should I bow? Curtsy? I settled for an awkward bob. "It's nice to meet you." Slipping into my seat opposite Rosamunde, I tried not to gawk at my surroundings.

Rosamunde's chocolate-brown eyes twinkled. "Questions?" She nodded toward the various beings moving about the room.

"I recognize the Linneans. Who's everyone else?"

"We hire many different races," she said. "Camlos are broad and muscular. The Weldens do not have legs but are very quick. The Kells are the ones with the beautiful eyes and sharp features. And of course, fauns, like Murray." She smiled at an older faun who placed a bowl of fruit on the table. "No Merripens—they are shape shifters—since they are unpredictable and our peace with them is tenuous."

After the serving staff disappeared into the kitchen, the king cleared his throat. "Let us give thanks."

Everyone else closed their eyes and raised both of their hands, and I scrambled to follow along. While he thanked the "Most High King for all abundance from His hand," I peeked, my gaze stalling on Erhardt. He sneered, eyes full of animosity.

Slamming my eyes shut, I resisted the urge to bolt from the table. Okay, he didn't like me. I'd give him space. After all, it was a big castle.

At the king's words, "So it is," everyone at the table responded, "So it is," and began passing bowls and platters of unfamiliar food. Lunch a distant memory, I took a serving of each dish. The light and fluffy rolls King Donalt called Kunkelsteuchen. A large platter held a boar lizard roast, which like the cliché, tasted like chicken, but had the consistency of pencil erasers. The gravy helped it go down easier. On another platter, an enormous grilled fish had been cut into servings, the head still intact. Serving myself a small piece near the tail, I tried to ignore its glowering, creepy eye. Carmeil salad sparkled in my mouth with the flavor of root beer, its slender leaves like green, yellow, and purple grass. Blue fruit with pebbled skin lay clustered in a bowl.

During the meal, the richness of the room and my dining companions' clothes weighed on me. My long-sleeved t-shirt was stained, and my jeans had been dunked in reservoir water. And I needed a shower. Rosamunde sat across from me, her long hair shining, in a beautiful red tunic with black scrolling embroidery. She took a sip of her pale-green drink, elegant even in the simplest actions.

Dad wasn't at the table. I swallowed my disappointment with a bite of salad. "How's my dad?"

The white foam at the top of her drink clung to her upper lip before she dabbed it away with a napkin. "He has been through a terrible experience. His wound is deep, and we are treating it to prevent infection. He cannot see anyone until the risk of infection passes. However, your grandmother is doing well. She ate a meal and is now taking a nap."

"Can I see her later?"

"That is acceptable. Perhaps you could send a letter to your father. Our physician Renke tells me he asked about you."

I nodded and finished my salad.

After the delicious meal, the king pushed back his plate. His penetrating hazel eyes, so like Erhardt's, studied me. "Brenna, how did you come to be in Linneah?"

Erhardt's hands stilled. The weight of his gaze pierced into me, through me.

"I had to."

Rosamunde and King Donalt leaned forward. Interest lighted their eyes.

Ignoring Erhardt, I cleared my throat. "My mother is missing, and today is my sixteenth birthday. My dad said I had to be in the portal today." I filled in my story: Grandma Helen battling big bugs at Big Rock, finding the portal guarded by more big bugs, my dad being attacked while my grandmother sucked the insects up in a tornado, and my grand finale: passing out in the portal. Exhaustion swamped me, tears stinging my eyes. "I have no idea what's going on."

King Donalt sat back, his expression thoughtful. "You said your mother is missing?"

"Yes. My father says she's missing here, in Linneah."

The adults exchanged a glance full of meaning. I hated that look—the way adults shared information without saying a word. "What?"

"What is her name?" Rosamunde stacked her silverware on her plate, then pushed it to the side.

"Sarah James. She's a native from here in Linneah but lives with us. At least she did until a couple of months ago. Can you tell me where she is?

The king didn't answer my question. "How did you make it through the portal without a jasper?"

Was it mere hours ago Dad had given me that gift? "It's in my bag."

Rosamunde raised an eyebrow. "You are fortunate the portal did not kill you. If you wear your jasper, it makes the experience bearable."

"I'll keep that in mind. Is that why my dad isn't doing so well?"

"No," she said. "It is the wound. Your grandmother provided protection enough."

"Outsiders do not often come through the portal," said Erhardt, his first words since the meal began. "Especially ones bringing trouble with them." His tone said he'd pay good money for my departure.

"Trouble?"

"The Largamants. Why are they with you? Are they spies? Who are you working with?"

I leaned back in my chair, putting more distance between us.

King Donalt's voice sliced the air like a steel sword. "That is enough. You will offer Brenna the same courtesy you offer our other guests."

"Our other guests do not bring wickedness with them, Father. The portals need to be guarded with more vigilance. We are in danger. How many visitors have come through the portal in only the last season?"

"This is not a discussion to have in front of guests."

Erhardt turned back to his plate, a muscle flexing in his tight jaw.

Rosamunde filled the awkward silence. "We can continue the discussion tomorrow after a full night of sleep."

"I just want to find my mom," I said.

Erhardt pushed back his chair with a disgusted sniff. "There is much I must attend to. If you will excuse me." Turning to me, he gave a mock bow. "A pleasure having dinner with you."

He left the room, taking the tension with him. But one nagging question remained since I rose from my nap. "Is there such a thing called the First Prophecy of Linneah?"

Rosamunde and King Donalt wore identical expressions—eyes wide, mouths partway open. The king recovered first. "Where did you hear of that?"

"During my nap, I had a dream. A large glowing person said I shouldn't be afraid, then mentioned a prophecy."

Rosamunde gave a start. "You received a visitation from the Sahale?"

"I thought it was a weird dream. Is it a big deal?"

The king's twinkling eyes had gone serious. "Yes, it is a very big deal, as you say. We Linneans call it a gift. It is rare to receive a visit or a message from one of the Lighted Ones."

The two adults exchanged another glance before he spoke again. "Perhaps I need to show you something. Come with me." He pushed back from the table.

Chapter Four

We walked down the main hallway, our footsteps echoing on the cobblestones. King Donalt stopped in front of a heavily carved wooden door. Opening it, he said, "Welcome to my study. I have a copy of the First Prophecy. Let me find it for you."

While he scanned a floor-to-ceiling bookshelf, I leaned against the doorframe. A fire smoldered in the hearth, giving the room a pleasant glow. Polished, honey-colored beams ran the length of the ceiling before meeting the rough stone walls. In one corner rested a beige fur-covered couch. The other corner held a sturdy desk with a matching chair. A few beautifully woven tapestries in rich jewel colors hung on the walls, most of them depicting calm, forested valleys or sea-swept beaches.

"Here it is." King Donalt pulled a gilt-edged book free from its place. "You should find it interesting."

I stifled a sigh. That kind of statement never preceded anything good. People didn't need to point out items of interest. They just *were* interesting.

He turned to me. "This prophecy is from many, many times ago."

"Times?"

"It is how we measure the passing of seasons." Rosamunde
sat on one end of the couch and crossed her legs. "A time is like
your year."

"The First Prophecy of Linneah." He laid the open book on
the desk and indicated the other end of the sofa. "Have a seat
while I read this. Then you may share your thoughts with us."

I sat. His powerful voice rolled over the words.

MANY DARK DAYS ARE COMING SOON,
BY THE LIGHT OF A TRAITOR'S MOON.
THREE WILL COME, BUT ONE WILL STAY.
VILE FOES TAKEN AWAY.
FROM DEEP WITHIN AND DEEP WITHOUT,
COMES ONE OF POWER AND OF DOUBT,
WITH THE SOURCE OF HOPE AND FIRE,
BENDING TO A WILL FAR HIGHER.
MIGHTY WORLD AWAY WILL PASS,
BY DESTROYER'S HAND AT LAST.
THE SACRED VEIL WILL DISAPPEAR,
SEARCH THE DARK WOOD, DESPITE YOUR FEAR.
VEILED ENEMIES WILL FIGHT ALL MEN,
AS BULL ATTACKS FROM FOREST GLEN.
TAKING LINNEAH'S FATE IN HAND,
THE RAVEN'S SHARE CAN SAVE THE LAND.

When he finished, I nodded. "Interesting." And it was, sort
of. "But what does this have to do with me?"

"Brenna, what is your talent?" Rosamunde asked.

I can quote large portions of dialogue from all the Star Wars
movies. Not helpful. "I'm not sure. My dad said you could help
me discover it."

"Are there any unusual occurrences you remember?"

Queasiness snaked through my stomach. Memories of the
burned cheerleaders' pom-poms reduced my voice to a whisper.

"I, um, started a fire. It was an accident. A flame came out of my fingertips. In the school hallway."

She laid a reassuring hand on my shoulder. "You are most likely a Firebrand, dear."

"What does that mean?"

"You can produce fire, flames, and heat with either healing or destructive properties. With study, you will be able to control those impulses according to the situation. The different fields of study—healing arts, defense, scientific realms—hold many opportunities."

Shooting flames out of my fingers was considered normal here?

"I am more interested in your visit with the Sahale," King Donalt said. "She mentioned the Prophecy. Why? What exactly did she say?" His narrowed eyes studied my face as though the answers were scrawled across my forehead.

Nervous, I crossed and uncrossed my restless legs. "Only what I told you. I don't remember anything else. Maybe they visited because I discovered I'm part Linnean."

"Perhaps. But some puzzle pieces do not fit, one of which is the enemy presence at the portal. Nevertheless, we have been waiting for the fulfiller of the First Prophecy for many times. Linneah will continue to wait." The king sat back in his seat with a sigh. "And you are untrained. An untrained Firebrand is a hazard."

Rosamunde and King Donalt exchanged another glance, and I bit my tongue. It wouldn't do any good to ask what those looks were all about—I had no leverage to demand information.

"You will begin training tomorrow," Rosamunde said.

"Who's my trainer?"

"I am," she said. "We can talk more in the morning. Would you like to see your grandmother? She is in the room next to yours. I can take you to her if you would like."

"Thanks, but I can find my own way back." I offered a smile to soften my refusal. "Could I have some paper? I'd like to write my dad a letter."

King Donalt handed me a box with a large, etched "D" on the front. "You will find what you need in here. Please leave it outside your room when you are finished. The couriers will return it." He closed the book and placed it back on the shelf. "I will be up for a while before I retire, Rosamunde. I have a few things to attend to."

She nodded, then followed me into the hall. "Leave the note outside your door. A castle courier will take it to Renke first thing in the morning. Good night and sleep well."

I nodded, mumbled something like "Good night" back, and headed down the hallway.

As I walked up the staircase, the words from the prophecy swirled in my head. No way had those words referred to me. At the top of the stairs, a rush of air carrying the scent of wood smoke, moist earth, and sea salt filled my nostrils. On my left, a door to a small balcony stood ajar, letting in the fresh night air. A guy about my age stood near the balcony's iron railing, his dark head bowed. Half of his face and his profile were lit by the hallway torches. Dark, mussed hair, square jaw, and a straight nose—but the solemn set to his mouth drew me.

Was he okay? I could—you know what? None of my business. I started to turn away.

My plan to continue to my room vanished when I saw the knife clenched in his hand. He studied it, tracing the blade, fingering the grip. That couldn't be good. Was he going to stab someone? Stab himself? He didn't look like a criminal—but then you could never tell. The seriousness of the situation gave me courage. I stepped onto the balcony, holding the king's stationery box like a shield.

"Hey, how's it going?" I got ready to run in case he turned the wicked-sharp knife on me.

With a start, he slipped his hands behind his back.

"Nice knife you have there."

His jaw tightened, and he shot me a glare. "I prefer to be alone."

"Yeah, good luck with that."

Heaving a sigh, he gazed at the shadowed scenery. From opposite sides of the horizon, two bright, glowing bands bisected the night sky. The twinkling stars gleamed through the rings before scattering to meet the shadowed black cliffs in the distance. Nearer the castle, the tiny glimmers of the surrounding city glittered, pinpricks of light.

"Wow. That's incredible." I pointed to the shining display. The whole scene was wonderfully romantic, but here I was, stuck with a knife-wielding weirdo. Really cute, but still a weirdo.

"The Petrus Rings. They encircle the planet." Several beats of silence passed before he spoke again. "You are not going to leave me alone, are you?"

"No, probably not. I don't want you slitting your throat or jumping off this balcony. Or both." I paused. "Though that might be a little difficult to do at the same time."

A chuckle escaped him. "I am not intending to harm myself."

"Good. Then put the knife away, and we'll all feel better."

Slipping it into the sheath at his waist, he held up his hands. "Better?"

"Yes, thanks."

His biceps flexed when he crossed his arms and leaned against the iron railing, his eyes attentive. "My name is Baldwin, and I am guessing you are one of the new visitors. The whole town is talking about your arrival."

I startled, my eyes wide. "Why?"

"It is always an event when strangers visit, but your entrance was epic."

Great. In the dim light, maybe he wouldn't notice my blush. "I'm Brenna."

"Brenna." He said it like it was a different language, trying out the vowels and consonants together. "Nice name. What do you think of castle life so far?"

"It's different. We don't have many castles at home."

"It is always interesting to hear about other alternities. Although when outsiders appear in the portal, it increases the number of guards." He gestured to the stone wall below.

"What do you mean?" I leaned over the balcony. Lanterns lined the castle wall, their yellow glow illuminating half a dozen guards walking its length.

"Any unknown visitor could pose a threat, so security will be increased for a while. More often than not, foreigners die from the portal experience." He looked at me with something like approval. "Since you were not wearing a jasper, you must be tougher than you look."

Nice. A left-handed compliment. I ignored it. "Have you met Sarah James? A tall woman with dark hair, red hairstreak, would've arrived here about two months ago?"

"Yes, but she has been gone for over a season now. Some issues arose in the Northern Province, and she left to mediate." His smile made his eyes come alive. "You resemble her. Is she your mother?"

I nodded. "Where's the Northern Province? And please don't say north."

"But it is. It borders the Kasek territory, north of Linneah."

"Is it dangerous?"

"You have no need to worry. Her mission was a peace-keeping operation to settle misunderstandings that had developed."

The words echoed. Mission. Peace-keeping. Misunderstandings. Mom, a government operative? I cleared my throat to relieve the sudden dryness. "What kind of misunderstandings?"

"Lady James is the best Sensitive Linneah has. With the rumors of uprisings, we had to utilize her ability."

"Sure," I said, as if I knew all about my mother's talent. She was a Sensitive. What did that even mean? "How come you know so much?"

He shrugged. "The nephew of the king tends to hear a lot, especially if his cousin is the adviser."

"Rosamunde is your cousin?"

"No, Erhardt."

I raised an eyebrow. Hard to believe this guy and the stone-cold soldier were related.

He chuckled, most likely from the look on my face. "We are nothing alike in almost every way. It happens sometimes." He turned and slipped through the doorway. "Nice meeting you, Brenna. See you tomorrow."

"Baldwin?"

He turned, his eyes curious.

"What were you going to do with that knife before I showed up?"

"Nothing. It is my father's. He gave it to me before he left three seasons ago. Sometimes I feel closer to him..." His voice trailed off, and he looked at the floor. "I guess that sounds childish."

"No, it doesn't. I get it."

He looked up, and understanding passed between us. In the past months, I'd carried the same burden—sadness and worry overlaid with fear. I handled my memories of Mom with care, hoping they wouldn't crumble like old photographs. "Stop playing with knives, okay?"

With a quick grin, he turned and walked down the hall.

I watched him go until I realized I was staring with a goofy grin on my face. Turning, I studied the night sky. The glowing gold and silver-blue rings twinkled. A colder edge crept into the night air, and I shivered. The guards continued their silent patrol. Murky shadows shifted near the steps of the castle. A light had burned out in that area, and I squinted, looking closer. After a moment more on the balcony, I gave up. Nothing to worry about—maybe guards at the entrance. Or someone back from a late walk.

Instead of going to my room, I walked past it and stopped at the room next door. Tapping on the open door, I peeked in. "Hi, Grandma."

She looked up from her book. "Brenna! I'm glad to see you. Come on in."

Dressed for bed in a long flannel robe, her gray hair flowed long and loose, out of its usual braid. Her red hairstreak flamed bright against her pale face.

I sat on the edge of her bed. "How do you feel?"

"Better. I overdid it a bit. Nothing that couldn't be cured by a good nap." She put aside her book. "What do you think of Linneah?"

"Well, everyone seems nice, though they talk weird. No contractions. Does everyone talk like that here?"

"All Linneans do. Races from other parts of the Jasper Territory don't. And your mom and I have adopted a less strict way of talking."

"On my way here, I met Baldwin, the king's nephew. He's nice." I paused for a moment. "Oh yeah, and his cousin Erhardt hates me and thinks I'm evil."

Grandma smiled and waved away my comment. "He doesn't hate you. Erhardt's a good kid, if a little high-strung. Must be his Warrior talent coming out."

"Speaking of Warrior talent, what did you do at the reservoir? Wind and tornadoes and bolts of lightning?"

"It's my Weatherbrand talent, but I wasn't very successful this time." She frowned. "I'm sorry it didn't work for Harrison. How is he?"

"They won't let me see him until he's better. I'm going to write him a note."

She patted my hand. "Your dad's healthy and strong, sweetie. He'll be better tomorrow."

"Baldwin said Mom's a Sensitive. What is that?"

"She can feel people's moods, knows when they're lying, that sort of thing. She's one of Linneah's best."

No wonder I was never able to fool her. Mom always caught my lies, soothed my temper, and lifted my sadness. I missed her beyond words, and my sadness and worry tightened my chest.

After a few minutes of small talk, I said goodnight and walked to my room to write a quick letter to Dad. By the time I finished sealing and addressing the note, my eyes burned, my lids heavy. I placed the letter and the king's box outside my door and got ready for bed.

Maybe tomorrow wouldn't be so weird.

The next morning, I woke earlier than I expected. After a huge stretch, I pulled aside the tapestry. The promise of the sun granted the gray glimmering sky a yellow peach skyline.

Inside my door lay a bundle wrapped in brown paper and tied with a simple brown string. I tore off the paper, and a blue tunic and black pants fell into my hands. Velvety soft yet light, the supple material felt like rose petals. The cobalt-blue tunic tied with a black leather belt and was embroidered on the back with black satin thread. I ran a hand over the pretty scrolling flourishes. Designs like these decorated many of the fabrics in the castle. Although the black pants would've looked better tucked into boots, all I had were my Converse. Maybe I could buy some boots later.

On impulse, I rummaged in my backpack for my pendant. In the new light of the morning, its facets flashed red fire. Placing it around my neck, I checked myself out in my room's mirror. A cooler version of me gazed back, comfortable in her own skin.

I checked Grandma's room—empty, quiet, and messy. Strewn over her bed were several open maps. A stack of books teetered on the edge of her desk, scraps of paper bookmarking important pages. I pushed the unsteady stack farther back on her desk and left.

Hurrying down the hallways, my stomach rumbled. Maybe they'd be serving breakfast now. I craved a Belgian waffle, but I didn't think Linneans had those. At least not yet.

I'm not sure how many floors were in the castle. Empty bedrooms occupied the third floor, and the second floor remained a mystery. The first floor housed the king's study (now with a closed door), a dining room, a massive ballroom, a comfortable sitting room and library, and an airy, octagonal room with graceful curving arches. I know because I peeked into just about every room I passed. Gorgeous didn't even begin to describe it. A beautiful collection of carved chairs encircled the perimeter of the final room.

The giant stained-glass window drew me in. When I moved closer, it shifted, changing like a kaleidoscope before settling into a striking piece of art. Trees shaded a winding road that disappeared into a rising sun. I had been there before, knew it well, yet couldn't place it. Turning to go, I came face to face with the old faun I saw the night before at supper.

"S-sorry."

"No, it is fine." He waved away my apology. "We did not get the chance to become acquainted last night. I am Murray."

"I'm Brenna. Is it okay if I'm in here?"

"You are always welcome."

"What is that a picture of?" I pointed to the stained glass. "The place looks familiar."

"I do not know. This is a Vision Window."

"A what?"

"A Vision Window. Whatever your question, the answer will be shown there. I cannot see what you are seeing. My vision, my need is different. But here in our Gathering Room, we can look for answers to our questions."

"So this place is like a church?"

"Yes, we praise the Most High King here for His goodness and blessings. Even in the midst of these confusing times, we are thankful."

He seemed lost in his own thoughts until I spoke.

"Confusing times?"

"Linneah is beset by troubles not seen in many times. The neighboring provinces are restless with rumors of war, dead men appear in our portals, and the weather is changing, shifting. Even the residents of Linneah report unhappiness and trouble. Thievery, anger, and drunkenness are becoming the norm."

I raised an eyebrow, thinking of home. "This is unusual?"

"Why, yes. Linneah has been most fortunate. In our past, we had wars, but those times have gone. The Most High King created a peaceful existence for the Jasper Territory. But now rifts have developed between the territories. We have never experienced problems of this magnitude before." His eyes fixed on the stained-glass window in a blind stare.

He began to shift from side to side, his voice a whisper. "Our universe is in flux, there is nothing to be done. The ground will shift, a river will run. The Great Serpent rises from the deep, then grown men wither, and families sleep. We must weather the storm, weather the storm."

He continued to stare, swaying back and forth. After a moment or two, the rocking stopped. When nothing else happened, I tired of waiting and snapped my fingers in front of him. "Murray?"

He jerked, his eyes focusing. "Oh, terribly sorry. And on an empty stomach, at that. Come, let us find the morning meal."

"What just happened?"

The older faun reddened. "All races in the Jasper Territory are gifted. I am a Visionary. I see things that are yet to happen."

"Whoa." Impressive. And a little weird, especially with the swaying and whispering deal. "Shouldn't you tell someone?"

"I will report to King Donalt after breakfast. Not that it will make any difference."

"What do you mean? It sounded pretty important."

"When one has made many mistakes, his credibility can be harmed, despite honorable intentions."

"But—"

"There have been enough visions that have not come to fruition."

"Yet," I said. "You said you see things that are 'yet to happen.'"

He gave me a sideways glance. "Your confidence in my talent is warming. But perhaps I am an inefficient Visionary."

"Has the Most High King ever made a mistake?"

"It is not possible."

Well, that settled it. "Then it would seem your gift isn't a mistake."

Hope brightening his face, he turned and trotted down the hall toward breakfast.

I smiled and followed him.

Chapter Five

My breakfast consisted of an unidentifiable jelly on unrecognizable toast and a bowl of brown seeds that tasted like popcorn. My thoughts drifted from the unappetizing fare.

The Great Serpent? The ground will shift? Murray's words were ominous, but who knew when it would happen. It could happen tomorrow or two hundred years from now.

Grimacing, I took another bite of toast, the fruit spread too sweet. It couldn't compete with a Belgian waffle, but I'd have to give up on that dream for a while. I finished breakfast, and Baldwin ambled in and grabbed a piece of fruit from a bowl on the table. My face heated. He was as cute as I remembered. No, scratch that. He was even cuter in bright daylight. Dark-brown hair swept back from brilliant green eyes, his smile growing when he spotted me. I melted a bit and tried to remember how to breathe.

"Good morning. I am surprised to see you up already."

"Yeah, I couldn't sleep."

"Do you need a more comfortable room?"

"What? Oh no, I'm fine. I mean, I slept fine. I just couldn't sleep more. This morning." I pressed my lips together. Me + Cute Guy = Nervous Babbling.

He smiled again as if he could read my thoughts. "Are you ready?"

"For?"

"A tour of Linneah. Nobody is going to be up for a while." He didn't wait for my response. "Come on."

Stepping into the clear, blue day cured me of any leftover morning fuzziness. Early morning rays gilded everything with yellow light. The portal fountain sprayed high, its droplets a glittering curtain. Smelling of the sea, the scented air rode the breeze all the way to the castle. We walked down the castle steps and followed a well-worn path set between the castle and another nondescript stone building. A low-arched entryway bridged the gap between the two buildings.

Baldwin started down a set of stairs, and I followed, charmed by the meandering ivy that curled around the railing. "Where are we going?"

"To see the city. This is one of two ways to the residential area of Linneah. The other is a path that goes past the portal entrance."

When we reached the bottom of the twisting staircase, we entered a mega-pavilion formed from thick branches, heavy leaves, and ivy. The walls, gargantuan tree trunks planted close together, had several cement archways open to the outside.

"The Linnean Gardens," he said, gesturing to the lush shaded acreage in front of us. "We often have festivals here. In fact, the next one is the Shaverim Festival. Maybe you will get to see it."

Nearby, a green pond bubbled and gurgled like a mad scientist's potion. I leaned down for a closer look. "What's this?"

"A natural spring. It heats the castle and the other buildings."

"Along with the glowfish?"

"Right. You have been doing research."

Ferns, moss, and leafy shrubs edged the cobblestone footpath. A few Linneans wandered some of the other trails while a small group of Kells practiced something like Tai Chi. Their angular features were set in serious expressions of concentration. The footpath ended at a row of wide arches leading to the outside.

We cleared the cement doorway, and Baldwin stopped. "And this is the village of Linneah."

I gasped. "Whoa."

Massive trees, their trunks about twenty feet in diameter, supported tree houses. With the flattened yet dense green leaves, the sturdy branches were the perfect structure for a tree house, something the Linneans used in most of their buildings, including the castle.

"You can find the shield tree everywhere in Linneah. We use the upper level for sleeping quarters, while the living space is below in the hollow trunks. Someone at the castle could take you in to see one, if you are interested." He leaned against the entryway.

"But what about winter?"

"What about it?"

"Don't you get cold weather here?"

"Some. During the Silent Season, it gets colder and windier. But the trees are very warm."

"You don't get snow?" My new hobby, snowboarding, required snow. A landscape without it? Impossible.

"It snows farther north."

"How much?"

He shot me a dark look. "Do you ever stop asking questions?"

Ouch. "I just wondered. Forget it."

"I have not traveled much." Pressing his lips together, he turned away.

Silence filled the space between us. Awkward.

After a moment, he looked at me and took a deep breath. "Sorry. My lack of travel experience is a sore spot. But not your fault."

"It's okay."

"Not really, but thank you. Please, ask anything you want."

Still curious, I returned to our previous—and safe—subject. "So why build in trees?"

"We have always done so. There used to be a flood season, many times ago. The heavy rains flooded this area about twice a time. So the sleeping areas also include living spaces. And of course the myth of the serpent comes into play, too."

What was it about these people and snakes? Yet I couldn't help myself. "What does the myth say?"

His voice became dramatic. "Once every five hundred times, a serpent will rise to terrorize Linneah. Due to its immense size, only residents high above ground will survive."

"You guys are in trouble."

He chuckled. "It is a myth."

Continuing our walk, we skirted the residential area. The rising sun warmed the back of my head. Wooden fences meandered over fields and hills, separating crops to be harvested from fields of baled hay. Dominating the landscape, the castle complex and lower gardens created a feeling of safety and community.

I loved the way each step revealed something new and different. Nothing like Pennsylvania.

We followed a path to a field a good distance from the castle. To the right were cliffs, and beyond that, a distant sea glittered in the sunlight. Ships with bright sails dotted the pale-blue expanse with cheerful spots of color.

As we neared the field, the sounds of clanging metal filled the air. Men and women wielding bulky shields and weapons practiced in groups of two or three. The bright sunlight reflected off the arcing silver swords. Off to the side, a smaller group practiced with double-edged axes, staffs, clubs with spikes, and bows and arrows. They were all handled with terrifying skill.

One of the men with a staff broke off training and strode toward us. "Baldwin, greetings!"

Baldwin dropped to one knee. "Emperor Rexson."

And there I stood. The feeling of community dissipated like a puff of dandelion seeds.

"You must be one of our visitors." Emperor Rexson's rugged face split into a warm grin. "Welcome to Linneah."

With a great degree of formality, Baldwin stood. "Brenna James, I am pleased to introduce you to Emperor Rexson, ruler of the Jasper Territory."

My brain scrambled to place this new member of royalty. King Donalt was—right, the ruler of Linneah. So Emperor Rexson was pretty much King Donalt's boss.

"Pleased to meet you." I gave a little bow, hoping a curtsy wasn't required. Unnerved at meeting someone so important, my ADHD took over. "Why are you training soldiers if Linneah is so peaceful?"

Baldwin's strained voice cracked. "Brenna!"

"I mean, uh, sorry." Sheesh.

The emperor handed his wooden pole to Baldwin. "Have a round with Fisk." He nodded at the brawny man who stood waiting. "Fisk, do not kill him."

Swallowing hard, Baldwin walked toward his doom.

Emperor Rexson grasped my forearm. "Allow me to welcome you with the formal greeting of the Territory. I am pleased to see you in Linneah."

Did he know Mom? Maybe I should ask. *No, don't be an idiot.*

"Do you like your homeland? We have been waiting for you to visit."

"I'm American. Born in Vermont, actually."

"Ah, but your heart is looking for a place to belong. One day you may consider Linneah your true home, the home of your heart. It is similar to America, correct?"

"Sure." Minus the prophecies, and the weird food, and the different races...

He grinned, the smile reaching his eyes and causing them to sparkle. "You are a strong young lady. Linneah could benefit from your leadership, if you allow it."

I gawked. Leadership? I didn't plan to stick around. I'd find my mom and go home.

He grasped my forearm again. "It was a pleasure meeting you, Brenna."

"Same here."

The emperor strolled toward Fisk and Baldwin. The two fought on a corner of the field, a beautiful display of power, agility, and spinning staffs. Despite the older man being twice Baldwin's size, Baldwin held his own. After a short jab to the chest, Baldwin recovered with a spin and a return strike. After a few more dizzying maneuvers, Fisk swept his staff down, knocking Baldwin's feet out from under him. With a smile, Baldwin stood and shook the older man's hand. He handed the staff to Emperor Rexson, bowed, and jogged back.

"You're alive."

"I am fine." He rubbed his ribs. "Fisk only got me once."

"So, why *is* Linneah training soldiers?"

"Why did you ask him that?"

"It was the first thing I thought of."

He didn't look at me, instead focusing on the archers at the archery range. They didn't miss, each arrow hitting the target with a loud *thunk*. "We need to be prepared to help our neighbors resist attacks or to defend ourselves. Although it has not happened in many times, King Donalt believes it is good to be prepared. Anyway, this is what I wanted you to see."

Turning, he pointed at a huge stone building, about the size of the castle, but relegated to two floors. In the center of the building rose a tall glass dome.

"What about it?"

"Wait."

A minute later, a creature the size of a large SUV appeared at the corner of the building. My mouth dropped open, and I took a step back. It. Was. Huge.

The magnificent dark-brown beast had an aquiline beak, smallish tufted ears, and intense, intelligent eyes. Massive feathered wings melded into the powerful body of a mountain lion. It began to run, its muscles bulging and the wings unfurling. With a leap, it climbed high into the sky.

"Wow. What is it?"

He grinned. "A griffin. That is Riothamus, the alpha leader. He leads a strong, healthy tribe of griffins that picked Linneah as their homeland over five hundred times ago. Some bond with our warriors, some with other talents. Often, one pass through the tribe is all it takes for a griffin to choose."

"After you bond with them, then what?"

"You ride them," he said, as if I were slow.

"So it's like a horse."

"No, you cannot own a griffin. He is a loyal, intelligent companion. A friend."

"How do they know who to choose?"

"They simply know. They are very wise, sometimes able to look into the heart of a man."

I didn't need anything or anyone poking around in my heart. Still, my curiosity won. "Can I see the others?"

"Sure. This building is their sleeping quarters, but many of them will spend their daylight hours behind the building."

We rounded the corner, and I gasped. Griffins of every size, shape, and color littered the area. Some played while others dozed in the sun. Baldwin explained traditional griffins were half-eagle and half-lion. Others had different features—all eagle but with the tail of a leopard, or a cheetah with eagle wings—but were no less beautiful. Regardless of their features, when we stepped closer, each griffin became aware of our presence. No sneaking up on these creatures.

Baldwin pointed to a golden griffin lazing in the sun. "That is Lev Leon-ahren. He chose me three times ago."

I stopped, my legs turning to useless stumps.

He frowned when he noticed me lagging behind. "What is wrong?"

"I'm close enough."

"But you can come closer."

"It seems disrespectful, and they're a little intimidating."

"You are safe. They will not hurt you."

A griffin the size of four-door sedan rose to its feet. My reply dried up in my throat. His features were all feline, except his powerful wings. Fur the color of soot covered his body, the edges of the dark-charcoal wings tipped in silver. He prowled closer. The sunlight sparkled off the metallic feathers.

When the creature stopped in front of us, Baldwin lowered his head in respect. I did the same. "We are sorry to intrude. This is a visitor, Brenna James. She wanted to see the tribe."

The griffin's low voice bordered on a rough growl. "She is not a visitor. She belongs. I am Arvandus Leon-ahren." Squirming under the griffin's solid gaze, I welcomed the break when he knelt in front of me. "I know you, and you will know me. You may ride."

"No, thanks."

Baldwin gasped, the sound deafening in the tense silence.

The griffin's feathers sparked silver flashes. "You are rejecting the vinculus?"

I took a step back, my eyes wide. The thing could shoot silver sparks? "No, no, of course not." I turned to Baldwin. "What's a vinculus?'

"It is the bond between a griffin and its rider."

"Oh, well, I've never ridden a griffin. I haven't been trained."

"There is no training for this," Baldwin said. "It is not needed."

"A vinculus does require trust, but I will not harm you." Arvandus waited for my decision, a silent leonine shadow.

Stepping closer to the griffin, I laid a light hand near his wing. His powerful muscles rippled underneath his fur. "Where do I sit?"

"The only place there is. Between my head and wings."

Grabbing a handful of fur, I tugged, slipped, and grunted my way on. Patient, the griffin stood, his muscles tensing for flight.

Amusement danced across Baldwin's features. "Since Lev is here, we can—" A piercing, brassy sound drifted over the clearing. His eyes widened, emerald bright. "The battle horn. Something is wrong." Before he finished speaking, Lev knelt in front of him, waiting for him to mount.

Searching for a place to put my hands, I followed Baldwin's example by burrowing my fingers into the fur near Arvandus's neck.

"Quick, to the castle," Baldwin said.

"Wait. Don't I need to—"

We took off. I swallowed the scream lodged in my throat and tightened my thighs at the quick jerk of power. Falling off my griffin on my first flight would be bad.

The trip, a short, dizzy rush of wind and speed, was a trial by fire. Relax and enjoy the view? Not happening, due to my white-knuckled grip in Arvandus's fur. Every dip, turn, and burst of speed convinced me—I was going to die. In a parallel alternity. On a griffin.

In minutes, the griffins landed near the castle. Guards guided civilians off the castle grounds, and the village merchants closed their booths. More guards formed a perimeter around the fountain. People hurried for the safety of their homes.

I slid off, stumbling and breathless. I freaking loved it. And I needed to get better, lots better. "Thanks, Arvandus. Can we ride again soon?"

The griffin nodded once. "I look forward to it."

He took to the sky, his wing tips reflecting light. Hurrying to catch Baldwin, I ran up the steps and slipped through the huge castle doors. Inside, a somber mood filled the hallway. More than a dozen guards stood in front of doors and entryways. In the rooms behind them, people clustered in groups, whispering and crying. Rosamunde and Erhardt stood outside the king's study.

Erhardt drew Baldwin to his side, and his gaze impaled me where I stood. "Father is dead. Murdered."

Before I could speak, two guards materialized on either side of me. Erhardt's voice dropped the temperature in the corridor by several icy degrees.

"And here is our murderer."

CHAPTER SIX

THE GUARDS SEIZED MY wrists.

"What? No! When I saw him—"

"Yes, last night. You came here to murder our great leader, bringing your spies with you!"

I struggled to break free from the guards' iron grip. "No, Rosamunde and I left his study at the same time." Looking to the woman for support, my anxiety rose. She wouldn't look me in the eye.

"That is true." Her voice was quiet.

"And then," Erhardt said, "you came back to his study to murder him with your foreign magic. We have no use for that here. How did you do it?" He advanced on me, but I had nowhere to run.

"I don't know magic. I—" One of the guards clamped down on my wrist, and I winced. A tingling heat speared through my fingers. Oh, no. Dread sprouted in my chest. Starting a fire in the castle would *not* help. I tried to take deep, calm breaths. "I went back to my room to write a letter to my father."

Baldwin's face had gone white. "Yes, I saw her after she left Uncle Donalt's study."

"She has seduced you with her act," Erhardt said. "You are young and impressionable. I see her for what she is—a criminal and murderer."

I started to panic. They were going to throw me in jail or a dungeon, if they had one. It'd be damp and moldy, I'd be limited to old bread and stale water, and my cell would be filled with spiders, rats, and an incessant dripping noise that would drive me insane... "Wait, I don't know how things work here. But where I come from, you need to have proof."

"You are not at home. This is Linneah." Erhardt's sneer twisted his pale, strained face. "Here, we do things our way."

"Erhardt, stop. Allow her to speak." Rosamunde nodded at me. "Go ahead."

"After I left King Donalt's study, I met Baldwin. We talked for a few minutes, then I visited my grandmother. I spent some time in her room, talking. Afterwards, I went to my room, wrote a letter to my dad, and went to bed." I swallowed hard. It wasn't much of a defense. "King Donalt seemed like a great leader. He was kind to me and my family. I have no reason to kill or hurt anyone here. Someone killed him, but it wasn't me."

Erhardt continued to glare at me. Rosamunde stepped forward, blocking me from his furious gaze. "Did you see anything unusual on your way to your room?"

Deny it. After all, who would believe me? Still, I had to try. "Last night, the far torch on the castle wall had burned out. I thought I saw a shadow near the main door. I didn't say anything because I figured the guards would catch anyone sneaking around."

"A perfect story. How convenient for you," Erhardt scoffed.

She turned to him. "We have no proof tying her to King Donalt's death."

"That does not mean she did not do it."

"It does not mean she did, either. She does not have the strength to knock out the guards, and then rush back to the study. Furthermore, she does not have the knowledge to bleed someone like that."

Her words caught my attention. "Bleed someone?"

"My father had no blood in his body. He had been bled dry, his blood taken." Erhardt's voice broke on the last word.

Eww. My stomach flipped.

She turned to the guards. "Release her, please. She is not to be arrested or detained until further evidence indicts her."

Both guards dropped my wrists. Although I rubbed them, they still ached.

Erhardt stalked off.

With a grimace, I turned to Rosamunde. "He really hates me, doesn't he?"

"Give him time. He will come around."

"I don't think I have that much time. He's starting to scare me."

Baldwin spoke. "He will not hurt you. Erhardt gets angry, but he never becomes violent." Despite the unshed tears, his eyes glowed with a fierce light. "I will not let him hurt you."

The warmth unfurling in my stomach alleviated some of the awkwardness. "Thank you."

He ducked his head, a flush staining his neck before he trudged down the hall after Erhardt.

"So that is how it is." Rosamunde raised an eyebrow.

"He's a friend." And one I'd had for less than twenty-four hours. Still, I trusted him.

"The funeral will be held tomorrow. It would be wise to attend."

"Of course."

She nodded, approval shining in her eyes. "Also, your grandmother wishes to see you. And your father has been cleared for visitors. The infirmary is on the second floor."

"Thanks!" I hurried to my grandmother's room.

When I poked my head inside Grandma's room, it reminded me of a hospital. No personal touches, neat, clean enough to eat off the floor. A big change from the last time I'd seen it.

"Brenna, I've been waiting for you," she said from the bed.

"Sorry. I was visiting the griffins." And trying to stay out of jail. "I've got a griffin now. Weird, huh?"

"I'm not surprised. What's the griffin's name?"

"Arvandus." I sat next to her.

Her eyes sobered. "Did you hear about King Donalt?"

I nodded. "Erhardt accused me of killing him."

"What?"

"It's okay. Rosamunde and Baldwin stood up for me."

"Good. I'd hate to leave if you were having problems."

"Leave?"

"I have to go home. If your mother arrives at the house, I want to be there."

"What if they arrest me for killing King Donalt?"

"Send a note to me right away. The castle couriers will get it to me. I'll come back if you need me." She patted my hand. "But I don't think it'll come to that. Erhardt's upset by his father's death, and he lashed out. Don't worry."

Easy for her to say. Rather than debate, I changed the subject. "How would Mom get here and use the portal without being noticed?"

"There's more than one portal into the Jasper Territory." She pulled a book from her nightstand and flipped it open to a marked page. A colorful map of the Jasper Territory sprawled across two pages, the edges decorated with graceful scrolling and a fearsome purple sea dragon lurking at the bottom of the page. "Here's Linneah." She pointed to the dot labeled *Linneah* on the left page before shifting to the right. "But over here's Wildamek, Lennor, Kelda Hills, and Ginselwyn." She pointed to the other cities marked and labeled the same way. "They all have their own portals. There's also a separate portal system for citizens traveling between the cities."

"What's beyond the Jasper Territory?" I pointed to a shaded area at the top of the page.

She frowned. "That would be the Kasek Territory. It's dangerous up there." Closing the book, she handed it to me. "You should read this overview of the Jasper Territory. It might answer some questions you have."

"Are you sure you have to go?"

"Yes, I want to be there for your mom. You and your dad stay here. Then no matter whether she shows up in Pennsylvania or Linneah, someone will be waiting. Once she's found, we'll meet at the castle." She gave me a hug. "Let's go visit your dad."

At the infirmary, Renke and his assistant Dirk worked on a patient with a broken arm.

"Hi. Can I see my dad, please?"

Renke looked at Dirk and jerked his head. The young assistant nodded, then motioned toward a bed where Dad lay, resting. "For a short period."

We approached his bedside, and his eyes flickered open. "Brenna! Helen!" His voice was rusty, brown stubble covered his chin, and his pale face held a faint tinge of yellow.

"How do you feel?" I sat on the edge of his bed.

"I've been better. Thanks for the note." He tried to lean forward but grimaced, his eyes darkening.

"Dad, I'm so sorry. If I'd come alone—"

"Then you'd be in this hospital bed. No, we're here now. That's the important thing." He shifted, gritting his teeth against the pain again. "Tell me what's been going on."

We gave him a general summary of events. Judging from Dirk's pointed glances, we didn't have much time left in the infirmary. I didn't mention being accused of killing the king, hoping I wouldn't have to defend myself again. By the time Grandma Helen finished telling Dad about her plans to leave, Dirk stood beside us. "You can visit tomorrow."

"I love you, Dad. Get better, okay?" I gave him a kiss and a careful hug, then walked to the hallway. Wiping away a few tears, I tried to pray. The words wouldn't come. Grandma's voice floated into the hallway as she said goodbye to Dad.

She came out a minute later. "Walk me to the portal in say, half an hour?"

"Okay, I'll meet you at your room."

After kissing my cheek, she strode down the hallway in the opposite direction.

I walked toward the staircase that connected the floors. At the landing, something between a moan and a groan stopped me in my tracks. Although I didn't believe in ghosts, a chill skittered up my spine. Again, the sound came, a wail carrying the agony of someone in pain. I peeked in a few of the rooms, trying not to be too nosy. The first two were empty.

In the third sparse bedroom, a middle-aged woman sat on the bed, rocking back and forth. Lines bracketed her narrow lips. Deep grooves radiated from emerald eyes fixed on a far point in the room. A jade hairstreak adorned her spiky blonde hair like a punk Tinkerbell. Whimpering and muttering, she grabbed the thin knitted shawl lying across her shoulder and wrapped it around her skinny frame.

I started to back out of the room. The woman jerked, her eyes finding me in the doorway.

Busted. "Hi. Do you need help?"

She stopped rocking, her eyes clearing. "So you have come."

"Um, yes." And now I'd be going.

A look of sorrow crossed her face. "A Firebrand will deliver us. It has begun."

"What?"

The woman glared at me. "Leave and do your work." She pounded a bony fist against her chest. "Do not waste time with Mariel. There is much to be accomplished. Go! Go," she said, her voice harsh.

"Sorry, sorry." I backed out of the room and bumped into a young woman carrying food on a tray.

She frowned, her eyes suspicious. "What are you doing?"

"I asked if I could help her. She was moaning like she was hurt."

"Mariel is King Donalt's sister. We have not given her the news of his death, but perhaps she knows anyway." At my confused look, she continued. "She is the most accurate Visionary in the kingdom. People think she is crazy, but her visions allow her to see too much, poor thing."

She brushed past me. I left, the woman's cheery voice echoing into the hallway. "Mariel, lunch is ready. It looks delicious."

Halfway up the stairs, Mariel's words hit me. *A Firebrand will deliver us...*

"No, no, no." Dread expanded in my stomach like a bag of microwaved popcorn. It had to be another Firebrand. But, Mariel seemed to recognize me.

In my room, I flopped onto the bed. Now would be a good time to look for my mom. I had transportation in the form of Arvandus, my griffin. After the king's funeral tomorrow morning, I could start my search. Maybe when I returned, another Firebrand would've delivered Linneah.

CHAPTER SEVEN

A LONG TIME AGO, someone had carved a set of stairs into the rocks. Stairs I now followed down to the windswept shoreline. Living in the landlocked states of Vermont and Pennsylvania hadn't prepared me for the crashing, white-tipped waves. The roaring surf struck the beach, the calmer eddies rolling in to soothe the battered sand. A stiff breeze threw my hair into my face. After enjoying the scenery for several long moments, I moved toward the mass of people gathered for King Donalt's funeral.

The body, covered with a beautifully embroidered, dark-blue cloth, had been laid on a wooden raft. Townspeople and castle employees who came to pay their respects passed in front of the raft before assembling in a solemn gathering.

I hung back and people-watched. Grief hung heavy over the crowd, some people quiet and still others crying outright. King Donalt's family and the residents of the castle stood closest to the front. Many of them wore white armbands, bright against the dark jewel tones of their clothing. The wealthier residents were next in the crowd, identified by extensive embroidery on their tunics and pants. Common laborers at the back wore tan pants and simple neutral-toned shirts of gray, beige, or brown. I lingered behind them, in no hurry to be hemmed in by the crush of strangers. Grim-faced guards, wearing silver breastplates embossed with an eight-pointed star, stood at attention near the front of the crowd and around the family. Two dozen more patrolled the edges of the crowd.

A man stepped forward and played a song on a flute-like instrument, the haunting melody beautiful and poignant. After the last notes faded, Murray shared a eulogy. I couldn't hear much of it, due to the size of the crowd and my place near the back. He finished with what looked like a prayer, his arms raised and tears on his face. Baldwin, Erhardt, and Mariel filed by, placing garlands of ivy on the cloth-draped body. Rosamunde joined them, then each one grasped a corner of the wooden raft and carried it the few feet to the sea. They dragged it into the ocean, wet to their knees. Erhardt held a lit match to a corner, and the perimeter of the platform burst into flame. A minute later, a mighty swell pulled the raft out to sea, beyond their reach. I swallowed the lump in my throat and turned away.

Climbing the shallow, carved steps, I hurried to the griffin house to visit Arvandus. We didn't know each other very well, but a long trip would be a perfect get-to-know-you activity. Dad didn't know about my idea to search for Mom, and because Grandma Helen would discourage me from going, I hadn't mentioned it to her, either. Yesterday, we'd walked to the portal. She'd given me a hug, smiled, and stepped onto the stone circle. I blinked once, and that was it. She was gone.

Before I reached the griffin house, Arvandus stepped from behind the building. "Greetings, Brenna."

"Yeah, greetings. How'd you know I was coming?"

"I could smell you."

"Really?" I did a sniff check. "But I bathed this morning."

"We have an acute sense of smell. Do not take it personally."

Nice. "Do you know a Sarah James?"

He stretched his wings before settling in front of me. "Your mother. She is bonded to Campion, although she did not take him with her when she left for the Northern Province."

"I've heard she's in trouble."

"So have I."

"You have? From who?"

A growl rumbled from deep in his throat. "Rumors circulate among the tribe as they do elsewhere. We have no proof."

"I want to find her and help her come home. Can you take me?"

His ears twitched. "No."

"No?"

"It is not wise. The Northern Province is a dangerous trip, particularly for a young, unskilled one."

"I'm sixteen."

"You are young. Without question, unskilled in combat or control."

I could win this argument. "You'd be surprised how quick I learn. And it wouldn't be smart to leave my mom locked up in the Northern Province."

"How do you know she is locked up?"

"My grandmother traveled with her but came home first. When Grandma arrived, she said Mom would be back soon. That was two months ago. What other explanation is there?"

He said nothing, his feline face impassive.

"She loves me."

"I am sure she does. But forcing your way into the province before you are ready will not bring her home sooner and may, in fact, cause her harm."

"So what do we do? We sit here and hope she shows up? I came here to find her, and now I'm supposed to do nothing?" I threw up my tingling hands, sparks flying. "Unbelievable!"

He reached over with a giant paw and batted me back a few feet. Stumbling, I landed on my backside. A blazing fireball the size of a cantaloupe landed with a dull *thump* where I'd been standing. It fizzled out, a quick death in the dirt.

"A Firebrand must be able to control her talent. You would be signing your death certificate."

Stunned, I eyed the charred circle. "I, uh, thanks."

"It was nothing. You will learn."

"What if I don't want to be a Firebrand?"

"Why would you wish to be anything else? It is an impressive talent with promises of power."

"Forget power. I want my mom." Crossing my legs, I picked at the hem of my pants. "This is hopeless. My mother's missing, my dad's injured, my grandmother's gone, the king's dead, and Erhardt wants to throw me back in the portal. If it wasn't for my mom, I wouldn't even be here."

"But you are here. There is a purpose for all things."

I nodded without enthusiasm. Knowing that didn't make reality any better. "Have you heard about the First Prophecy?"

"Yes, one will come and help Linneah in a time of chaos. Some think it will be a Warrior talent. I would not worry, Raven. There is no chaos here."

"What did you call me?"

He blinked once. "Raven. That is what Brenna means."

The Raven's share can save the land. How did one avoid fulfilling a prophecy? "I'd better head back."

He didn't respond. His feline eyes focused on the horizon, his muzzle up.

"What?"

"The air smells...evil. Something is coming."

Before I could answer, the ground shifted with a jittery shake. I clutched Arvandus's fur while a low rumbling like a train filled my ears. Loud cracks split the air. Giant trees near the edge of the field toppled.

He knelt. "Climb on. Now." He turned his head and released a roar that left my ears ringing.

I didn't need another invitation. The griffin took flight, climbing higher, the breeze cool on my face.

Below, the destruction occurred in slow motion. Trees fell over with a maelstrom of leaves. Shaken from their moorings, houses split open or collapsed. One side of the city wall fell in, the large stones crumbling like dry cookies. A large swath of farmland cracked, the gaping holes yawning in the landscape.

Our flight path followed the coastline of Linneah. Boats moored in the harbor bobbed in the choppy water. Near the rocky cliffs, chunks of rock fell and plunged into the roiling sea. The tides pulled away from the coast, leaving a few fishing ships beached on the ocean bottom. I leaned forward and yelled over the wind. "We have to get the fishermen out."

"Why?"

"The waves will be back, higher than before, and people will be killed. We don't have long."

Arvandus banked and flew to a few griffins nearby. He roared, the message sending the creatures to the doomed fishing boats.

"We need to warn those on land, too. They have to head for higher ground."

He roared again, bringing other griffins to his side. Communicating with a deafening mix of growls, roars, and shrieks, the immense creatures split into several groups. One group flew toward the castle, and the rest set out for the more populated areas of the city. Arvandus increased his speed, flying toward the castle, until my eyes watered from the whipping wind. When he landed, I slipped off his shoulders and raced for the carved doors. The main structure hadn't crumbled, but the wide windows in the dining room facing the sea had shattered. I ran into the main hallway, dodging the cracked statue in the entryway and the broken paintings on the floor.

"Rosamunde, Baldwin! Murray! Anyone?" My yells brought a crowd of people to the hall. Some sobbed while others stood, eyes wide in shock. "We need to get to higher ground. The sea has pulled out. It'll return with bigger waves, much bigger. People will die. We need to move." I took a much-needed breath.

A voice cut through the crowd like an ax. "We will not follow this child anywhere. She knows nothing."

Erhardt. My heart sank. "I'm not making this up. I'd invite you to check the ocean for yourself, but there's no time. We may have ten minutes or twenty, but we have to go."

"Minutes?" His brow furrowed.

What a time to suffer a language barrier. "We need to get going. Griffins are waiting to help." The shrieks and snarls outside became louder, penetrating the thick castle walls. "Erhardt, come on. Everyone here will die."

"Will you kill them with your foreign spells?"

"No, I—"

"She knows of what she speaks. We must move." Mariel stood in the middle of the crowd, her thin frame supported by Baldwin. They had the same green eyes and firm jaw. "Lead the people to the cliffs. It is the highest and closest spot. Those of you with griffins, ride them." She stopped, her edict given.

After a slight hesitation, Erhardt herded the group in the hallway toward the front entrance of the castle. "Everyone, follow me."

Rosamunde appeared next to me, directing another crowd of people outside.

Were there enough griffins? "How many people can ride a griffin?"

"Three, if the griffin is big." She held out her hand to assist an elderly man shuffling toward the exit.

Baldwin called over the clamor of voices. "Double and triple up on the griffins if you have to."

"I am going to help evacuate the castle." She took off at a jog, disappearing down the hallway.

He walked over to me. "Is Lev outside? He can carry me and my mom."

"Yeah, go ahead. I have to get my dad." Turning, I hurried toward the stairs.

Baldwin caught up with me on the second floor. "My mom will be okay with Erhardt. Renke will need help with the patients."

When we arrived at the infirmary, two patients needed to be moved. My dad insisted on walking out under his own power. Renke scurried about the room, throwing supplies into a bag while Dirk prepared to transfer the other patient to a litter. Baldwin and I helped Dad down the stairs while Renke and Dirk carried the last man out on a stretcher. Our quick footsteps echoed in the wide stone hallways. Under my breath, I muttered prayers for more time.

When we reached the clearing, Lev and Arvandus remained. Renke and Dirk maneuvered the other patient onto Lev's back. I turned to Arvandus. "Can you handle three riders?"

"Where are we headed?"

"The cliffs."

"Yes, it is a short flight."

After Dad and I climbed on, I motioned to Dirk. "We have room for one more."

He sauntered over, his stride easy. "I do not see why we have to hurry. The tide is still out."

"It's not a tide. It's a wave due to the earthquake." I grabbed his hand and pulled him up, my stomach jittery with nerves. "And it'll be bigger than anything you've ever seen." The thunder of rushing water filled my ears. I looked up. "Like that!"

A flood of muddy water breached the low wall and poured into the clearing.

CHAPTER EIGHT

I clutched Arvandus's fur. "Go, go, go!"

The griffin unfurled his wings and rose into the air with a growl, his muscles straining and silver sparks flickering from his wingtips. The water's angry foam licked at his underbelly. Dirk leaned over the side, fascinated by all the water pouring into the clearing.

"Dude, knock it off." I yanked on his sleeve. "You're going to get hurt."

He sat up. "This is amazing. How did you do it?"

"Do what?"

"All you Weatherbrands are the same. What spell did you use? Regular talent would not create this kind of force."

"I didn't do this." With a sickening *snap*, a majestic tree fell and disappeared under the turbulent flood. The continuous incoming wave inundated the landscape, then tumbled into a fissure on the eastern side of the castle.

"Arvandus, what's that gap on the other side of the castle?"

"A new river, created by the tremor."

The water hadn't yet reached the populated area behind the castle, but there'd be a death toll. I prayed for a low body count.

Dirk tapped my shoulder. "Erhardt says you know powerful magic not seen here in many times."

I was *so* not up for this right now. "He's an idiot. I'm not responsible for this."

"You can tell me. We can work together."

Leaving the flood waters behind, we flew toward the clearing on the cliffs. I twisted around and spoke clearly so he didn't miss any big words. "I. Did. Not. Do. This. Got that?"

He raised his eyebrows.

"I'm a Firebrand, okay?" I turned back around. This conversation was over.

He remained quiet until we landed. After he slid off, he helped my dad down, then turned to me. "Let me know if you change your mind. A Weatherbrand is a powerful talent, and I can help you manage yours. After all, we do not want another disaster."

I glared at his retreating back. "Aagh!" Throwing up my hands, a puff of smoke escaped. A quick check to the sky revealed no surprise fireball.

"Relax," Arvandus said. "He is a fool with a fool's knowledge. But he is correct about the cause. The tremor and the wave were not natural events. I smelled the air. Those spells were evil born." He stalked away to share the information with Erhardt.

After I made Dad comfortable near some rocks, Baldwin arrived with Mariel. He made introductions, settled Mariel next to my dad, then turned to me. "Everyone is talking about you."

Great. "Why am I not surprised?"

"You and the griffins saved most of the castle employees." His eyes darkened, changing to the color of a mysterious forest. "But I have not seen Rosamunde or Murray."

"They'd be safe in the castle, I think. Most of the water swept around the castle and fell into the river on the other side."

"But Linneah does not have a river."

"You do now." My dad and Mariel's conversation carried above the crowd's noise. They were talking like old friends. "I didn't know you and Mariel were related."

"She is my mother. Have you met her?"

"Yesterday. She said something about a Firebrand and doing my work, whatever that means."

"She is not crazy," Baldwin said, lifting his chin.

"No, I don't think she is. I just didn't get what she was saying." An indecipherable look crossed Baldwin's face. "What?"

"You are a Firebrand?"

"Yeah. So?"

"My mother gave the First Prophecy of Linneah. She believed it referred to a Firebrand."

I smirked. "It was given 'many, many times ago.' Or so I heard. How old is your mom?"

"She will be two hundred fifty times in two seasons."

I started to laugh, but he held up a hand. "I am not joking. How old is your dad?"

"Forty-one."

"Oh. Well, everyone is different. Including you, Brenna."

I shook my head.

"You could be the one."

I was not talking about this.

"You could bring healing to Linneah." His face brightened, his eyes glittering with excitement.

"Linneah doesn't need healing. It's fine. There hasn't been a war in ages or times or whatever you call it."

"Things are changing. This chaos is the beginning, and you are a part of it."

Amazing. He was a triple threat. Good-looking, obstinate, and annoying. "It could be anyone, Baldwin. It could be you or Erhardt."

"Some scholars feel the fulfiller is a female."

"Okay…" I resisted the urge to smack him. "It could be Rosamunde or any other female in Linneah. It's not me."

"Why not?"

"Because I just got here." I'd held the fear and desperation inside. Now, I cracked like a concrete sidewalk, buckling under too much pressure. "I don't want this. I can't be the fulfiller. I just want to find my mom."

He shook his head before I'd even finished. "Almost every phrase of the prophecy fits you. *From deep within and deep without*—you are part Linnean, yet you call another place home. *Comes One of power and of doubt*—I have not seen your power yet, but I can see you are full of doubt. *With the source of hope and fire—*"

"Stop!"

His monologue abruptly ended.

"I'm not the fulfiller of the First Prophecy. Period."

"You may not have a choice in the matter." His comment hung in the air between us.

I walked away, flexing my tingling hands. Tiny embers flickered from my fingertips.

Erhardt issued orders for returning to the castle, but I ignored him. I needed a long walk, far away from all the crazy talk about fulfillers and prophecies. There were others who could fulfill the prophecy much better than I could.

If I didn't do it, wouldn't someone else step in and save Linneah?

A good distance from the crowd, I found a quiet hollow to be alone. Tall rock walls formed a secluded nook, the rocky ground strewn with boulders. Off to the right, far in the distance, a tidal sandbar bridged Linneah to an island. The marina was empty, the boats tossed about like forgotten toys. Closing my eyes, I pulled up peaceful, happy thoughts—warm maple syrup with Belgian waffles, fresh snow on Christmas morning, my mom home after too much time away.

Not working. All my frustration and confusion welled up like a geyser. I held out my hands, tiny flames sputtering from my fingertips. A stone about the size of a basketball lay on the ground with other rocks. Power coursed through my arms and into my wrists, leaving my hands shaking. A pulsing wave of fire burst from my palms, the recoil knocking me on my butt. With a loud *snap*, the rock shattered into giant shards.

The gratifying release made me a little giddy, and I scrambled to my feet to do it again. My next target rock was bigger, about beach-ball sized. I squinted, concentrating.

Crack. A twig snapped like a gunshot.

The wall of fire blasted from my hands, going wide and exploding several rocks. A fist-sized fragment grazed my cheek with a slicing sting.

A familiar roar came from behind me. I turned. Arvandus stood like a statue, his wingtips shooting bright silver sparks. I couldn't stop staring. He was absolutely terrifying. Vibrant red caught my eye, and I tore my gaze away from the sparks. Near his wing, a large cut welled with blood. I gasped. What had I done?

"Brenna! Do be careful when others are near. Have you not learned Rule Number One during training?"

"I, um, haven't been trained. At all." I swiped at my cheek. My hand came away smeared with blood. Great.

"Saints and sinners, that stings!" His feathers flashed silver in the sunlight. "What do you mean you have not trained? Rosamunde is training you, correct?"

"Yeah, but with King Donalt's death, I think things got busy for her."

"That is not right. When you arrived, training should have begun without delay." He growled, his displeasure clear. "There is no help for that now. Come closer. Your first lesson will begin immediately."

"You can't train me."

"Why not?"

"Because Rosamunde—" I stumbled and fell to my knees.

While I braced my hands on the ground, the world spun in crazy circles. Arvandus sighed. "And the vertigo would not be occurring as well, had you been trained."

Chapter Nine

After a few minutes, the world stopped tilting. Vertigo sucked. "Sorry."

"No apology necessary. To answer your question, yes, I can train you. Rosamunde is not the only one with the ability to teach. Griffins know much, and while we do not often instruct, these are unusual circumstances. Let us see to your cheek and my wing."

"I don't have any bandages or anything."

"You do not need them. Your gift can create a healing warmth. With focus, you can heal anything."

"I can heal myself?"

"It is possible. Let us attend to my wing first."

He sat, his injured side facing me. "When you use your gift without training, you will get dizzy and drain your own energy. This first time, we will use your jasper. The pendant stores a little energy. Put the pendant between your hands. Let nothing distract you. Make the blood clot first, and then heal the skin. The muscle did not tear, which is good."

Blood from the cut near his wing oozed through his fur and dripped from his feathers, the dark stain on the ground growing larger.

"Cup your hands together, the pendant between them. Focus on creating heat between your hands. When you feel them begin to warm, place them on the injury."

"Right on the cut?"

"Yes."

"But what about germs?"

"Do not worry about cleanliness now."

Placing my hands together, a tingling began in my fingertips, back through my palms, and into my wrists.

"Be patient. Allow time for the healing to occur. You will know when the blood vessels have knit together."

My hands warmed, and I dropped the jasper. Arvandus flinched at my first touch, then remained still while I applied the lightest pressure. Everything slowed and took on a dreamlike quality. The air turned dense and sluggish, cloaking me in a heavy haze. His pulse thrummed under my fingers. With a sudden, inaudible click, the air lightened, and time began to move at a normal speed. I blinked a few times to clear mental cobwebs. "Well, that was weird."

"What did you experience?"

I explained the sensations, and he nodded. "The blood coagulated, and the vessels healed. Now concentrate on mending the skin. Keep the edges of the cut together."

Focusing on the wound, I covered it with my hands. Once more, the slowing sensations flowed over me, enveloping me in a gauzy, unhurried bubble. The skin tightened, almost writhing under my palms. When it stopped moving, time resumed its ordinary pace. I removed my hands. Under his fur, a thin line marked the place where skin met skin, like stitches placed along a seam.

"Now, place your fingers to your cheek. Just mend the skin because you are not bleeding anymore."

I hesitated, hating the cloudy slowing of time that occurred during healing. "Do I have to?"

He tilted his head. "It is a bad cut. Without the healing, you will need to see Renke for stitches."

That'd leave an ugly scar. Closing my eyes, I touched my cheek. For the third time, minutes stretched while my skin healed. I withdrew my hand when the sensations stopped.

Arvandus nodded. "Very good."

"There's a difference between healing and creating fire. I don't know what it is, but it feels different."

"You must control your gift when healing. With fire, less finesse is needed."

Pulling my hair back from my face, I sat down. "Are we done?"

"Yes, for now. You did better than I expected."

Wait, what? The meaning of his words sunk in. I straightened, frowning. "Is that why we worked on your wing first? In case I screwed up?"

His shrug spoke volumes. "I was a better choice to be your first."

"Better for who? What if I'd messed up? There you'd be, a mangled mess, and I wouldn't be able to do anything. You wouldn't be able to fly. And it would've been my fault."

"Raven, if you are uncomfortable with being wrong, you can give up now."

I bristled. "What's that supposed to mean?"

"It means you are not perfect. I think, by the grace of Elyon, you will be able to hone your talent into a powerful force. But you will make mistakes. You will have to live with them like the rest of us." He paused, flexing his wing. "But my injury feels much better. It should soon be stronger than before."

"Why stronger?"

"Forgiveness, redemption, and mercy are powerful healing forces, particularly when given by the one who caused the injury. It would be a good idea to rest now. Three healings in a short time is a lot for a beginner, although I do not think you will get dizzy.

The jasper's power helps with that, of course. You will not need it once you make your decision."

"What decision?" The endless parade of weird events never stopped. I sighed, letting weariness seep into my pores.

"As a rule, we would have this talk before you used your talent, but circumstances have dictated otherwise. The jasper contains a small amount of power for your use. It is so with each person until they have decided who they will serve."

"I have decided. I'm serving Linneah, all my power at its disposal."

"Sarcasm does not become you." His look was severe. "It is an honor to be chosen for such an important task. Perhaps it is not what you would have chosen for yourself. And I am beginning to see why."

"What if I choose not to save Linneah? What if I walk away and let someone else fulfill the First Prophecy?"

"I cannot see the future."

I raised an eyebrow and waited.

"The possibility of someone else stepping in to take your place will never happen. Each individual is important with a unique role to fill. Therefore, substitutions do not work. Parts of the prophecy, such as the promises of chaos and death, would be fulfilled. Thousands of Linneans would perish. Some scholars claim the kingdom would disappear."

"Are you sure about that?"

"I just said I was not a Visionary."

"Well, then how do you know?"

"Much study has been done on the First Prophecy. Certain assumptions can be made if one makes a foolish choice, for instance, choosing not to fulfill a prophecy meant for them."

"Easy for you to say. It's not your life."

"I would do it without reservation for the Most High King." He snorted, the sound a gunshot. "You are immature and childish, which can be forgiven due to your age. But you are also selfish to the extreme. Linneah is in jeopardy, and you are upset you were chosen. In the future, you would do well to remember it is not always about you."

Immature? Childish? I'd had enough of his lecture. I wanted to quit. But I never quit—anything—so I decided to dig for a little more information. Especially since I wasn't getting up anytime soon. "So, who is it about?"

"Sometimes it is about those who are the most in need."

"An incompetent Firebrand won't help them."

"You will learn, Raven. From what I have seen so far, you will be powerful. That power will require you to make wise choices."

"I'm not so good with that."

"Fine. Then you will be careful, too."

"I'm not so good with that, either."

"As I said, you will learn. At some point, you should choose who you will serve. Linneah is not your master. Neither is Emperor Rexson nor Prince Rune. Your master will be Elyon or the evil He fights."

"I've met Emperor Rexon. Who's Prince Rune?"

"He is the ruler of the Kasek Territory."

"It's a good bet I'll never meet him. I'm staying here."

"Your residence does not matter to Rune. He is determined to become the next ruler of the Jasper Territory, regardless of how he comes to power. The more followers and power he has, the happier he is." The low rumble in his voice carried a warning.

"What aren't you telling me?"

He stretched, paws extended and hind end up, before he sat. "Prince Rune and Emperor Rexson were once close friends. When Emperor Rexson became the ruler of the Jasper Territory, Rune searched for a way to be more powerful than his friend. He created Shadow Power, a power source in direct opposition to what

Elyon has provided. It is an addictive substance, and his followers number in the thousands."

"He's more powerful than Emperor Rexson?"

"No, Emperor Rexson's power comes from Elyon. Rune will never match it, although for him, it is a constant quest." He sighed. "Remember, your ability could make you valuable to many people."

"Why can't I be neutral?"

"By not choosing the one, you are endorsing the other. It is that way with some things."

"When I met Emperor Rexson, he asked if I would consider Linneah my home." The memory was a warm spot of sunlight.

"Rune will not do that. Any ties you feel to Linneah, he will consider a threat. He will require your loyalty to him, not to family, country, or any other god."

"That's pretty extreme."

"If you choose to serve Emperor Rexson and Elyon, it will make you a target. Rune will try to kill you."

I swallowed hard. That wasn't much of a choice.

He stood and stretched his wing again. "Very good work, Brenna. It feels a little tender." He turned to face me. "You have some time. Everyone makes their decision when they are ready. Some make it very young, some wait until their deathbed. Due to your power, it would not be wise to wait long."

"Why did you choose Emperor Rexson?"

"Because he accepted me, despite my shortcomings."

"I didn't know you had any."

His golden eyes narrowed. "Flattery, eh? No, I am not considered a true griffin, due to my feline features. While most griffins are tolerant, a few are disrespectful. My opinions matter little to the tribe leader."

"I'm sorry." Any respect I had for Riothamus disappeared.

"Do not be. Emperor Rexson looks at my heart, not my heredity." Before I could reply, he padded away, his leonine head held high.

CHAPTER TEN

AT THE CASTLE, I helped sweep up broken glass and install boards to cover shattered windows. Erhardt walked the castle and its grounds with a checklist, assessing the damage. Some of the missing came forward. Others were found among the dead. Although Rosamunde and Murray had remained safe at the castle during the disaster, several employees had been out when Arvandus and I gave the warning. They were still missing. Before lunch, I took a break at the new river's edge.

The muddy mess under the castle didn't look like the Linnean Garden I had toured with Baldwin. Ferns and ivy dripped with mud, and standing pools of dirty water littered the grounds. The quake had ruptured the earth near the castle's foundation, creating a riverfront view for the lower level. According to castle speculation, the new river's source was located much farther north. Downed trees, pieces of houses, and other unidentified objects churned and tumbled toward the ocean. I stood at the edge, transfixed by the raging waters.

"If I may have a moment?" Erhardt's voice stirred me out of my stupor.

What had I done wrong now? "Sure."

"I would like to apologize for our earlier disagreement. I have never let my personal feelings jeopardize my people. Your information saved many citizens." Erhardt's gaze drifted somewhere over my left shoulder, his cheeks flushed.

"I'm glad we saved those we could."

His eyes finally met mine. He blinked, and his face grew pale. With a single, awkward nod, he turned and left.

So weird. At least he wasn't accusing me of creating the disaster this time.

I walked to my room to wash up. While I soaped my hands, I gave my reflection a quick check. The flash of red made me look again. A scarlet hairstreak shaded the first couple of inches of my dark hair. I dried my hands and touched the vivid strands. Silky, identical to the rest of my hair. It was like Mom's hairstreak, but why now? What was different? Tucking the strands behind my right ear, I arranged my other hair to hide it. Maybe nobody would notice.

In the dining room, I settled next to Baldwin for lunch and released a sigh.

He glanced at me. "You okay?"

"Yeah, just hoping for some normalcy." I filled my plate with carmeil salad and sliced meat and cheese. Added to the flaky flatbread in the basket on the table, it would make a delicious sandwich. "Nothing has been normal since I got here."

"You have that effect." He grinned.

I stuck out my tongue at him, then took a bite of the carmeil salad.

Baldwin began to peel the pebbled blue skin off a piece of fruit. "Hey, I see you discovered your talent. When did that happen?"

Gasping in surprise, I choked.

His brow furrowed. Patting my back, he pushed my water glass toward me. "Take a drink."

Although I did, a full thirty seconds passed before I could speak without coughing. "How did you know?"

"Your hairstreak." He shrugged. "It happens all the time around here."

"So that's why it showed up." Erhardt sat one table over, so I lowered my voice. "It freaked Erhardt out. He looked at me as if I'd grown three heads."

"He thought you were an imposter."

"How does that work? I have a Linnean mother."

Rosamunde hurried into the room and rushed over to Erhardt. "It is gone." She twisted her hands in front of her.

He stood, concern etched into his features. "What is?"

"The Veil. It is not in the safe. The lock is broken. It is gone." She grasped Erhardt's arm, her knuckles white. "Gone!" Her eyes rolled back in her head, and she slipped to the floor in a dead faint.

He caught her before her head hit the hard floor. Baldwin and I slipped out of our seats and hurried to his side.

Erhardt glanced at us as he cradled her. "We should take her to Father's study. We can lay her down there."

While he carried Rosamunde, Baldwin and I opened doors and cleared his path. She stirred when he laid her on the couch in the king's study. "Erhardt, it is gone."

"Shh, Rosa. Relax." He brushed her hair back from her forehead.

"But he promised not to do this! It was not supposed to be this way."

"He who?"

She closed her eyes, tears leaking out from behind her lids. "'The Sacred Veil will disappear.' It is done." Her eyes flew open, finding me in the small room. Paralyzed by her fierce gaze, I couldn't have moved even if a giant Largamant came at me. Of course, that had already happened with a less than successful finish. "You. You are the fulfiller of the First Prophecy. Go find the Veil."

Yeah, I'd run right out and do that. "Um..."

"You must," Rosamunde insisted. "You must!"

"She is a child." Erhardt took her hand. "She is young, un-trained."

Baldwin stepped forward. "I will go with her."

I loved being talked about like I wasn't here. "I'm not going anywhere."

"If you go, I would ask to go with you. Please."

Erhardt ushered us out of the room. "Give us a moment, please."

We cleared the doorway, and I rounded on Baldwin. "What was that all about?"

"Look, Rosa said it. You are the fulfiller of the First Prophecy, whether you like it or not. That means you have to find the Veil. But you will need help with the local customs and social groups. I know a few languages, too."

"But I haven't agreed to anything!" Nobody was listening to me. "What about my dad? I can't leave him here alone."

"He is living in the castle. That hardly makes him alone."

"I wouldn't be here."

"He does not need you to be. Linneah cannot afford to send valuable men and women to accompany you on this trip. We are still rebuilding and cleaning up from the flooding."

I crossed my arms. "Why would I pick you to accompany me? After all, I have Arvandus."

His shoulders slumped, and he looked at the floor before shrugging. "Oh. I thought you would appreciate having a friend along."

"I do. I mean, I would—will." I sighed, the sound a dead weight. "Whatever. Okay, so what is the Veil?"

He brightened. I guess I'd just told him yes. "The Sacred Veil is used in the ceremony when the new ruler is crowned. Elyon gave it to the first ruler of Linneah to show approval. He continues that tradition with every ruler He chooses. If the Veil is missing or stolen, He cannot present His choice to the people. That has to happen soon. We cannot continue without a leader."

"You can't get a new ruler until you have the Veil?" I asked.

"Well, whoever has the Veil could rule Linneah. It carries immense power."

"But no one has come forward, claiming to be king."

"Whoever stole it knows he will have to fight all of Linneah for the position. We will not surrender without a battle."

"What if Erhardt took over? He seems to like telling people what to do."

Baldwin didn't respond to my snark. "No, if Linneah chose to nominate their own leader, Elyon would see we have not trusted Him to provide. That could prove disastrous. We need to get the Veil back."

"So, you have all the answers."

He shrugged. "Erhardt and Uncle Donalt often talked politics."

I peeked into the room and came face to face with Erhardt leaving. I backed up. "Sorry."

"Rosamunde is adamant. The two of you leave in two days to find the Veil." A muscle twitched in Erhardt's jaw. "I understand you are the fulfiller of the First Prophecy. But I do not like it. You are female, an untrained talent, and too young."

I bit the inside of my cheek and prayed for grace, patience, paralysis, anything to slow the anger building in my chest. "I can't do anything about my gender or my age. Arvandus has begun my training."

"He is a wise griffin. You could learn much from him, provided you do not give him trouble."

Baldwin coughed, his eyes lit with mirth. I shot him a withering look.

"Erhardt." I tried to keep my voice even. "I've been patient, giving you time to get used to me and my family. I am part Linnean. I should've been welcomed here with open arms." He began to speak, but I held up a hand, praying I wasn't digging my own grave. "I traveled through a portal I couldn't see, watched my family battle giant bugs, was nominated to fulfill a prophecy I know nothing about in a world I've never visited, and am now bonded to a griffin, which I didn't think existed. Why can't you give me a break?"

"Perhaps my welcome left something to be desired. I apologize for that. However, I will not apologize for wanting to keep the citizens of Linneah safe. My father, may he rest with Elyon, did not grasp the enormity of the problems facing Linneah. We do not have the luxury of leniency. But as I mentioned before, your warning system after the tremors was impressive. I hope you are a fast learner." He turned on his heel and left the two of us in the hallway.

Holding my tongue, I headed down the hallway with Baldwin at my side. After speaking my mind, at least Erhardt hadn't banished me to a dungeon or whatever it was they did to outspoken teens. Maybe he was waiting. *After* I fulfilled the Prophecy, *then* he would throw me in the dungeon.

"This is great." Baldwin grinned, his eyes sparkling. "We should lay out a plan and decide our first step."

"I have no idea." Panic sprouted in my chest. "None. See, this is why I shouldn't be involved in the First Prophecy. I don't even know how to plan for this trip. Why do I have to go when I don't know anything?"

His smile slipped. "First, relax. Now, think. What does the First Prophecy say?"

After finding a copy of it in the history book Grandma Helen had given me, I had it memorized. "'The Sacred Veil will disappear; search the Dark Wood, despite your fear.'"

"Silvastamen. Also called the Dark Wood."

Great. Happy, happy. The one place everyone said we shouldn't go.

"Between us, our griffins, and the First Prophecy, we can figure out a plan," he said.

"Okay. But first I need to tell my dad about the trip."

"Can I come with you? I should talk to him, too."

"Yeah, that's fine. He'll go all paternal on you." At his blank look, I said, "You know, 'Take care of my daughter,' and 'I don't want any funny stuff going on.' Stuff like that."

"Funny stuff?"

My cheeks warmed. "It's just the two of us. He won't like it." Did I have to draw this guy a picture?

"What about Lev and Arvandus?"

"True, but I think he'll want human supervision." Maybe Baldwin wasn't interested in me. No matter how cute he was, I wasn't looking for a boyfriend. The last few days had been so chaotic, I'd funneled most of my energy into other areas. Like trying to stay alive.

"After my next birthday, I will be considered an adult," he said.

"But Erhardt keeps saying you're young."

He waved away the comment. "He is behind the common opinion in Linneah. He feels I need a father figure."

"Is your dad still gone?"

He grew quiet, his face pensive. "In the Steen Mountain Range with Emperor Rexson's men. He should be home soon. The routine missions do not last long." His flippant words didn't match his tone.

I nodded, knowing from experience nothing I'd say would reduce his worry. We didn't say another word until we reached the infirmary.

In the infirmary, I found Dad dressed, packed, and his bed made. "What's up?"

"I'm healing quickly, so they're sending me to a separate room." His voice quieted. "They need every bed here."

Cots full of the injured and those close to death lined the wall. The small room smelled of desperation.

Renke handed my dad a sheet of instructions. "Directions for your healing. See me if you have not improved by next week or if the pain worsens."

"Thanks." Dad attempted to give the man a fist bump. Frowning, Renke tried to take part in the foreign gesture.

We walked to Dad's new room on the third floor. He moved slowly, his steps tired.

Matching my pace to his, I slipped my hand into the crook of his elbow. "How do you really feel?"

"Okay. I'm improving every day."

Maybe I could heal him. But what if I screwed up? Despite my lack of confidence, I had to make an attempt. "Um, can I see your injury?"

He shot a look at Baldwin, who feigned great interest in the cobblestone floor. "Renke wrapped it this morning. I'd like to keep it covered until it's a little better."

Wrong time, maybe even wrong place. The whole thing was too awkward. I changed the subject. "We've had some excitement while you've been recovering. Baldwin and I have to leave the day after tomorrow."

"What? Why?"

"The Sacred Veil of Linneah was stolen. Everyone is busy rebuilding and cleaning up. They can't spare anyone else, so we have to find and return it." I didn't mention the First Prophecy. Identifying me as the fulfiller was ludicrous, simply wishful thinking on the Linneans' part. "Baldwin's going along to help, since he knows his way around the Jasper Territory."

"The two of you by yourselves?"

Baldwin met my dad's cool eyes, not an easy task. I had to give him credit for bravery. Or maybe he was just stupid. "Lord James, I will protect Brenna and keep her safe. You have my word."

"Who will protect her from you?"

"Uh—" Baldwin flushed and glanced at me.

"Dad, it's not like that. Our griffins are going, too."

"It's not enough. I trust you, Brenna, but I can't lose you, too." His voice hardened. "It's not safe. Let me talk to Rosamunde about this. Where is she?"

That meeting wouldn't go over well. "You can talk to her. But Erhardt already did, and Rosamunde didn't budge."

"Can you pick another person to accompany you on your trip? Someone else to go with both of you?"

Baldwin brightened as if someone had handed him a get-out-of-jail-free card. "Yes! Anyone you think is appropriate, Lord James."

"Why don't you ask Murray if he could spare the time for this?"

"I will do that now." He turned to leave.

"Meet me at the griffins' field when you're done," I called.

Baldwin raised a hand to indicate he heard me.

Dad's bedroom was close to mine, a few doors down and like all the others. A simple bed, a wooden chair and desk, and a small bathroom nook. "I won't be here that long," he said. "I have to get back."

"Why?"

"The university expects me, Brenna. I have to teach classes on Tuesday."

I sighed. "Then why do you care what I do? You're leaving anyway."

"Not fair, kiddo. You have good people who care about you here. Rosamunde is your trainer, Arvandus is a great griffin, and you've made friends. Look at it like summer camp."

At summer camp, the most dangerous thing was poison ivy.

Before I left Dad's room, I gave him a hug, positioning my hands over his wound. I didn't experience time slowing, but when he pulled away, he shook his head. "I must be tired. My back's tingling. I think I'll take a nap."

As I walked down the stairs to the ground floor, a collection of voices drifted up the stairwell. Two men in long traveling cloaks stood in the hallway, talking with Erhardt and Rosamunde. The tan material flapped with their hand gestures. Was that suede? How could I get an awesome-looking cloak like that? But I was in no mood for conversation, so I intended to dash past with a quick wave. Before I could move, Rosamunde spotted me.

"Brenna, come meet our new guests." She motioned me forward. "This is Hedeon, and this is Talus."

The first man, Hedeon, spared me a glance before his dark eyes slid away. Bald with small, close-set eyes, he stood broad like a linebacker for a football team with no neck and chunky arms. His cloak fit him like a tent.

The second man she introduced, Talus, was Hedeon's opposite. Tall and lean, his bright-blue eyes missed nothing. His collar-length black hair gleamed in the hallway light, his copper hair-streak shining. He gave me a big smile, his charisma almost tangible. "It is a pleasure to meet a fellow visitor. Have you come from far away?"

"Yes, but Linneah's very welcoming." I ignored Erhardt, the exception to Linneah's hospitality.

"I look forward to enjoying their kindness." He smiled again, and something about it seemed familiar. When I left for the griffin's field, his grin wedged in my mind like a pebble in my sneaker.

Chapter Eleven

I MET ARVANDUS OUTSIDE the griffin house. "Smelled me coming, huh?"

"Something like that."

"The Sacred Veil has been stolen. You and I, Baldwin and Lev, and maybe Murray are being sent to find it."

"Wait, please. I will return with Lev." Arvandus appeared moments later with Baldwin's griffin. Both of them settled in front of me. The golden Lev and the charcoal Arvandus sitting side by side were an impressive sight. Why would my dad worry with these two along?

I told them about the missing Veil and how I'd been "promoted" to go get it. "One small problem. I have no idea where it is, who took it, or anything like that. Any idea where to start?"

"According to the prophecy, our destination is Silvastamen, toward the Northern Province," Arvandus said. "Before we leave, we could send out informants among the townspeople to see if there are rumors. A theft like this will be an accomplishment. The thief may find it hard to hold his tongue."

"The Northern Province?" Too good to be true. My mom had disappeared there.

"Careful, Raven. Remember your commitments."

"What?" I tried for a look of total innocence.

"You will need to find the Veil first, your mother second. In addition, we will need to start your training. Tonight."

"We already did that."

"Not talent training, arms training. Have you ever wielded a sword, staff, or bow and arrow?"

"Uh, not much need for that in high school."

"This is different. Prince Rune and his followers will make any former adversaries seem trivial. I assume nobody wanted to kill you in high school."

Before I could answer, Baldwin arrived. "I have arranged for Murray to travel with us. He is excited and already packing."

"Good. That will make Dad happy."

"We need to stop at the smithy before the evening meal. He finished your sword this morning."

"Don't you have to order something like that in advance?"

"King Donalt ordered it the day after you arrived. The blacksmith has been working on little else since."

"Oh." Me, flinging a sword around? Bad idea. "I'll start packing for the trip." I turned to Arvandus. "And after supper, I'll meet you for weapons training."

"Come when you are finished. There is much you need to learn." Arvandus and Lev both got up and stretched. "We must hunt, so unless you have need of us..."

"No, go ahead. Get supper." I waved them on.

Baldwin and I headed back toward the castle, where the blacksmith's shop was located.

I matched my strides to his. "Since my hairstreak showed up, I've been thinking about the different talents: Visionaries, Sensitives, Warriors, Firebrands, Weatherbrands. What others are there?"

Baldwin wrinkled his brow. "There are Waterbrands, who work with water in all its forms, Wisdom Trainers, like Rosa, who teach and seek knowledge, and Builderbrands, who build and repair our city. Story Shapers create and record stories. There are many other talents, each with different abilities. It would take too long to list all of them."

"So which one are you?"

"Does it matter?" He slanted an eyebrow, his jaw clenched.

"No, not really." What had turned this conversation into a landmine? "Just, um, curious about your gift."

"I do not know." He ducked his head, his lips pressed together.

"You don't?" Strange. He was older than me.

"No, I do not, but I should, and it has been an unending source of frustration to me and everyone who knows me. I waited for an emerging talent, tried any number of jobs, and took tests. And I discovered that while I am good at many things, none of them are my talent."

"But you received a jasper."

"Yes, but that does not tell you what your gift is."

"But it means you weren't forgotten. Maybe your talent is an unusual one."

"I have already passed through my youth. No talent, unusual or typical, has emerged. I am older than you. Perhaps I have been forgotten after all." We stopped in front of the blacksmith's shop. "I would prefer not to talk of this anymore."

Heat rose in my cheeks, and I nodded.

We entered the shop, and a bell above the door jingled. A voice called above the chaos. "We are closed for the day. Nobody is here. Come back tomorrow."

The room rang with the clanging of metal on metal and the roar of the furnace. A blond-haired young man pulled a long, thin piece of metal from the furnace, its tip glowing red-hot. His muscles bulged when he swung his hammer, and sparks flew. The blast of the furnace fire burned white, bright yellow, orange-red. An assistant worked a set of bellows to make the flames burn hotter.

The intense heat irritated my eyes, making them sting and water. We moved toward the back of the well-lit shop, leaving some of the heat and noise behind us.

A handsome Camlo in his mid-twenties emerged from a storage room and strolled toward us. "I said nobody—oh, Baldwin. For you, I will be here. Nice to see you again." A grin flashed on his dark face. His gaze shifted to me, and his grin vanished, replaced by something like awe. "And you are Brenna James, the fulfiller of the First Prophecy." He fell to one knee, bowing his head.

Awkward. I gave Baldwin a pleading look.

He rolled his eyes. "Brenna, this is Adrik."

"It's nice to meet you," I said to the top of his bald head. Sheesh. "Please stand up."

The man rose to his full height, his dark eyes intent on my face. "It is an honor to prepare a sword for the Firebrand who will save Linneah."

"Linneah doesn't need saving." Maybe if I said it enough times, people would stop calling me the fulfiller. "And if it does, all Linneans will band together to save the city."

Adrik stepped back, placing a hand over his firm chest. His large biceps flexed with the move. "Ah, she is courageous, beautiful, *and* wise."

"Brenna needs her sword," Baldwin said. "Now."

"If it's ready," I added. Baldwin was being a jerk. I tried to catch his eye, but he wouldn't look at me.

"Of course." The blacksmith moved to the benches along the wall, where several wrapped bundles lay. He picked up a long parcel swathed in red velvet. Bringing it forward, he laid it on a small table and began to unwrap it. The room started to swim. Blinking a couple of times, I took shallow breaths until my surroundings steadied.

Made of a gold metal, the scabbard was etched with a beautiful floral design that shimmered in the low light. "The sheath is brass."

He pulled the sword out of the sheath with a slight ringing *swish*. "The sword is made of vladlen steel, a very rare metal."

The room tipped again, this time nausea making a guest appearance. A cold sweat broke out between my shoulder blades.

"Where did you find it?" Baldwin turned the scabbard in his hands, studying the etched design.

"Several Kells came through with twenty-five pounds to trade. I took advantage of the opportunity." He grinned. "There is no stronger metal than vladlen. It is powerful and very sharp."

Did it also make you sick? Because I was about to make a big mess on the shop floor.

In the bright lantern light, the floral-etched blade of the sword gleamed. The simple hilt was wrapped with silver-braided wire. Adrik turned and handed me the sword.

I struggled against the weight, the sword's point tipping toward the floor. Through sheer force, I hefted it and took a few practice swings. I'd never held anything more unwieldy.

Watching my struggle, the blacksmith frowned.

"Once you finish arms training," Baldwin said, "it will feel more comfortable."

"Sometimes it takes several seasons to build a relationship with your weapon." Adrik gave me an encouraging smile.

I didn't have the heart to tell him I didn't have several seasons. "This is beautiful. Thank you."

He captured one of my hands, his grip warm. "I am more than happy to lend my skills to such a beautiful woman." With a little bow, he gave me a roguish wink.

My mind went blank.

Baldwin tossed the velvet cloth to me, and the embarrassing moment ended. "Wrap the sword so we can be on our way."

"Brenna." Adrik's voice was low. "Please allow me." Taking the cloth from my hands, he swaddled the weapon in velvet, all the while explaining the basics of how to care for my sword. Finishing, he stepped close and handed me the bundle. "If there is anything else you need, anything at all, please do not hesitate to call on me. I can make time for any of your requests." His gaze was just this side of a leer.

Hmm, Adrik needed to find a hobby—one that kept him far away from me. "I don't think that'll be necessary. Thank you again. It's a beautiful sword."

Baldwin pulled me out of the shop before I had a chance to say goodbye. He released my arm and marched ahead of me on his way to the castle steps.

Okaaay. "Baldwin, wait up. I—"

He walked faster, fists clenched at his sides.

I stopped in the middle of the path. "What is with you?"

He stopped, turned, and stared over the top of my head. "I am not sure what you mean."

"You've been stomping around like a spoiled two-year-old since we left Adrik's shop."

"You acted just like a...like a girl." Baldwin's face flushed.

"Hello, I am a girl, in case you didn't notice."

"Well, Adrik did."

"I can't help that."

"You were fawning all over him. He is probably thinking what an advantage it would be for a blacksmith to be married to a Firebrand."

I snorted. "I'm not marrying Adrik."

"In two times, you will be old enough to become a wife in Linneah."

"Right. But I didn't flirt with him or anything." I headed for the steps, shifting the sword to my other hand. The thing was heavier than a brick.

"'Oh, Adrik,'" he said in a falsetto voice. "'This is so beautiful. Thank you so much.'"

I slapped his arm. "You don't think it's a gorgeous sword?"

"There have been other swords with nicer grips."

"That's not what I asked."

"Okay, it is nice." He seemed to struggle with the words.

"It is beautiful. And I thanked him. What would you like me to do? Spit on the floor of his shop?"

"No, but—"

"You were rude, so I overlooked your behavior, thanked him, and managed to ignore his flirting. Now, is there anything else you can think of that I should've handled better?"

"I guess not." He gave me a mischievous grin. "Are you sure they do not call you a Firebrand because of your temper?"

A low growl slipped from my throat. Laughing, he sprinted up the castle steps. I tried to catch up, but carrying my sword made my steps drag. By the time I arrived in the dining room, supper waited, steaming and fragrant.

Chapter Twelve

I ATE A SMALL dinner, the roasted meat and savory vegetables sticking in my throat. The nerves in my stomach over weapons training had morphed into something close to terror. My mind offered the many ways I could hurt myself—nicking an important artery, falling on my sword, or cutting off a needed body part. Each disaster would leave me bleeding to death.

I arrived at the griffins' house in a state of panic.

Arvandus paced in front of the building, muscles rippling in his flanks. "Why are you worried?"

"What makes you think I'm worried?"

"A griffin can sense the moods of his rider."

"But I was all the way up at the castle."

"You did not answer my question."

"I don't like blood."

He shook his head. "There will not be any during training. You will use one of these." He nodded at a small collection of wooden sticks with handles. "It is called a waster. Every trainee uses one." He walked to an overstuffed scarecrow. "This is your target for now. You will use your own sword and spar with real people after your training. I will set up a session for tomorrow morning."

"Tomorrow morning?" Panic was back. Big time.

"A small joke, Raven."

"Ha-ha. Not funny."

For the rest of the evening, Arvandus taught me the parts of a sword, a guard position, and a basic thrust and parry move. Many hours later, I flopped on the ground next to a big wheelbarrow tipped on its side. I threw my waster into it and rested my head on its wooden edge, exhausted. "What time is it?"

"Close to midnight."

The Petrus Rings glimmered, their light silvering his fur. Despite the dark night, the training area glowed with large plants that looked like mushrooms. "What are those?"

"Helli plants. They give off light after it gets dark. We planted these, but they are native to Linneah and grow wild in many places. The smaller ones are often used in lanterns."

"Can you eat them?"

"Not if you want to live."

"Good to know." Avoiding the handles, I leaned back in the wheelbarrow, relishing the cool breeze on my overheated skin.

"Will you be able to make it back to the castle?"

"Sure. Give me a minute." I closed my eyes.

I awoke to darkness. After a minute to two, my eyes adjusted. The wheelbarrow was gone, and I lay on the floor. A thick layer of scratchy straw poked through a thin blanket. Wood-paneled walls, ceiling, and a wide-open doorway finished the room.

"Arvandus?" When I didn't hear anything, I rolled to my side to get up. Big mistake. Every muscle screamed, my nerve endings on fire. I bit back a moan. Although my arms ached, a few careful stretches loosened my muscles.

Taking particular care, I stood and braced myself against the wooden paneling to keep from falling. Muffled snoring came from several other open doorways, and the earthy smell of wildcat wafted in the air. I shuffled to the doorway of my sleeping area, a stark fifteen-foot square filled with straw. Most of the stalls were the same size, occupied by other griffins. Between the stalls, a long corridor led to the large double doors on my left. A broad staircase connected to the second floor of compartments on my right. The center of the massive building showcased an atrium, the high ceiling created of glass and silver girders. Snatching my sword from the floor, I wobbled and fell. My arms throbbed, a reminder of my demanding exercise earlier. I pulled myself up again and limped for the open door. Outside, a crescent moon lit the landscape with a hoary gleam. A soft breeze blew, threaded with the scent of the sea.

"Hello, Princess."

The darkness, Arvandus's training, and fear pooled together. I spun around, my sword drawn. It's a miracle I didn't stab myself.

The guest I'd met earlier—Talus, was it?—froze, my sword point wavering inches from his throat. A flicker of something glittered in his eyes before he gave me an easy smile and raised a dark eyebrow. "Playing soldier?"

"Uh, no. Sorry." I lowered my sword, fumbling to slide it back into its sheath.

"You do not strike me as the warrior type."

"I'm not."

"And yet there you stand, witlessly waving a sword."

"We can't be good at everything. And why are you walking around in the middle of the night anyway? Looking for someone to irritate?"

He laughed, giving a casual shrug. "Sorry, Princess."

"Do *not* call me that."

He held up both hands, his handsome face full of mock innocence. "Sorry. Perhaps we should start over." He placed a hand on his chest. "I am Talus Trennen, traveler of the provinces. It is a pleasure to meet you, Brenna James."

"Yeah. Whatever. Why are you out in the middle of the night?"

"I could not sleep. A walk clears my head." He spoke in the precise formal speech favored by most Linneans.

"You may be a traveler, but you speak like a Linnean." And looked like one, too, although his copper hairstreak had disappeared in the moonlight.

"Yes, my parents were Linnean. But because of my travels, I am fluent in many languages. Something that might be helpful during your trip to the Northern Province."

How'd he know about that? Only a few people had been told. He began walking toward the cliffs. I fell into step next to him. "We don't know where we're headed yet."

"You are an incompetent liar. I overheard Murray talking with Erhardt. Do not worry—your little secret is safe with me. Did you know there are several dozen dialects in the Northern Province alone?"

The roar of the sea filled my ears as we drew closer to the cliffs. "I don't have time to learn them all."

"No, you misunderstand me. I am offering my services. I could help you and your group. The Northern Province is a dangerous place."

"So I keep hearing."

"Who do you have in your little band?" Without waiting for an answer, he ticked off the individuals on his fingers. "A geriatric faun, a youth impatient to prove himself, a reluctant heroine, and two small griffins."

"Try again," I said. "How about a wise Visionary, a bold and loyal young man, and two impressive protectors?"

"And what of yourself?"

"I'm here because Rosamunde insisted."

"Now *you* are wrong." His eyes shone black in the shadowed hollows of his face. "You are the most important individual of this group. A Firebrand—one of the most powerful talents joining the expedition. But I believe you are being wasted here."

Go away. "Thank you, O Wise One. Do you have a point?"

"Listen, Brenna." He stopped and gripped my arm with a firm hand. "Your group will need assistance in the Northern Province. I am offering to help with the languages and the dangerous terrain. Since I am Linnean, I have a stake in this, too. And after the expedition is over, my leader would be interested in meeting you to discuss other opportunities."

"I've already met Emperor Rexson."

"No, I was speaking of Prince Rune."

Rune? Sweat broke out under my arms, and my heart surged to my throat. I fought to keep my voice level. "Interesting. I've been told he wants to kill me."

"That is unlike him. He is a wise leader, bound for kingship one day. He would be interested in meeting someone with your talent."

I opened my mouth but was saved from answering.

"I am sure he would." Arvandus materialized from the shadows. "Prince Rune loves to use and abuse whatever talents are available to further his own cause."

Talus stiffened. "He encourages gifted individuals to grow and learn great things."

"But they must never question. Rune kills for that crime."

"Loyalty is an important virtue."

Arvandus growled a warning. "Yes, something he would know nothing about since he betrayed the one who loved him like a brother."

Talus sneered, his lip curling. "Emperor Rexson expected blind obedience to a small god. He dissuaded Prince Rune from learning and exploring. And when he became more powerful, Rexson feared his old friend's new power."

"Emperor Rexson is not afraid of Shadow Power, no matter what unspeakable things are done."

"Power is power, Arvandus. Prince Rune has the followers to prove it. Does Emperor Rexson?"

"Yes, faithful ones. He does not follow his own path, but the path of Elyon. He cares for each of his followers, regardless of their talent, and extends mercy to those who ask it. Emperor Rexson has never killed followers who failed, nor tortured enemies until they went mad."

"The tales are nothing but legends and folklore."

Suspicion snaked through me, and goosebumps broke out on my arms as their rapid-fire discussion swirled in my head.

Arvandus advanced on Talus until he stood mere inches from him. "My father was tortured by Prince Rune," he growled. "He went insane and was never heard from again. That is the truth, not a legend. Because of it, I will never serve Prince Rune."

"And that will be your undoing. Whoever chooses not to support him will be in an unfavorable position." He turned to me. "These stories are gross exaggerations. You are young with so many choices and decisions in front of you. As a show of good faith, Prince Rune wants to help you with your biggest obstacle. You will owe him nothing in return."

A tiny flicker of doubt sprang to life within me. Maybe I was overreacting... If Prince Rune was such a bad guy, why would he offer to help me?

Arvandus snorted. "Empty promises."

"Brenna," Talus said. "What do you want more than anything?"

"To find my mom." My voice squeaked, and I cleared my throat. "She's missing in the Northern Province."

"Prince Rune could dispatch soldiers at a moment's notice to help you search for her. You could be reunited by next week."

Arvandus shook his head. "No. Brenna promised to find the Veil."

"What?" I glared at Arvandus. "What difference is a few days going to make?"

"You made a commitment to find the Veil and bring it back so a ruler can be crowned. Time is of the essence."

"What a shame." Talus shook his head.

"Maybe when I get back from my trip." Hope and desperation leaked from my voice like helium from a balloon.

"Allow me to find out if that would be acceptable." Talus turned toward the castle. "I will send a letter tomorrow. But now I must go to bed. It is quite late." He disappeared into the shadows.

"Thank you," I called after him. "Thank you so much."

My elation faded when I saw Arvandus's expression. Disappointment and sadness mingled on his feline features. Hours later, while I struggled for sleep, his expression continued to haunt me.

CHAPTER THIRTEEN

THE NEXT MORNING OVER breakfast, Baldwin and Murray consulted maps of the Northern Province. Morning sun streamed through the windows, bathing the dining room with light. My crystal glass, filled with rain-fruit juice, glistened light blue. Rain fruit, seedless but sweet like a ripe peach, made a fantastic juice and was my new favorite. I nibbled on my toast and wished for a Belgian waffle. At the other end of our long table, Talus and Hedeon ate their breakfast and talked with Rosamunde and Erhardt.

"Because of my Linnean heritage, I feel it is my duty to help you in this troubled time," Talus said.

Erhardt frowned and took the last bite of his breakfast biscuit.

The lavender bruises under Rosamunde's eyes spoke of her grief. "It has been difficult. We greatly miss King Donalt."

"Do you have a need for workers? Hedeon is strong, experienced in construction."

The hulking man nodded but kept his beady eyes focused on his breakfast. Eggs and a rare steak swam in its own blood. He took a vicious bite, chewing with relish. When he noticed me staring, he gave me a menacing smile. I turned back to my toast.

Erhardt assessed each man before leaning toward Talus. "Who were your parents?"

"Linnean commoners. They both left at a young age and never lived here in the castle. I am sure you do not know them."

Pressing his lips together, Erhardt steepled his fingers. "We could use Hedeon and any other help you may offer."

"Allow me to offer my assistance to your group heading to find the Veil. Their course may take them into the Northern Province. I am fluent in many languages, including the Northern dialect of Syeira and the language of the nomadic Kells."

Tuning in to the discussion, Baldwin spoke up. "I have covered that side of the trip."

"I have traveled to the territories beyond Silvastamen. Has your travel experience taken you far beyond the castle walls?" Talus offered him an innocent smile.

Baldwin glared, a muscle ticking in his jaw.

"While we appreciate the offer, we do not want to inconvenience a guest," Rosamunde said. "Baldwin is more than capable."

Talus placed a hand over hers. "Please let me help."

Her cheeks colored. Erhardt's gaze sharpened. "It would be good to have another guide with the group. Be prepared to leave soon."

I took the last bite of my toast to hide my shock. Maybe Erhardt didn't know Talus followed Prince Rune. Maybe it didn't matter. Looking up, I opened my mouth to speak, but my eyes met Hedeon's. The big man leaned forward with a venomous look, his bloody steak knife clenched in his hand. Fear gripped my throat, and I sat back. For now, I'd keep my mouth shut but my eyes open.

We didn't leave until two weeks later.

Baldwin and Murray checked their maps, worked out safe routes, and gathered supplies, while Arvandus continued my talent training during the day. Weapons training took place in the evening, and I spent any remaining time asleep. A week earlier, Grandma Helen had returned to escort Dad through the portal. After offering tons of unwanted advice, they both promised to come back when I returned from my trip.

My last night in Linneah, I hurried toward the griffin house after supper. I needed to train often with Arvandus to strengthen my growing skills. A mild breeze blew off the ocean, blending the smells of salt and wood smoke. The sun hung low, and the Petrus Rings were mere echoes of their usual late-night display.

Baldwin, my sparring partner, waited for me with Arvandus and Lev. Hefting the small silver shield I'd picked up from the armory, I unsheathed my sword. I took a deep breath and let the dizziness wash over me. It happened every time I touched it. Not ideal, but there was no time to get something else. Arvandus and Lev stood off to the side while Baldwin and I trash talked.

"I'm going to whip your butt."

He snorted. "So do it. You fight like a girl."

"Yeah?" I grinned. "So do you." I snaked out a foot, hooking his heel. Stumbling, he regained his footing and delivered a jab.

After a five-minute match, I lost my shield when I tripped over a root. In seconds, Baldwin pointed his sword at my stomach. I huffed out a breath. "Man, I'm dead. Again!"

"Yeah." He gave me a smug smile.

"Whoopee, good for you. It'll be amazing if I come out of this trip alive."

"The possibility of you ever needing these skills is slim," Arvandus said. "It is a safeguard, a precaution. And you have been improving by great measures, Raven."

Right. Instead of a quick, violent beheading, I'd probably die a long, painful death from tripping and falling on my sword.

We cleared the training field before flying back to the castle on the griffins. Once in the air, the dusky sky took on a quiet stillness. A singular evening star appeared, the sky darkening to twilight blue. The Petrus Rings grew brighter, the gold and silvery blue bands sparkling. In the distance, the castle towers stood tall, the river rushing by the new wall being built. Linneah spread out to the left of it, a patchwork quilt of forests, tree houses, and farmland.

Below, the peaceful scene shattered, chaos erupting on the ground. People ran from house to house, their screams faint at this distance. Before I could ask Arvandus to get closer, he spoke—in my head. It was his voice, gravel purr and all. *Going in, Raven. Be prepared to use your sword.*

A huge serpent came into view, winding its way through the residences of Linneah. My breath caught. Five feet in diameter and about fifty feet long, it had a round head and bulging eyes. Its dark-gray, iridescent scales shimmered in the low light. People tried to hide or run to safety, but the monster overtook them, swallowing them whole.

Sickness coiled in my gut, quickly replaced by burning anger. This creature was going down.

Arvandus flew toward a small clearing amid the forested landscape. Leaves and broken branches littered the ground.

Baldwin drew his sword. "Go for its head and eyes, Brenna."

I nodded. My ability to hyperfocus, a symptom of ADHD, kicked in. Every distraction but the monster was pushed aside. Dropping in low, Arvandus slowed. I slid off, my ankle twisting when I landed. Ignoring the pain, I drew my sword. My limbs trembled, but I shook it off and tightened my grip. The snake-monster thing hadn't seen me yet. I sidled closer, and Arvandus sent another message. *When I distract it, move in for the kill. Do not get eaten.*

Thanks. Real helpful.

I ran toward its head, using trees for cover. Arvandus swooped toward the creature's back. Baldwin had dismounted and stayed even with me on the other side of the monster. One step closer, and it saw me. Its dead, flat eyes bulged wider. Instead of waiting for it to strike, I charged. At the same time, the griffins ripped into its back with their claws, leaving gaping wounds. The snake turned toward its injury, and I stabbed him in the throat. Pulling back, my hand slipped. The sword stuck. I came away empty handed.

Great.

When the snake turned on me, I started praying. Baldwin stabbed the creature from the other side, drawing its attention. Fisting my hands, power surged in my fingers. I turned a palm outward and unleashed a fireball at the creature's head. Above his eyes, the flames exploded in a direct hit. The rank odor of burning flesh wafted through the air. My stomach flipped. When Arvandus and Lev attacked again from above, I grabbed my sword and pulled. Nothing. I pulled again. With a final yank, the sword sprang free. The snake turned and snapped. Its yellow teeth were like a row of sharpened swords. I struck a blow under its eyes. The smell of sewage and rotting meat punched a blow to my stomach. Gagging, I backed away.

A wave of fatigue swamped me, and I stumbled. Though the creature trailed blood, he continued to attack. We couldn't stop now. Baldwin yelled from his low perch in a shield tree. The serpent turned. He thrust his sword into its eye, driving the blade in all the way before jerking it out.

I winced but couldn't look away. The creature writhed, flipped, and slithered away from us while we tried to stay close to its head. Sliding through the trees, its whipsawing tail jarred houses from their lofty foundations. Even though we ran to keep up, the snake outdistanced us. Its trail of destruction ended at the river's edge.

Bending at the waist, I nursed a stitch in my side. My sore ankle throbbed.

"Back to the river," Baldwin said, panting.

At a grassy area, I wiped off my blade while fighting my gag reflex. Disgusting. "He won't live, will he?"

"I hope not."

Limping to a nearby tree, I leaned against it to give my aching ankle a break. "Murray had it right. He predicted the ground would shift and the Great Serpent would rise from the deep. The myth came true."

He shook his head. "Unbelievable. I always thought it was an old story parents told to misbehaving children."

Arvandus and Lev landed amid the devastation of broken branches and a shattered house. The owners were gone.

Still favoring my ankle, I leaned against Arvandus. "Are you okay?"

"Fine. You did well, Raven."

"I lost my grip on my sword. That thing disarmed me."

"You are alive. You used your talent. And you retrieved your sword. Consider it a good day."

"We should go back," Baldwin said. "It is dark. I need to report what happened to Erhardt. He will want to check on the residents."

Climbing back on our griffins, we continued on. The adrenaline rush drained me, and all I wanted was my soft bed.

When we arrived back at the castle, I said goodnight to Arvandus and Baldwin and stumbled up the stairs to my room. Before I drifted off, Arvandus's new way of communicating with me invaded my sleepy thoughts. I'd have to ask him about that.

The next morning when I got up, my tight muscles complained. While I dressed, I flexed my tender ankle, relieved it wasn't swollen. Then I sat on the bed and closed my eyes. After gathering the curing warmth in my hands, I pressed them to the sore area. Minutes slowed while I mended. The knock at my bedroom door shattered the hazy bubble.

"Brenna, are you up?"

"No." Rolling my eyes, I opened the door. Baldwin stood in the hallway, wearing a cloak. A bag hung across his shoulders.

"We're leaving? Now?"

He nodded. "Say your goodbyes. Meet me at the far side of the fountain. We need to leave. No more delays."

I seized my empty bag from the corner. It had been packed two weeks ago, but over time, I had used things and forgotten to put them back. I gathered my deodorant, my hairbrush, a few hair elastics, and an extra pair of underwear and threw them in my bag. Toothpaste and toothbrushes weren't used in Linneah, but they used a paste for cleaning teeth. I tossed a small jar of it into a side pocket. Jamming my feet in my Chucks, I snatched my gray cloak—totally awesome that I finally owned one of these beauties—and my bedroll and ran downstairs. No time for breakfast. I grabbed the package of food supplies from the kitchen and two pieces of fruit and nut bread. Stuffing one slice into my mouth, I hurried outside.

Dawn lightened the sky to a creamy shade of gold, and the crisp air carried the scent of fall leaves. I pulled my gray traveling cloak tighter around me. Rosamunde had given it to me, along with three money chains, in preparation for my trip. Slipping my hand into my bag, I checked for the chains tucked at the bottom. Right there. I fingered one of the pretty filigree coins hanging from the chain before letting it drop again. I wouldn't find a mall anywhere in the Jasper Territory, but carrying a little Linnean cash was a good idea. Rosamunde, Erhardt, and the rest of our group loaded the griffins while children from the castle played tag in the clearing. Their families stood in groups, talking among themselves.

I placed the last item, my bedroll, on Arvandus and turned to Baldwin. "Kind of early for the little kids, isn't it?"

"They are seeing the fulfillment of the First Prophecy. The Sacred Veil represents Linneah and our future."

So this trip symbolized future success for the residents of Linneah. Great. Nothing like big expectations to lower stress. While they were thinking about the future of the city and the fulfillment of the First Prophecy, my goal was to come back alive, hopefully with the Veil.

"Brenna," Arvandus said, "meet Reina." He nodded to another griffin, a powerful tan creature with the head of an eagle and the hindquarters of a lion. "She will be carrying Talus and Murray."

Reina nodded back, her golden eyes piercing. I looked away, uneasy with the griffin's ability to see below the surface.

Baldwin put his final bag on Lev. "Because Reina has two passengers, we will have to divide their bags between us. You packed light?"

"I did the best I could."

"What about the money Rosamunde gave you?"

"It's packed."

"And the food?" He plucked the last bite of bread from my fingers and popped it into his mouth.

"Hey!" I glared at him. "Packed. You're worse than my dad. I'm not stupid."

"We will be unable to turn around if you forget something."

Grumbling under my breath, I walked toward Arvandus. His insistent orders pounded through my head. *Climb on. We have to fly. Time is short—*

No lectures, thanks. I threw up a mental wall to cut off his nagging. After hugging Rosamunde, I waved goodbye to everyone gathered. With a brave smile, I climbed on Arvandus, who glared at me.

"Okay, now we can fly," I said in his ear.

Do not do that again.

Grinning, I blew a raspberry.

Rising in the air, Arvandus replied with a threatening growl. A few silver sparks flickered from his wingtips. The little kids waved and yelled as if we were pilots going to war.

Once we were in the air and everyone had settled in a rhythm, I patted Arvandus's neck. "Okay, big guy. What's going on?"

"Our informants from Linneah found no clues, so we will fly along the Galt Cliffs and land in West Linneah. Two from our group will head into town to gain information. A lead or two should surface."

"That's not what I meant. What's with the your-thoughts-in-my-head thing?"

Ah, you mean this. It is part of the vinculus, the bond we have. Over time, it will get deeper. Sharing our thoughts is one way we can do this.

"Don't you think you should've asked first?" I shifted in my seat. "It's invasive."

"It is a shared ability. Send me a message."

Closing my eyes, I took a moment to focus. *You know, this whole thing weirds me out.*

Very good, Raven. But please, do not block me. It is rude.

"So is nagging. I wanted to say goodbye. Who knows when we'll see everyone again?"

"This trip is not supposed to take long, maybe a week at most. After all, we have to have the Veil by the Shaverim Festival."

"We have a deadline?" I glared at the back of his head. "When do we have to be back?"

"Two weeks."

"Two weeks? Why didn't anyone tell me? And why didn't we leave two weeks ago?"

"This is not a trip to take lightly. It required planning."

"But a deadline of two weeks doesn't give us much time. If I'd known—"

"Will you try harder to find the Veil?"

"Well, no, but—"

"Then there was no point."

Out of all the griffins in Linneah, I got this one. "What is the Shaverim Festival?"

"It is an annual celebration. Linneah invites rulers and citizens from other cities in the Territory to share the blessings of the time. For three days, the town offers tournaments, games, music, and storytelling. On the first day, a feast is held on the castle grounds. This time is more important, due to the death of King Donalt. We will crown the new king or queen the first night of the festival."

"Why?"

"Linneah appears weak without a ruler. Unrest brews in the other territories, and rumors of a takeover are rampant."

"In Linneah? I thought it was peaceful." I buried my fingers in his warm fur.

"Things have changed."

"Do we have to use the Veil? Couldn't we crown the ruler Elyon provides, but without the Veil?"

"It is not possible. The Veil is a crucial part of the ceremony. We should not try to modify tradition, although it may seem easier. If there is no Veil, there is no ruler and no blessing."

We didn't talk again until we landed in a field not far from the main road through the small town. A short stroll dropped us into a hollow, offering some protection. Off to one side stretched a broad meadow. The woods behind us hid the view of the Linnean harbor. We could make camp here if it became necessary.

The sun hadn't brightened the day. Low-hanging clouds cluttered the gloomy sky, showing off their distended gray bellies. I pulled my cloak tighter around my body. Baldwin opened his mouth to say something when Talus spoke.

"It is a mere mile or two into town. Who will join me?"

Baldwin's eyes darkened. "I was not planning to send you."

He sneered. "The little boy wants to be in charge. Who is the leader of this expedition?"

Murray held up his hands in surrender, claiming no ownership, while Baldwin and Talus glared at each other.

Speak up, Brenna. You must take charge. There is no one better to lead them.

Shaking my head, I burrowed deeper into my cloak.

Raven.

This time, my mental wall wasn't strong enough. Though muffled, Arvandus's persistent voice pushed through. *You are the most logical choice. Talus is not trustworthy and will not accept Baldwin's leadership. You must take the responsibility. Please.*

But I don't know where we're going!

You know more than you think.

"Who do you think you are, little boy, to challenge me?" Talus clenched his hands into fists.

"You are a guest on this trip," Baldwin shot back.

"Guest? I am Linnean, fluent in languages, knowledgeable about the terrain. You are disposable."

Raven, now.

The tension in the air and Arvandus's badgering undid me. "That's enough! I'm making an executive decision."

Both of them gave me a blank stare.

"I'm the boss for right now. What I say goes. And I say Baldwin and I are going into town. Murray and Talus, you stay here with the griffins. We'll be back before lunch."

With a glare, Talus stepped forward, but I held up a hand. "Please don't ask me who I think I am. I'm Brenna the Firebrand, fulfiller of the First Prophecy." I drew a deep breath, praying for oxygen mixed with courage. "For better or for worse."

Chapter Fourteen

WE WERE QUIET DURING our walk into town. Hiking across the meadow and over a rocky outcropping, we skidded down a small hill to a dirt path that cut through the forested land. The well-worn track held few people at this time of day. Baldwin remained sullen and pouting, but I wasn't in the mood to make nice. If he and Talus were going to fight like toddlers for this whole trip, I'd find a new traveling buddy.

When the outer wall came into sight, Baldwin turned and pulled his hood over his head. "Keep your hood up while we are in West Linneah. It will give you a measure of anonymity." He handed me a card. "This is your entrance pass. Do not lose it."

I read the rolling script.

This certifies that *Brenna James*, owner and controller of this pass, is a Linnean from the Jasper Territory. Said person is permitted to come and go from all businesses and residences as needed. Said person will conduct him/herself with due responsibility and care befitting a Linnean, furthering the Kingdom and its Causes.

Signed, Rosamunde Kedar.

In the corner next to her signature gleamed a silver holographic seal in the shape of an eight-pointed star.

Baldwin had walked ahead, and I hurried to catch up. "Hey, are we okay?"

"Of course."

Which meant no.

When I tugged his sleeve, he gave me an annoyed glare. "Baldwin, someone had to step in back there, or you and Talus would've killed each other."

"I would relish the job."

"Not yet. We have to get along with him for the next week or so until we find the Veil. So, since you guys hate each other, I'll make the decisions."

"But you do not know anything!"

Hurt bloomed in my chest, even though he was right. "Wow. Thanks. Why don't you tell me how you really feel?"

"I mean, I am capable of handling this mission."

"Not with Talus, you're not. He won't let you. But I have the First Prophecy behind me which gives me a certain bit of leverage." I sighed. "We have a problem. You want to lead, but Talus will fight you. I don't know enough to lead, but he won't challenge me. If we work *together*, we can get through this alive, get the Veil, and get out."

Baldwin crossed his arms. "I am not working with him."

"Then work with me."

He didn't say anything.

I rolled my eyes. "Look, you have to. Or at least pretend to."

He set his chin at a stubborn angle. "We need to keep moving. Follow me."

He led the way, stomping up to the gate with all the grace of a tank. A tall, bony man with a thin face and even thinner brown hair sat near the gate. His wispy purple hairstreak dangled near his cheekbone. Sitting slumped in the small booth, he propped up his head with one hand. "Entrance pass?"

Pressing the seal with his index finger, Baldwin then handed him the card. "Baldwin Marek," came the recorded voice of Rosamunde.

"Clear." The gatekeeper waved him through.

The same thing happened with me. I pressed the seal, Rosa's voice pricked the air, announcing "Brenna James," and the gatekeeper motioned me through. After clearing the gate, I joined Baldwin. "How did she do that?"

"Rosamunde is a Wisdom Trainer. Although she is a teacher, she also continues to learn new ways of doing things. During one of her trips, she learned this practice. Now she uses it for the business district passes. It is difficult to forge."

The main road bustled with activity. Vendors called to shoppers, their voices adding to the commotion. People led wagons filled with various goods down the road. A woman with a stall on the side of the road sold candles, soap, and fresh eggs, while another stall held fishing nets, crab traps, reels, sinkers, and hooks. We passed another booth, and the heady fragrance of fresh flowers wafted out. On the corner, farmers' market booths filled the air with the scent of fish, spices, freshly baked bread, and roasted chicken. I stopped in front of a booth selling a dark, savory meat roasted on a skewer. It sizzled as the man pulled it off his makeshift grill. My stomach gurgled, reminding me of the light breakfast I'd eaten hours ago.

Baldwin nudged me. "Quit staring."

"Sorry. I can't help it."

"Try to blend in."

Uh-oh. "Baldwin, look at my shoes."

"Where are your boots?"

"I don't have any. All I've got is my sneakers."

"You have to get rid of them."

"No way! These are new Chucks. I saved my allowance for a month to get them."

"You look like a foreigner. Nobody will tell you anything. So you will have to buy something else. Take off your shoes." He motioned to a tent with a red-and-white-striped top. "We can stop here."

He led me around to the back of a tent so I could pull off my sneakers and stow them in my bag. Then we walked to the front of the stall where row upon row of boots and shoes stood.

"I like these." I pointed to a leather pair of boots with the scrolling Linnean embroidery on the shaft.

"You would. They are the most expensive pair here."

Sensing a paying customer, the seller approached us. A short man with a receding hairline, his dark little mustache wiggled when he talked. "These are hand-embroidered in Linneah. The best boots for your money." He gestured to the black pair I'd been eyeing.

"How much?"

"Five money chains."

"Thank you, no. I do not have enough money," I said in a formal tone. Dork central, right here.

"Ah, then perhaps this pair would fit your needs." He held up a pair of brown boots that strapped together with a dozen buckles. "Four money chains."

Cool, but I didn't want to jangle when I walked. And they were too much. I shook my head.

He scanned his goods for another pair to interest me, his gaze sweeping the tent before it stalled on my stocking feet. "Where are your shoes?"

"Um. They were stolen. In the night. While I slept." I slammed my mouth shut to keep from blurting out any more stupid comments.

"You will need to be fitted. I can have them ready next week."

I didn't have time to wait. "I will take whatever you have that fits me."

He looked at my feet. "They are very big."

Baldwin choked, a cough covering his laugh.

Turning, the man found a pair of plain brown boots and held them up. "One money chain. An amazing value."

A strap of leather at the top circled the shaft and knotted on the side. I loved them. But was it a good deal? I glanced at Baldwin, unsure. He nodded once. Guess that meant yes. Or hurry up. Or something. Whatever.

While I tried them on, the little man furrowed his brow. "I have heard many reports of stealing. Everywhere," he insisted, his arms flapping to encompass a vast area. He knocked over a pair of boots but didn't even pause. "These thieves," he said, the words a curse, "take anything that is not locked up. Nothing is sacred. Nothing!"

"Have they stolen from you?" Baldwin picked up the boots and put them back on the shelf.

"No. These men are not interested in a pair of simple boots. They want things that will give them power. After altering the object, they then pervert that power to serve their own purposes."

"What have they taken?" I flexed my feet, wiggling my toes in my new boots.

"Uh, I have heard stories. From others who have not fared well." He turned away, avoiding my eyes. "The stories are no doubt exaggerated. Would you be interested in a pair of gray silk boots, too?"

Shaking my head, I paid for the brown boots. Well, I'd messed that one up. Hopefully the next merchant would be more talkative.

We strolled back out to the main road. Baldwin pulled me close, the heat from his hand stealing through my tunic sleeve. "Stories of stealing powerful things? For example, a veil?"

"Yeah, the sellers would know. Theft is bad for their businesses. They'll hear stories in the local taverns and share it with their friends. Help me buy a shirt, too."

"Brenna, I am not going shopping with you."

"Today you are. Follow me on this. If it's a dead end, we've lost nothing." He followed me to a tent selling exquisitely embroidered clothes in vivid jewel tones. We walked among the colorful choices hanging on the tent walls and folded on a small table. The seller, an elderly woman with gray hair and a pale-blue hairstreak, gave me a friendly smile.

I smiled back. "These are beautiful. Have you made them all?"

"Yes, it keeps my hands busy and food on my table. Elyon has blessed me and my family."

A beautiful scarlet dress stopped me in my tracks. Silver thread stitched into flourishes glittered against the crimson cloth. The full skirt glimmered with more silver scrollwork, while crocheted silver lace peeked from the scooped neck. Absolutely beautiful, but I had no place to wear it. Still, it was too gorgeous to pass up. After checking the price, I released a silent sigh of relief. It'd cost me one more money chain, and I'd have an extra left. If we got information with it, it'd be a bargain.

I turned to the woman. "I love this one." I pulled the dress from the display. "Do you do special orders? For example, if someone had a piece of cloth they wanted made into a piece of clothing?"

"What kind of cloth?"

"It is a fine knit. A powerful, sacred object."

"I do not work on sacred objects. I told the other woman that this morning."

"Someone else wanted you to do that? You must be doing well to turn work away."

"I try not to. Most of my customers are fine people. This woman's request carried too much secrecy, too much"—she paused, searching for the right word—"darkness. After close to one hundred and fifty times on this planet, I have learned to trust my instincts. I am not a Sensitive, but this woman gave me a bad feeling."

"Did she say what she wanted?"

"She claimed a friend had something sacred he wanted made into a tunic." She shook her head, her eyes unfocused while she thought. "I cannot imagine what that might be, but it is wrong to alter sacred objects. Bad things happen. I told her I was very busy, and it would take a long time. That was not what she wanted to hear. So she left."

"Do you know her name or where we might find her?" Baldwin leaned forward.

Her eyes narrowed. "Why would two respectable young people be interested in someone like that?"

"We are interested in righting a wrong, recovering a stolen object. We will find it, with Elyon's help."

She raised her eyebrows. "Young man, you are going to need it."

He said nothing, waiting her out.

"I do not know her name. She mentioned heading deep into the Northern Province, toward Silvastamen and beyond to the new lake that formed there since the big wave." She sat back, her features shuttered.

I gave her a thankful smile. "This is beautiful. I cannot wait to wear it."

"Perhaps, young man," she said in an undertone to Baldwin. "You need to give this charming young lady a reason to dress up."

He flushed. "Yes, my lady."

After I paid and she wrapped my purchase, we headed to the main road again. Feeling pretty good about what just happened, I punched Baldwin's arm. "Woohoo. Good stuff, huh?"

"Keep your voice down." He hustled me past different vendors' booths and into a deserted alley.

"Sorry. What now?"

"I am not sure. We might find out the customer's name in that tavern"—he nodded toward a nondescript building—"but I do not think you should go in there."

"Why not? I can handle it." I gave it a once-over. Looked harmless to me.

"It is not a place for a girl."

"You could say I'm your sister."

"The owner knows me."

"Oh. How about a distant cousin?"

Our eyes met. His green eyes held gold flecks, stars on a backdrop of emerald. Smiling a private smile, he shook his head. "That would never work."

My breath caught in my throat. I looked away and focused on a hangnail on my thumb. "Then what do we do next?"

"Go back. Maybe Murray or I could return and visit the tavern later tonight. That means we will have to camp here." He frowned. "We need to get going."

"Tell Lev."

"What?"

"Tell Lev you need him to send Murray. We'll meet him on the way. You and Murray head to the tavern, and I'll walk back to the camp. You get the information you need, hurry back to camp, and we'll leave before night sets in."

"Wow. Smart. Why did I not think of that?"

I grinned. "Thanks. Not bad for an airhead, huh?"

The gentle tug he gave my braid was almost a caress. "That is not the name I would use."

I bit my lip, unable to ignore the warm glow surrounding my heart.

We trudged back to the main road, Baldwin quiet amid all the bustling hawkers. Finally, he turned to me. "I contacted Lev. Murray is on his way."

"How will he get down that steep slope? You know, the one we slid down?"

"If you follow the road a little farther, it leads to the meadow we crossed. He can follow that path. It takes longer, but it will be safer for him."

We strolled through the market, knowing it would take Murray some time to get to us. We met him not far outside the city gate.

"You do not need to stay. I can fill him in while we walk," Baldwin said.

"Will you be all right on your way back?" Murray frowned.

"I'll be fine. It's a short walk from here."

When they disappeared through the outer city gate, I pulled in a deep breath. No big deal. I walked around Cloverdale by myself all the time.

This was just another alternity, a place I'd never been before, with dangerous thieves on the loose. I swallowed.

The lonely dirt path stretched before me.

Chapter Fifteen

ALTHOUGH THE PATH DID lead back to the meadow, it took a lot longer to get there. Maybe because I turned around every ten seconds to satisfy my paranoia. After about fifteen minutes of walking, the rocky ridge on my right leveled out to the meadow. Leaving the path, I walked through the tall grass toward the hollow where we'd set up camp. A wind sprang up, pushing some of the gray clouds away. The surrounding woods held dark-green shadows. Sunlight broke through the remaining clouds, sending shafts of light spearing through the trees.

Small clusters of blue flowers grew along the edge of the forest. The sapphire color matched my friend Tiny's eyes. She would've loved it here. At home, every walk with her became an adventure, a new discovery. Too bad she'd never see this place. Mentioning a portal or a parallel alternity would make her think I'd lost it.

A blur of movement among the evergreen leaves stopped me. What creatures hid in these woods? The snap of breaking twigs ricocheted through the forest. My hand drifted to my jasper, its presence reassuring. Rustling leaves raised goosebumps on my arms.

Something was in there.

After a few agonizing seconds, an animal with canine features cleared the underbrush. Built slender and wiry, it had long, ash-blond fur and a narrow muzzle. I couldn't identify the breed, but then this was Linneah. Maybe it wasn't a dog at all, but a vicious woodland predator.

The creature hobbled toward me, its right front leg marred by a wide gash and hanging limp. When he tried to use it, a sad whine slipped from his mouth. The animal lay down several feet away and panted with sad eyes.

"Hey, buddy." My muscles tightened with fear. Weren't injured wild animals aggressive? "You're hurt pretty bad."

His pathetic whimper melted away my fear.

"Let me go get some help for you."

The creature shot to his feet, scuttling backward.

"Okay, bad idea. Maybe I can heal it for you." I'd improved a little with my ability, but I still lacked confidence. "I'm willing to try."

The animal came back to its original position and gave me a sideways glance before sitting.

"Come here, boy." After a quick check, I rephrased my command. "Come here, girl." She crept closer, still wary, then settled in front of me. The gray eyes blazed with intelligence.

"You seem to understand what I'm saying, which is weird. Anyway, I don't know how this is going to go. Your leg might be broken, and I'll need to touch your leg to fix it. It might hurt a little." I sat on the ground, my back to a tree.

The creature growled, her little teeth a warning.

"You want to get better or not?" I held up my hands. "This is all I've got."

Pressing my hands together, the healing heat built. Clearing my mind of everything but the little animal's leg, I placed my hands on it. She jerked, then went still. I frowned, concentrating on the bone. A simple split, but deep inside, a mass with a squishy marshmallow texture had settled. An infection. Closing my eyes, the languorous dream-like fog enveloped me. Time slowed to a crawl, minutes ticking by like hours. After the fracture fused together and the wound closed, I focused on the infection, using heat to pull it from her system. When time resumed its normal pace, my vision cleared.

"Rest, okay? You can test it in a minute."

The animal refused to put the paw down until I suggested she try walking on it. In minutes, she pranced around, her tail wagging. I leaned against the tree and watched her chew on tree roots. She was cute. Too bad I was allergic.

Dusting off my pants, I stood. "Maybe you should find your owner, if you have one." I glanced up, but the creature had vanished.

"Reefstars! Can you teach me how to do that?"

Spinning toward the voice, my hand clutched the jasper at my neck. There stood a short girl with clear gray eyes the color of storm-tossed waves. Her dark-blonde curls held an ashy tint and hung in disarray. She wore a zip up floral hoodie over a cropped tank top and ripped board shorts. "Who're you?"

"You-you just healed me. Are you a mage?"

"No, I healed a dog-like thing."

She pursed her lips. "That was a beach coyote."

At my blank look, she grinned, the smile startlingly beautiful. "You're not native, are you? I'm a Merripen, a shape shifter. Thank you for healing me—you literally saved my life."

"It was just a fracture."

She gave me a side-eyed glance. "That's drift talk. You removed my infection. Without your help, I would've been tail-tied in a couple days."

Tail-tied? That sounded like a bad thing. "How'd you get injured anyway?"

"I fell climbing on the beach rocks, and I, uh, didn't want to go home."

"Why not? Your mom or dad could've stitched you up."

She shook her head. "Bad idea. Anyway, meeting you was shell fine."

"Well, glad I could help." I started to walk away.

"Salt it down." The girl held out a hand to stop my departure. "Isn't there something I can do for you, to repay you?"

"No, you don't need to. I mean, anyone would've done what I did."

"Then why, after seeing six people this morning, are you the only one who stopped?"

What is wrong with people? I frowned. "I don't know."

"Look, let me hang out with you. I'm pretty wavewise to have around. You won't even know I'm here."

I glanced toward the hollow where we'd set up camp. "I'm traveling with some people. Maybe they should decide whether they're okay with adding to our group."

She nodded enthusiastically. "Great."

As she fell into step next to me, I gave up trying to ditch her. "So, what's your name?"

"Annalise Annalice."

I turned my laugh into a cough. "Seriously?"

She grimaced. "As serious as a riptide. You can call me Anna or Annalise. What about you?"

"I'm Brenna."

"We have a dolphin named Brenna."

I stopped. "What?"

She blushed. "Sorry. Was that rude?"

"You own a pet dolphin?"

"Well, she shows up on our side of the island every year and has her calves nearby. She kinda feels like family. We even protect her when terrorists get too close."

My heart thumped once. "You have terrorists?"

She smirked. "It's what we call the tourists. You can never tell if they're going to flip the fin."

Talking to her was giving me a headache. "Flip the fin?"

"Oh, sorry. It means to do something unexpected."

Her comment reminded me of the leaf peepers that came to Vermont every fall, and I nodded as we began walking again. "I experienced that at my old home. Most were nice, but some were an accident waiting to happen."

"Where's that?"

I shook my head. "You've never heard of it. It's a place called Vermont."

"Shells and shimmer, you're from Earth?" Awe enveloped her features, and she stared at me with wide eyes and an adoring look on her face. "I'm totally addicted to television. And pop music. And french fries."

"You've been there?"

"Every time I have the chance. My last trip was four weeks ago. When my mom caught me, she banned me from using any portal for a moon. I missed so much in those twenty days." She sighed. "Which is why I can't go home like this. My mom worries, like, all the time. This trip was to prove I could be 'responsible." She air quoted the word and rolled her eyes.

Nodding in sympathy, I said nothing. Mothers were the same, no matter the alternity. We soon cleared the hill, our camp coming into view. Before I could see him, I sensed Arvandus.

You have returned. Who is that with you?

I messaged him back. *How do you know I have someone with me? She smells.*

Right. Annalise Annalice, a Merripen. I'll fill you in later. I hoped he didn't share Rosamunde's bias against Merripens.

Talus stood over the campfire, roasting meat on wooden sticks. At our approach, he looked up and gestured to the sizzling food.

"Reina caught us some lunch. Are you and your friend hungry?"
With a sideways glance, he gave Anna a leering once over. It was
kind of disgusting.

"I'm starved. Talus, this is Annalise. I met her on the way back."

He gave a low bow. Wow, a little over the top, dude.

I looked at Anna, and my eyes widened. Her smile stunned with
its brilliance, and her shiny hair curled in waves down her back.
A spotless khaki jacket draped effortlessly over a pair of killer gray
leather pants.

"It is a pleasure to meet you, Talus."

He returned her smile with a smarmy one of his own. "The
pleasure is mine. Allow me to get you some food. Please, have a
seat."

Gross.

I studied Anna while Talus scrounged in the packs for bowls.
Plopping on a nearby stump, I lowered my voice to a whisper.
"Okay, so which one is the real you?"

She hitched a shoulder but avoided my gaze. "I like to put my
best foot forward. It makes people more comfortable when they
meet someone who's pretty."

"No, I think it makes *you* more comfortable when you're pretty
and meet new people."

"What's the difference?" She accepted a plate from Talus, giving
him another dazzling smile.

Too hungry to argue, I wolfed down the mystery meat, rather
than identify it.

Talus threw another log onto the fire. "We need more firewood.
I will be back."

After he left, Anna turned to me, her expression serious. "Snap
your scales, Brenna."

"What?"

"Pay attention. He's wind slick, for sure, but I don't trust him."

"You just met him."

"Yeah, but he smells different."

"What is it with you people and smell? Everyone smells different."

She lowered her voice. "He smells like Shadow Power."

"I've heard of that. What is it again?"

She grimaced then took another bite of her lunch. "It's an addictive drug that gives power to its users. Prince Rune created it for his followers. Those who use it smell like it. It's much better to stick with your talent, whatever it might be."

Prince Rune again. Great. "What's yours?"

"I'm a Finder."

"What do you mean? Do you find lost people?" Hope sprang to life within me. Maybe she could help me find Mom.

"No, more like things or objects you need."

The hope crumbled into dust. I covered my disappointment with a wobbly smile. "Like lost car keys?"

"Oh!" She brightened. "I love cars. They're so foamed out. I wish someone in the Territory would build them." She stopped speaking, her eyes focused somewhere else.

"Anna?"

She giggled, a blush rising on her cheeks. "Sorry. I can't find missing things, just 'necessary' things. Like important stuff you might need later. I end up keeping a lot of the things I find because I never know when someone might need something."

"Where do you keep all of it?"

"In a bottomless bag strapped to my leg. I bought it off a Kell a time ago."

Arvandus strolled over, his gold eyes keen. "I am Arvandus Leon-ahren, Merripen. Who are you, and why are you here?"

He said it without malice. Coming from anyone else, it would've sounded rude.

"Annalise Annalice, from Matana Island. I owe Brenna my life. She healed my broken bone and infection."

"You are fortunate Brenna is gifted with healing. Are you joining our expedition?"

I waved away Arvandus's question. "I haven't told her anything about that. The whole group should vote on whether or not we can take on another traveler. We had to bring Reina because Talus joined. If the griffins have to carry another traveler, we'll have to rearrange bags."

"No," she said. "I can shape shift, remember?"

"So you can change shape into a griffin?"

"Well, nothing shell fine that like, but I can shift into a hawk or a Steen falcon." She grinned. "So you wouldn't need to make concessions. I love to fly."

"That helps. When the guys get back, we'll take a vote."

Her face brightened, obviously excited at the idea of traveling with us. "Okay. I'll wait."

An hour later, Baldwin and Murray returned. Baldwin slumped onto a wooden stump. "Nothing concrete. A few shared rumors about a woman traveling to the new lake. Maybe we should follow. Anything else would be chasing ghosts."

"Perhaps you should do more thorough investigating," Talus said.

Murray intervened before Baldwin could reply. "We did, but people were not talking. We stopped at the inn, the tavern, and a few of the farmers' market stands, but all we heard were rumors or stories. Our choices are limited in a town the size of West Linneah."

"Before we decide where we're going, let's vote on whether or not Anna goes with us," I said.

"Ooh, that's my cue." Anna jumped to her feet.

"You could visit the griffins." Baldwin pointed toward the rocks. "They are over there, enjoying the last rays of the sun."

She smiled her thanks and walked away.

"We should not add another person to this group," Talus said. "We do not have enough griffins or supplies."

"We've got an extra blanket for sleeping and plenty of food. And we won't need a griffin for her. She's a shape shifter," I said.

"A Merripen!" He crossed his arms. "They are unreliable. You have not known her long."

"I haven't known you very long either, yet here you are." I crossed my arms, mimicking his stance.

"It is not fair to judge someone based on their ethnicity." Murray shot Talus a disapproving look. "She has been pleasant and courteous. Therefore, I vote yes."

"I vote no," Talus said. "She is an unknown and will talk of our plans and ruin our success."

"She owes me," I said. "She's not going to stab me in the back after I healed her."

"Probably. I vote yes," Baldwin said.

"Me, too." I grinned. "That's a majority."

I walked to where Anna sat, chatting with the griffins. Judging from the bits of overheard conversation, she had won them over in a few minutes. "You're in. Why don't you go see Baldwin? He has a few supplies for you."

She shot me a beaming smile and hurried off.

After she'd strolled away, I sat next to Arvandus. "You like her?"

"She is an honest person and wants to help us, even though she does not know what our search is for."

Reina stood and walked to a dwindling patch of sunlight. With a catlike stretch, she arched her back, fanned her feathers, and lay down. Her eyes closing, her tail flicked once and was still.

I dropped my voice so I didn't disturb the griffin's nap. "Good, because she's going to be with us all the way to the new lake."

"It will take longer than just a few days."

"Do we have enough food?"

"Lev, Reina, and I can hunt for game. The Silent Season is not for four more weeks."

"And you can't get food then?"

"No. Everything goes into hibernation until the next season breaks."

"Okay, so how long will this trip take if we go all the way to the lake and all the way back?"

"I have not seen the lake, but some of the other members of the tribe saw it after the quake occurred, while they were hunting. It took Riothamus over a week to get there and back."

"That's a long trip for a meal," I said. "We've only got two weeks until the festival."

He nodded, his eyes serious.

Our conversation died there. We sat next to each other thinking and worrying. That's how Baldwin found us.

"We should camp here for the night. There is not enough daylight to head for Gibor Mountain."

"What about the deadline?"

He looked toward the horizon. "The sun will be setting soon. It is better to travel into this kind of territory in daylight. We will get an early start."

Chapter Sixteen

If I'd known what Baldwin meant by "early start," I would've protested.

When Arvandus woke me, the Petrus Rings still glowed against a dark-blue velvet curtain. *Wake up, Raven.* His unblinking stare roused me more than an alarm clock. Not a morning person, I stumbled through the motions of eating a light breakfast and packing bags. The bright bands in the sky faded under the rising sun. Baldwin consulted with Murray and Talus on the best way to our first stop, Gibor Mountain.

Anna stepped behind a large tree to transform into a Steen falcon. Standing off to the side, I finally asked. "Why?"

"Why what?"

"Why hide?"

"I can't explain it. Shape shifting without cover is like being naked in public. Very uncomfortable." She gave me a wary look. "Did you want to watch?"

"No, that's okay." I stepped away to give her more privacy.

In less than an hour, we were in the air. Baldwin, Murray, and Lev flew in the front, while Talus, Reina, and Anna brought up the rear. Looking down, the New River curled through a thick forested landscape with green shadowy crags and pockets. Gibor Mountain loomed large, its massive shadow threatening, though it lay a couple of hours away. I so wasn't in Kansas—or even Pennsylvania—anymore.

Arvandus?

Yes?

Why has nobody from Earth discovered Linneah?

It is a well-kept secret. Those who live here want to keep it secluded. The rigors of the portal were created to discourage visitors.

Was the Jasper Territory created by Elyon?

Yes. You are fortunate to have lived in the same place with His Son.

It's not the same place. Israel and Pennsylvania are never confused for each other.

He sighed with a touch of envy. *But His Son walked on your earth. Here, we read only the stories of His life.*

It's not a big deal on Earth anymore. Some people don't believe in God, His Son, or really anything.

Here, everyone believes, even if not everyone follows. Reality does not change to match one's belief. You discovered that truth with the First Prophecy.

We don't know how that's going to work out, Arvandus. His mention of the First Prophecy reminded me of a particular passage I'd puzzled over. *What does the prophecy mean when it says, "Mighty World away will pass by Destroyer's hand"?*

King Donalt's name means World Ruler or Mighty World. "Destroyer" refers to the murderer's name.

I didn't know much about names, even less about Linnean ones. If only we could've identified the Destroyer before King Donalt had been murdered.

Did King Donalt know he was going to die?

Everyone dies, Brenna. But I do not think that thought consumed him.

I sat back, a bit reassured. The scenery below blurred as my thoughts drifted.

After several hours, the griffins dropped in altitude, looking for a landing site. As we skimmed the treetops, a small meadow came into view. The bright sun blazed high in the sky, and my muscles were stiff from sitting. My stomach grumbled. I needed a break and food. The three griffins glided into the meadow. A cool breeze ruffled the tall grass, a fresh, green scent filling the air.

After dismounting, I removed the heaviest bags. Murray set out a snack of bread and cheese while others found a friendly bush. Grabbing the canteens, I walked toward the murmur of running water. The river ran close to our landing site.

This part of it flowed clear with little pockets of white, frothing rapids. The hushed rushing sound indicated a deep bottom. Fifty feet across with no way to the other side, it'd be a while before people built a bridge here.

I hung the canteens around my neck and wandered to a spot near the riverbank. Cupping my hands, I took a tentative sip. Delicious. I plunged in my hands and drew out several long swallows.

Arvandus appeared at my side, his paws silent. "You should not leave camp unattended."

"I did yesterday. After leaving West Linneah's city gates, I walked back to the camp alone."

"Unwise. You should have asked me to meet you. We are entering unfamiliar terrain, so you must be careful."

"Something tells me this trip's going to require me to do a lot of 'unwise' things. Won't there be times when we'll have to be apart to get more done?"

"We will discuss that if and when the time arises. What is that smell?"

Lifting my head, I gave an experimental sniff. Why did I bother? "I don't smell anything."

"Shadow Power. The odor is strong near the water." He lowered his quivering nose to the stream, then reared back. "It is poisoned."

"Um, I just drank that."

"How much?"

"A few mouthfuls. It tasted great."

"The Shadow Power is already compromising your system."

"You're overreacting. I'll fill these canteens, and we can get back to camp."

"Do not touch that river."

I shrugged. "Too late. Don't worry, I'm fine." Why was he freaking out? The water, poisoned? His imagination was working overtime.

I pulled a canteen over my head to fill it. My hands began to shake, and my knees went loose, collapsing beneath me. A knife-like pain ripped through my abdomen. Curling into a fetal position, I gasped as pain stabbed through to my spine. Tears streamed down my face, the agony relentless. *Please, let it stop. Let me pass out. Please...* Anything would be better than this.

Arvandus leaned back and roared. His powerful scream shattered the peaceful woodland. I chanted to myself, *Focus, gather the heat, heal the pain. Focus, gather the h—*

With another searing spasm, my concentration broke. The torture multiplied, shooting through my torso, down my legs, into my head.

Others from camp arrived, their voices flowing over me like water. Someone's arms gathered me close, then lifted and carried me. Time started to stutter. I drifted in and out of consciousness. Every time I opened my eyes, someone stood at my side, doing something—wiping my forehead, holding my hand, trying to get me to eat (bad idea), or pushing nasty concoctions down my throat that tasted like lighter fluid. That mixture was the one thing I kept down. And in the end, it saved me.

The next time I opened my eyes, the pain had subsided to a dull throbbing. I lay on a thin pad in a tent I didn't even know we had. Baldwin sat on the ground next to me and held my hand, tracing my fingers and caressing my palm. Despite feeling like road kill, his touch ignited tingles all the way up my arm. When he began to speak, I faked sleeping.

"Brenna, I do not know if you can hear me. Everyone says you can, but I have never seen you so still. It seems too quiet without all your questions. As usual, Talus is acting like a dictator. He tells us what to do, when to do it, and how. I have been ignoring him. Murray goes along to keep the peace. Anna spends a lot of time away from camp. She is worried about you. We all are. You have to get better. Please. You are important to Linneah."

Irritation flooded me. Just Linneah, huh?

"And to me."

My eyes flew open.

"So you need to fight this off." Looking up, his eyes widened. He dropped my hand. "You are awake."

Thank you, Captain Obvious. "It would seem so." *But* why *am I important to you?* I bit my lip to hold the question inside.

"Do you feel better?"

"Mm, I think so. I don't want to die so much." Looking around the tent, I squinted at the opening filled with bright light. "How long have I been out?"

"About three days."

"Three days?" I tried to sit up, but gravity sunk its teeth into me. "We've got to get going."

"Not an option. You need more rest. Murray's herbal medicine helped, but now time is the best healer. You shook hands with death, Brenna."

"Dramatic much?"

A muscle ticced in his jaw. "Someone wanted you dead."

"The drinking water was for everyone. I wasn't the target."

"And your dad expects me to watch—"

"I'm not two-years-old." Heaven forbid something should happen to me on this trip. "Don't protect me because you promised my dad you would."

"That is what I do for friends."

"Okay, but it goes both ways. We watch each other's back. And I would rather have you do it out of friendship than duty."

"I am not doing it because of duty, but I cannot speak for everyone else. Can we trust every person in this group?" He raised an eyebrow.

Talus's connections made him a suspect. But he was Linnean and would gain nothing if I died. Anna, on the other hand, we'd known for a mere day before my accident. Rosamunde had mentioned a shaky peace between Linneans and Merripens. Did she have a motive I didn't know about? I shook the thought away.

"This group is all we've got. We'll have to work with it."

"You need to be more careful."

Anger had me pushing myself up with one arm. "Quit the lecture, *Dad*. If I spend the rest of this trip being careful, what will happen? Nothing." I collapsed like a broken umbrella.

He stood, his features impassable. "Get more rest. Supper will be soon."

An hour later, the main dish turned out to be Mud Rat stew, which I didn't learn the name of until after I'd cleaned my bowl. Either I was getting better at eating unidentified food, or my taste buds were dying.

Later, all of us relaxed around the fire. Anna told folktales from her homeland, Matana Island, while I drifted in and out of sleep. Glad to be with the group, I blinked hard, fighting the urge to nap yet again. Talus sat across the firepit, frowning at me when he thought I wasn't looking. I didn't get that guy.

After another day of rest, I convinced everyone we should continue our journey. We had ten days left. Although I tired easily, sitting on my griffin was doable. Arvandus had to do all the hard work.

When I went to see him, he nestled his head in the curve of my neck. "I am glad you have recovered."

"Me, too." I ran my fingers through his dark fur. "Guess what? The river was poisoned."

"I will refrain from saying 'I told you so.' Murray found a good water source, so we are well supplied. However, I fear for the citizens of Linneah downstream. Once we get closer to the lake, we might discover the person responsible."

Talus sauntered up to us. "Are you feeling better, Brenna? Murray was scared for you."

"Yeah, me too. I'm done with the scary stuff."

"That will probably not be the case. Most trips through Silvastamen are fraught with danger and 'scary stuff.'" He gave me a condescending smirk.

I lifted my chin. Arrogant jerk. "I'll be ready."

"Glad to see you are up for the challenge." He strolled away, a bitter scent lingering behind him.

"What is that smell?" I wrinkled my nose.

"Shadow Power. He is a strong user of it."

"That's what Anna said a few days ago. I couldn't smell it. At least until now."

"Your exposure has made you sensitive. Perhaps he poisoned the river."

"Talus? I guess it's possible. But why would he do that? He promised to help Rosamunde. 'I feel it is my duty to help in this time of need,' blah, blah, blah. Baldwin and I wondered if it was Anna."

"No." He shook his furry head. "She was very upset when you fell ill. Her heart is honest. Not like Talus. He is a follower of Rune."

I was sick of hearing about this Rune dude. "So?"

"Rune is no friend of Linneah. I would not be surprised to learn he was the one who took the Sacred Veil."

"Why does he want it in the first place?"

"He knows it is a quick way to weaken Linneah. It is one of the three Sacred Objects of Power. Any one of them will make him even more powerful than he already is."

"What are the other two?"

"The Stones of the Spring and the Caelestis Staff. They are kept in other cities in the Jasper Territory."

Grabbing a bag, I placed it on Arvandus's back. When I tried to place another on him, he backed away. "You may carry that one."

"I didn't on the last flight."

"We are walking from here."

"Why?"

"It has been decided it is safer on the ground than in the air. In town, Murray heard reports of a large airborne predator that attacks other birds. One farmer had his entire flock of peacocks slaughtered overnight. The citizens call it the Dragon Demon. Because we are not prepared for an assault, we will walk. After all, Linneans do not travel through Silvastamen. They head northeast toward Syeira and Mount Malvern to avoid it. Very few men return from quests to this area. The few who do, go insane."

Chills shook me and gathered in my core. "And you're just now thinking to tell me this?"

"I did tell you it was dangerous."

"Dangerous and insane aren't the same thing. I can't believe you didn't tell me. Were you afraid I wouldn't do it? That I'd back out?"

He didn't look away. "The idea did occur to me. You have not been very excited about your leadership position in Linneah's future. I hoped the less you knew, the more willing you would be."

"Not likely." I stalked away, muttering insults. Hurt and anger burned in my chest. What else had Arvandus failed to mention? I kicked at a small cluster of dead leaves at the edge of the field. With time, I'd accepted the idea of being a Firebrand and the fulfiller of the First Prophecy. Having a definite skill had changed me from the airhead who zoned out in class to a Firebrand who could destroy or heal. So, why didn't my own griffin trust me? The question made me angry all over again.

"It is time to go." Baldwin's voice carried across the clearing. He met everyone in the center of the meadow, a map in his hand. "We will follow the river toward Gibor Mountain, fly over the summit, and arrive at the northern face of the mountain by nightfall."

"That is a relentless pace, boy," Talus said. "Did you know there are Blade Pines growing up here?"

"Here? Blade Pines?" Murray's face lost all color.

"They grow so thick in some places, a man must walk sideways to avoid being sliced like a roast," Talus said.

"What are Blade Pines?"

Murray didn't answer my question. "Then we should ride the whole way to avoid the pines. It would be safer."

"We discussed this already." Baldwin folded the map and tucked it into his bag. "We want to avoid flying as much as we can."

Murray's concerned look didn't change. "I have seen what Blade Pines can do. Talus's description is accurate. One brush from their needles will carve your skin wide open. And Elyon forbid if a nest of Blood Spinners is in the tree."

This story grew worse and worse. "Please tell me Blood Spinners are harmless."

"Hairy, red, eight-legged demons that smell blood." Talus's voice was grim. "They wait in the pines for their prey to be sliced open before they trap it with their netted columns. The nets are like fine steel blades, and when the prey struggles, it cuts itself on the unbreakable web. Then, while the prey bleeds to death, they will call to their brothers and eat."

I shuddered. "The griffins won't be able to get through."

"We will go as far as we can, then ride," Baldwin said.

Murray, Baldwin, and I went first. Anna and Talus followed us, while the griffins brought up the rear. Before long, my weakness became obvious. The farther we walked, the farther I lagged behind.

On Baldwin's third trip back to check on me, he couldn't curb his annoyance. "You need to stay with the group, Brenna. I cannot keep making sure you are with us."

I was doing the best I could, but I wouldn't whine. "Nobody asked you to. Arvandus is with me. We'll catch up at lunchtime."

"And what if you become injured?"

"I'll scream so loud, you'll hear me in the Kasek Territory."

With an irritated glare, Baldwin left me on my own.

The air turned colder the farther north we ventured. In a few places, small patches of snow lay gathered like eggs in a nest. A damp fog floated in pockets, and trees poked their bare branches toward the meager light. This place sucked, with its low clouds and creepy shadows. The sun couldn't come out soon enough.

Blowing a hank of hair out of my eye, I stumbled once, twice, before my knees gave out. Sweat dribbled down my back, pooled under my arms, then froze on the back of my tunic.

"Are you hurt, Raven?"

I pushed myself up. "No, tired. I need food."

"You are not fully recovered. We should have stayed in the meadow another day."

"We don't have another day. The festival is in ten days."

"Perhaps you should ride me."

"And be the weak link? No thanks. Besides, I have no idea where we're going. Baldwin's got the map."

When we caught up to everyone else, Murray handed me a sandwich made of a dry crusty roll and hard cheese. Despite my hunger, I would've traded it for a ten-minute nap. Talus finished his sandwich and walked over, brushing crumbs from his immaculate shirt. He was clean, neat, and pressed. I kind of hated him at that moment.

"We thought perhaps you took a side trip."

"No, a small tumble slowed me down a bit." I took a bite of my dry sandwich, the hard roll leaving crumbs on my shirt.

"Before we left, I received a reply to my letter regarding your mother. Prince Rune had some interesting information."

Hope rose. "What?"

"I intended to share it with you sooner, but we were in such a hurry to leave, then you fell ill..." He held up his hands in a what-can-you-do gesture. "Prince Rune heard rumors of a female slave, bearing your mother's description, being held near the western face of Gibor Mountain. A small nomadic band set up a temporary settlement there. It might be nothing." His tone said he thought otherwise.

Excitement built in my chest, and I fought to keep my voice even. "It's on the way, so it wouldn't take any extra time to check."

"That would be a smart move."

Despite my weariness, the good news gave me a jolt of adrenaline. Various daring strategies for my mother's rescue ran through my mind.

Baldwin pulled me aside. "You are pushing yourself too hard."

Tossing back a healthy swallow of water from my canteen, the cool liquid slipped down my parched throat. "I'm not used to hiking rocky terrain."

"That is not it. The poison left you weak. We think everyone should ride the griffins to Gibor Mountain."

I frowned. "Is that the royal 'we,' or does someone else agree with this idea?"

"Murray and I."

So they'd been talking about me behind my back. Rude. "Don't change your plans for me. Any special treatment is unnecessary."

"That is not true," he said, ignoring my protests. "You were near death two days ago."

"Yeah, two days ago. I'm getting better, almost normal."

"Brenna, we will never make it at this pace."

"So now it's my fault?"

"I did not say that."

"You didn't have to. All of you are up ahead, plotting how to make this an easier trip for the weakling slowing you down. I'll walk faster, okay?"

"You are being childish."

"Real nice, Baldwin. Thanks."

"What would you like me to say? I am telling you the best course of action due to your illness. You almost died." He closed his eyes and pinched the bridge of his nose.

"But I didn't. We're wasting time. Let's go."

"You are so stubborn! You argue with everything and do not do what is best." He turned to leave, mumbling under his breath. "This would be so much easier if you were not—"

"If I was not what?" I grabbed his arm and spun him to face me. "If I wasn't here?"

Color surged to his cheeks. He refused to meet my eyes.

"So why did you come, anyway? Nobody made you. Just go home. I'll find the Veil and fulfill the prophecy without your help."

One guilty look and everything made sense. A lead ball settled low in my stomach. "Your 'help' had nothing to do with me. You couldn't wait to get out of that stupid castle. Travel, experience, *and* fame by fulfilling the First Prophecy. That's why you came, isn't it?"

"Not true." He coughed. "Well, at first, yes, but then—"

I clenched my jaw. "Shut. Up."

I stalked away, hoping he'd choke on his lame excuses.

CHAPTER SEVENTEEN

NEXT TO A GROVE of evergreens, Arvandus and I sat side by side, away from the others. Low clouds blocked the sunlight. I poked at a small clod of snow with my toe, then stomped it into a liquid. The cold air seeped through my cloak. I was wet, tired, and annoyed with Baldwin the pinhead. He and Murray had left on a reconnaissance mission for Blade Pines in the area. I hoped Murray lost him.

Arvandus's quiet voice broke through my brooding. "Raven, I am sorry."

"For what?"

"I withheld information from you. It was wrong, and it will not happen again."

I sighed. "Forgiven, Arvandus. Give me a chance next time. I might surprise you."

He nodded, his gold eyes thoughtful.

Murray and Baldwin returned from their little journey. "Mount up," Murray said. "The Pines are too thick."

I raised my eyebrows. Whoa. The Blade Pines were *right here*? I thought they were up ahead, kind of like a line in the sand. *Here is where the Blade Pines start.* When I slung my bag across Arvandus's back, my arm brushed the branch of the pine tree next to me.

The sharp pain stung like acid. Blood rose from three thick, red cuts. Placing my hand on the gashes, I ignored the pain and focused on healing. Arvandus's harsh indrawn gasp broke my concentration. Four hairy, red spiders dropped from the tree. Golf-ball sized, each spider landed with a muffled *thump.* At lightning speed, they built a wide, glittering column around me from the forest floor to the high branches. Trapped.

"Raven. Do. Not. Move."

"Right." Forcing some healing heat into my palm, I stopped the bleeding and knit the skin on my arm. The spiders scuttled to eye level on the webs, scattering the hazy dreaminess from the healing. No way to escape. "Do these spiders bite?"

"Not much," Talus said. "Avoid their webs, and you will be fine."

One spider jumped, landing on my forehead. I stood motionless, whimpering. The other spiders followed suit, clambering down my arms and legs, looking for vulnerable places to attack. I noted little pricks, like bee stings, on my knee, on my collarbone, and another in the middle of my back. One made the mistake of trying to bite my hand. With a vicious slap, I killed it and let its disgusting little body fall to the ground.

In seconds, the other spiders dropped to the ground and began to devour their dead friend. Aiming well, I dropped my booted foot on the entire group and ground my heel for good measure.

"Do not move your foot," Murray said, his voice quiet. "The rest of the spinners will devour them when you remove it. They can detect blood and death from quite a distance."

"Okay, they're dead, but I need to get out of here."

"Nothing can get through those webs," Talus said.

"Thanks for sharing. Now, how about some problem solving?" My voice wobbled on the last word.

"Did you try your talent?" Murray moved closer to inspect the webs.

"I can't risk it. Everything around here is fuel." Being trapped while a fire raged? No thanks.

Using the dull edge of their swords, Baldwin and Murray cleared the area in front of the webs, scattering dead leaves and grass until they reached bare dirt.

The glistening webs' thick, silk edges reflected light with razor-wire clarity. I dropped my hands, palms out, and released a few small fireballs. They passed through the webs like ghosts, then sputtered to death in the soil.

Murray closed his eyes, his lips moving. I think he was praying.

"Can you give me your sword?" Baldwin held out his hand.

"Why don't you at least wait until I'm dead before you take my stuff?"

He rolled his eyes. "Your sword is vladlen steel, the strongest metal ever forged." The light in his eyes gave me hope.

Rather than pulling the sword out of its scabbard, I unhooked my belt and dropped the whole mess on the ground. With a flick of my foot, it slid through an opening near the bottom of the web.

Baldwin showed me his target, so I could avoid the lethal blade. I smothered a manic giggle, hysteria tightening my throat.

Taking a deep breath, he swung the sword in a mighty arc. The blade hit the webs, the grating clang of metal on the hardened silk echoing through the forest. No dents or cuts. My heart dropped to my feet. Baldwin set his jaw and swung again. And again and again. Silent tears tracked down my cheeks. On the fifth swing, the sword met the web, and with a discordant shriek, ripped a hole to the bottom. A final blow opened the gap large enough for me to escape. Gathering my cloak close to my body, I turned sideways and slipped through the ragged opening. I threw my arms around Baldwin in relief. He stiffened for an instant before his strong arms came around me in a tight hug. When Murray cleared his throat,

I yanked my arms down. Embarrassment flooded through me in a red tide.

"Thank you," I said to Baldwin's collar, unable to meet his eyes.

The rustling behind me made everyone retreat. Dozens of spiders converged on their dead buddies—mealtime for the rest of the Blood Spinners.

Baldwin returned my sword, and I buckled it back on with shaking hands. After several minutes, we reached a clearing rimmed with brightly flowered trees. "All right." He sighed. "Everyone mount up and fly to Gibor Mountain. Be on the lookout for the Dragon Demon. Once we get there, land on the eastern side, and we will hike to the entrance of Maron Cave."

While climbing onto Arvandus, I admired the beautiful trees. Showy purple and yellow blooms nestled among the glossy chartreuse leaves. We lifted off, and the tree line dropped away. I pulled in a few deep breaths, relaxing into the rhythm of flying. Anna flew near me in Steen-falcon form. Baldwin and Lev led the way with Murray, Talus, and Reina behind.

Below, the bright flowers lifted up and away from the tree line. A wild cloud of purple and yellow raced up to meet us.

Flying flowers?

A colorful blur slammed into my shoulder. "Hey!" The garish blossoms had morphed into feathery flying lizards with curved beaks. Neon yellow and purple feathers clung to my shirt. I brushed them off, startled when my hand came away bloody.

Arvandus, whatever that thing is, it got me. I'm bleeding.

Lean close and hang on. There are more.

I scanned the air, my fingers buried in Arvandus's fur. On my left, the flock appeared, a twisting whirlwind of colorful feathers. They scattered before converging into a formation that looked very much like...a huge dragon. I sucked in a breath and tightened my grip until my knuckles turned white. The image dissipated when they broke apart, aiming for Reina and her riders. Each individual creature came into sharp relief as they whipped by me. Their huge bat-like wings were tipped with sharp, skeletal claws. Slitted red eyes peered out of a leathery head covered in green scales. Each bird let out a *whirr* when it passed, a high-pitched buzz. I hoped it wasn't a call that meant *here's dinner.*

The birds surrounded Talus and Murray, although Reina shrieked and swiped with her talons, keeping some of the attackers at bay. Murray rode in front, wild-eyed, while Talus took swings at the birds with a small dagger. Anna, in falcon form, burst forward. I tracked her flight path as she swerved and dodged. She fled the crush of birds, her small form disappearing into the clouds.

Ahead, a bird slammed into Baldwin, knocking him sideways. His hands slipped, grasped air. I swallowed a scream. Grabbing Lev's neck, he pulled himself back on. A large flock on my right rushed toward us, dispersing our small group.

With a blizzard of feathers, the flock attacked Arvandus's flanks. Snarling, he veered right, then left. Shrieks, roars, and buzzes filled the air. Behind us, the birds refused to give up. I tossed a small fireball toward the closest birds. They emitted a decibel-shattering screech. A massive bird appeared out of the flock, its wings eating up the distance between us.

Go faster, Arvandus! Daddy bird's behind us, and he's gaining!

Arvandus flew higher and faster. Below, the landscape blurred, and icy wind tugged at my hair. Giving up, the great bird turned and dove for the trees. A few far-away shrieks from the griffins faded in the distance. We raced for Gibor Mountain, my eyes watering in the whipping wind.

He's gone. I flopped against his neck, wiped out. *You did great. What were those things?* I hoped he wouldn't say what I was thinking.

I assume Dragon Demons.

Yep. Called it.

But their name hardly matters. Silvastamen is full of unexplored horrors. That must be one of them.

Where are the others? We should make sure they're safe.

Reina said everyone escaped. Because we were pulled farther off course, we will have to take the western route. After we land, we will hike to the meeting place.

He reduced his speed and dropped back into traveling mode. While he flew, I healed the cut from the birds' talons. After a quick visual inventory, I scowled. They'd sliced a hole in my tunic. Darn it. I arranged my cloak to cover the rip. Arvandus had a large cut on his flank, but I couldn't take care of it until we stopped.

I shivered on Arvandus's back for about an hour, then glanced up. We approached Gibor Mountain's summit. My eyes drank in the beauty. The sun sparkled off the glittering snow covering the top of the mountain. Dark shadows lurked in the icy chasms. Farther down the mountain, evergreens grew thick. At the bottom of the western side of the mountain, we glided into a small clearing dusted with a thin layer of snow. Thick firs, their needles layered with powdery snow, gave the air the pleasant scent of Christmas. No pines. Good. I rolled my shoulders, releasing the tension. Massive boulders the size of cars lay strewn about beyond the clearing.

Sliding off Arvandus, I stretched to get the kinks out of my legs. The jittery shakiness from our chase had dissipated a half hour ago. After healing the cut on his flank, I gave him some water and a leftover chunk of bread from my bag. While I nibbled on bread myself, I paced the frost-covered perimeter of our clearing. My mom was less than a hundred yards away.

"Let's take a short walk over this rise," I said when he finished eating.

He licked his muzzle with a pink tongue and fixed me with his yellow-eyed stare. "Why?"

"The walk would do us good. I'm tired of sitting. Maybe there's a trail we can follow to Maron Cave."

"We should look for the others."

"If they took the eastern route, we'll have to wait for them to show up at the cave entrance."

"So then we wait. It will not be the first or the last time." He tilted his head. "What are you hiding?"

"Okay, here's what I know." I told him the information Talus had shared with me earlier.

"I do not know Talus well. Yet I know Prince Rune and do not trust him. And you expect me to follow you into this situation that will take important time from our mission?"

"But it's my mom, Arvandus. Please? It will take thirty minutes, tops."

"It is at best a wild goose chase or at worst, a trap."

"You don't know that." I still wasn't convinced Rune was such a bad guy. So far, he'd delivered on his promise. "Please? You'll be with me for security."

"What if I decline?"

"I'll go anyway."

He shook his head and growled. "Stubborn girl. Do not make me regret this."

I threw my arms around his furry neck in a quick hug. "You're the best."

After a brisk, silent walk, we climbed onto a snow-covered boulder. Over a rise, a meadow stretched before us, filled with tall, brown grass. Beyond it, two dozen houses lay clustered at the edge of the field. I dropped into a crevice and motioned for Arvandus to do the same so we stayed hidden.

"See those houses? I'll go in. You stay here and keep watch."

He snorted. "You are not going in there by yourself."

"Oh, no problem. A griffin is an everyday occurrence around here."

"That is not my concern. In case you have forgotten, you almost died when you went alone to the river."

"Thanks for the reminder."

"We go in together or not at all."

"Arvandus, I would love to have you next to me. But you're conspicuous, and no one would forget the girl who showed up with a black griffin. How about this lookout spot?" I patted the rocky ledge where we sat. "If things start to go south, you'll be nearby."

He didn't move, didn't blink. I stared at him until the silence got to me. "Okay, did you die? Or are you thinking?"

His eyes slitted into thin bands of yellow. "Thinking." Several more excruciating seconds passed before he sighed. "I do not like it. But I will wait." He climbed to the top of the rocky outcropping. *Check in often. And if things start to go south, as you so eloquently put it, I will be there before the first person touches you.*

Leaving my bag in a crevice, I walked toward the village. It was a lot farther away then it looked, and I picked up my pace. The footpath meandered next to the miniscule town, wooden houses in a neat line along the right side. Tidy garden plots lay snuggled between the buildings. To the left spread the wide-open field before it met the towering forest. I reached the first house and paused. *Arvandus, do nomads build houses and plant crops?*

No. Why?

I'm not sure Prince Rune's information was correct. This doesn't look like a nomad community. Or if they were nomads, they're not now. I'm going to the middle of town to see if I can find someone.

Careful, Raven.

The houses sat silent, the bolted, shuttered windows glaring as I walked by. No birds sang. A lonely wind whistled, dying out with a sigh. With a shudder, I shook my head. It was fine. I was fine. It was a normal, quiet town.

In the center of the village, the silence persisted. Dwellings lay hushed as if residents had paused during their normal routines. Subtle signs of life remained. A campfire smoldered near one. At another, a broom leaned against the doorframe. Off to the side, a gleaming steel fence encircled a large yard and house with paned windows and an etched door. The muted notes of a piano came from inside. Someone had to be home. I steeled my nerves and knocked on the door, my courage shrinking by the second. The sound of footsteps caused my pulse to beat double time. I schooled my features into a pleasant smile.

The door opened, and my smile slipped away. "Talus?"

"My dear! Come in." My resistance dissolved in shock as he placed a hand under my elbow and ushered me in. "I am so pleased you came to see me. Have a seat. Would you like something to drink?" He crossed the room to a built-in bookcase. With a flick of his wrist, he turned off the classical music coming from two tall, gleaming speakers. "It is not that nasty river water. This is clean and pure from a nearby well."

I sat, my mind reeling. The luxurious furnishings glistened bright white. A snowy sofa with two matching stuffed chairs filled the room. Pillows in pearl damask, white brocade, and ivory velvet spilled from the furniture. Thick-piled carpets underfoot and soft lighting invited me to sink into the most comfortable chair and never move. A realistic painting of the Petrus Rings hung on the eggshell-painted walls.

"Talus, what's going on? Where are the nomads?"

He laughed, his blue eyes lighting up before he turned to pour water from a crystal pitcher into a matching tumbler. "Brenna, you are delightfully naïve. Let me explain the situation. Sit back. Relax."

Not happening. Talus's face bore dashed tracings like trail marks on a map. Were they tattoos? Scars? The smell of Shadow Power overwhelmed me. I sat on the edge of an upholstered chair and dug my fingers into the overstuffed padding. *Arvandus, Talus is here. But things are hinky...*

I am coming in.

No, he's going to explain. Give me a minute.

He crossed the room and handed me the glass. "You and Arvandus made good time. Where is he, by the way?"

"Off taking a nap. I didn't want him to scare the non-existent nomads." The emphasized last words hung heavy in the room.

"Yes, the nomads. There are none. I had to lie a bit, so sorry. But all this is my creation." He waved his hands like a game-show host. "What do you think of my house?"

"It's all super. Where's my mom?"

"You can enjoy these deluxe accommodations during your stay."

I blinked, but his expression didn't change. "My stay?"

"Well, you do not need to stay, but it would help with scheduling. Prince Rune wants to start your training immediately. And these accommodations were the best I could do on such short notice."

"I'm already trained, thank you very much. Arvandus trained me himself."

"Rudimentary. Did you know you could learn to do so much more with your ability? Prince Rune is impressed with your talent, Brenna, and he would like to help you expand your gift. There are some great opportunities for you in the Kasek Territory. This veil 'quest,' if you want to call it that, is ridiculous."

"The Linneans don't think so."

"Yes, but what do you think? Does it not seem trivial? All this fuss about a silly piece of cloth when they could easily crown a ruler and be done with it."

"You know that's not how it works. Linneah needs to follow Elyon's leading to crown a ruler. And they need the Veil to do that."

"It will not matter in the long run. Prince Rune intends to make Linneah his first acquisition when he expands his kingdom. But he is interested in you, Brenna. You could help establish this larger kingdom." He paused. "It will need leaders like a powerful Firebrand."

"How's he going to acquire and rule Linneah without the Veil?"

"You are searching for it now. And if you fail to find it, the thief will be killed when he steps forward to take control. Prince Rune will be successful. And he wants you to be successful, too. Your family reunited, friends, love, money, access to the kingdom—all these things could be yours. You could help others learn how to use their talents with enhanced capabilities. You could mentor those who struggle and build Linneah into a place of learning and growth."

"And what about my mom?"

"He would release her."

Arvandus's story about Prince Rune torturing his father flitted through my head. "He's holding her? Where?"

"Ah, you have not agreed to help. We would—"

"Why would I help some psycho who's holding my mom captive?"

His voice sliced the air. "You would do well to hold your tongue. Prince Rune was unaware of her identity and assumed she was a spy. After discovering otherwise and learning of your search, he charged me with her safekeeping until you arrived. So here is our proposal. You agree to be trained by Prince Rune, and we release your mother."

"You're blackmailing me?"

"That is such a nasty expression. I prefer to use the term insurance."

Jerk. "What about the Veil?"

"After your extensive training, you can continue the search."

"I promised the Linneans I would find it by the Shaverim Festival."

"You do not owe Linneah or Emperor Rexson anything."

"But Linneah's a part of me." I shot him a glare. "And a part of you, too, I thought."

"Hmm. Well, one must move on and put the past behind him and all that."

"Right. I should really talk about this with my mom."

His blue eyes flashed. "You must make this decision on your own. But if you walk away from this offer, it is doubtful you will ever see your mother again. So can we make a place for you, Brenna?"

CHAPTER EIGHTEEN

STALLING, I TOOK A sip of water after a quick sniff. No Shadow Power. If I cooperated, I could get my mom released or find out where they were holding her. The blackmail threat hanging over my head turned my stomach. So much for my hope that Rune was a nice guy. Still, this assignment gave me a chance to find Mom. Emperor Rexson had never given me any indication he knew of her location. I could use this opportunity.

"Sure," I said. "Where do I sign up?"

Talus grinned, the handsome smile again seeming so familiar. His next statement stripped away my musing.

"We like to initiate newcomers." He placed a basket of clear glass spheres on the gold coffee table in front of me. "These are spiegel globes. With each globe, we can track or view a single person." He held up a globe, and it began to glow with a violet light. "Who do you see?"

I peered into the ball, and a faun trudging through a forest came into view. "It's Murray."

"Correct. Hiking toward Maron Cave." The purple glow died. He placed the sphere in the basket. Picking another, he held it out. "Hold the globe."

The cool glass warming in my hand, the fragile globe began to shine with a soft blue light.

Talus leaned forward, his eyes narrowed in concentration. "What about this one?"

In the center of the glass, Baldwin came into view, his brow furrowed, hacking his way through the bushes. "That's Baldwin." A sliver of worry pierced my heart. If this whole charade worked, he'd never talk to me again. I'd forever be known as the traitor, working with the enemy.

The blue gleam faded, and I put it back in the basket. He placed another globe in my hand. "Now, it is your turn. Concentrate on this globe. Imagine someone you would like to see, anyone at all."

My mom? No, I didn't like the calculated gleam in Talus's eye. Instead, I chose Rosamunde. With a stutter and a pop, the orb's borders began to glow with a weak, green light. Inside, a faint image of Rosamunde walked down a castle hallway, her brown hair shining.

He nodded in approval and handed me another globe. "You are a quick learner. Now, think of someone you dislike or have had problems with."

Erhardt came to mind, but again, something about Talus's manner made me choose someone else. Pink light gleamed from the perimeter of the glass ball. The clear center filled with an image of Dirk, the physician's assistant, filling bottles in the infirmary stockroom.

He frowned. "I was not aware there were problems with Dirk."

An uneasy prickle skittered up my neck. I said nothing.

"Very well. Gather your talent and force it toward him."

"Why? Will it hurt him?" Squinting, I focused on the globe. The pink light deepened to a soft red.

"Done right, it will kill him."

"Kill him?" Shock sliced through me. The glass sphere turned clear in my hand. "Why would I do that?"

"He is an obstacle to your path, someone who has caused problems for you. He deserves to suffer, to die."

Forcing the globe to glow again, I considered my next action. A pulse of energy would kill Dirk? Maybe Talus wanted to see if I would follow directions. Maybe the smallest amount wouldn't hurt him. I hoped. Creating a small burst of heat, I pushed it toward the image of Dirk. The globe swallowed the energy, the light deepening to cherry red. An insignificant puff of smoke billowed, then dissipated, behind the physician's assistant. My palms began to sweat.

"An excellent attempt. Try again to concentrate that talent." Talus's eyes glittered cobalt in the hollows of his face.

Amazing—the globe transferred talent. But should I do it? Dirk was an idiot, but that wasn't a crime. Seconds ticked by. There had to be an alternative to death. Maybe if I started a fire near Dirk, he'd be able to escape.

Wiping my damp hands one at a time down my pants, I gathered my talent and aimed for the area next to his feet. The globe absorbed the energy, and flames exploded under Dirk's feet. I gasped as the scene unfolded. Screaming, Dirk stumbled, the fire growing. A pair of hands came into view and beat out the flames with a cloth. The anonymous person helped Dirk to a chair and pulled off his boots while he moaned in agony. Too much. I swallowed against the rising bile.

Talus cut the connection by plucking the globe out of my hand. "You can do better. This is an important skill to utilize. Try again."

If I succeeded, Dirk would die. If I didn't succeed, Mom would die. A terrible choice, but I'd do it for her. Clearing my face of emotion, I trickled a small amount of energy into the glass. The orb flared scarlet before the scene became clear. Dirk lay on a bed, his inflamed burns exposed. Renke moved close to him and laid wet cloths on the blistered, peeling skin. I shuddered, and the red light flickered.

"Now, Brenna." Talus's voice grated in my ears.

"But—"

"Now!"

I jerked, dropping the fragile globe. It hit the corner of the coffee table and shattered. Splinters of glass glittered like razor-sharp gems on the gold surface.

His cold fingers gripped my chin and yanked up my head to meet his furious gaze. "That is your best?"

Jerking away from his grasp, I studied my fingers. What could I say? Even with my mom's life on the line, I was a lousy double crosser.

"You are either unwilling or unable to control your talent efficiently. That makes you and your precious mother expendable."

"My mom—"

"Your mother was a bargaining chip. She has served her purpose."

"No!" I shot out of my seat, desperate to bargain for her release.

He shoved me back into the chair. "And you are a nuisance. I cannot spend my time keeping a bastard child under control."

I gasped. All my world focused on that one word. "What did you call me?"

He balled his hands into fists, his face a vicious snarl. "Shut up."

Opening his fists, Talus released a blast of blinding light, and the walls of the house dissolved. The luxurious furnishings fell away, and I plunged into an enormous sinkhole.

Arvandus!

Raven? What is wrong?

A discordant grinding *crash* filled the air, and the ground shook. The steel fence surrounding the house shot up, the silver fence posts fusing together several feet above my head. I coughed. The odor of burnt spices drifted over me. Shadow Power, and a lot of it. Ugh.

On a steep bank beyond the bars, Talus stood, the hash-marked trails on his face startlingly clear. He grinned. "So, *Raven*, are you comfortable in your new bird cage?"

"Let me out." Gathering my talent, I pushed. A large fireball blasted past the bars, then shriveled into embers. Two more efforts yielded the same result. "Let me out, you parasite."

Brenna, I am coming in.

"I think not. Instead, I have installed a mirage to fool and conceal. You will slowly starve to death. The rest of the group will never find your body. Tragic to die so young." With another malicious grin, he tramped up the banks of the sinkhole and disappeared.

Slumping to the floor of the cage, I laid my head on my knees. *Arvandus, watch out for Talus. Hide so he doesn't see you. I'm trapped, and he might come looking for you next.*

Stay safe, Brenna. I will be there soon.

The steel bars were spaced about four inches apart, each one two inches in diameter. Maybe concentrated heat would weaken them. I grabbed a bar, forcing the heat through while trying to bend it. A few minutes later, I gave up. Since my sword was vladlen steel, cutting an opening might work. I unsheathed my sword and swung it like an ax. The clang of metal on metal reverberated in the sinkhole. After a few minutes of intense work, the bars showed minor nicks, and I was exhausted. If the bars weren't vladlen steel, they were a close cousin.

"Brenna?" Arvandus's voice broke through my fatigue.

"Over here, in the hole."

"Where?"

His face never appeared. I sighed. "Talus said he created a mirage. I guess you can't see me."

"Are you injured?" His voice was louder, closer.

"No, but I'm caged. There's no door, and my talent won't touch the bars."

"Even if I could find you, it would do no good."

"Don't you know any counter spells or something?" I leaned my forehead against the cold steel bars.

"I do not use spells, Raven. That is a dangerous path. Besides, if Talus enhanced a spell with Shadow Power, any counter spells could cause irreparable harm."

"So, I'm dead."

"No, there is always a solution." After a moment, he spoke, his voice firm. "I know of only one way to get you out. We need to contact Emperor Rexson."

"Why?"

"He has dealt with Shadow Power spells before. He would be able to free you."

Bad idea. I had joined Rexson's worst enemy, then attacked an innocent man. Emperors did not drop everything to help criminals. "What about Rosamunde? She's closer."

"She has not worked with Shadow Power spells. That is a forbidden area for all but the most skilled. I heard Emperor Rexson was in the Steen Mountains. It is a large area, but I will go look."

"Be careful you don't run into Talus."

"I saw him, walking north. Everyone else will be meeting at Maron Cave."

Except me. But I couldn't say it out loud. "How long will you be gone?"

"One day, maybe two." He paused. "I could meet the others, then look for Emperor Rexson. But it will take more time."

Part of me wanted to tell him to meet the others so they could look for me. And warn them about Talus. But what could they do? They wouldn't find me, couldn't see me. And I couldn't help them. Should Arvandus take the extra time to warn them? What if Talus tried to trap them, too?

"Are the others in danger?"

A beat of silence, and then, "No. I believe the fulfiller of the First Prophecy was Talus's first and only target. And I am not sure you can spare the extra time."

"Then don't bother. Use the time to travel. I don't have any food or water."

"I will hurry."

"Thanks, Arvandus."

"Raven? Pray. Elyon will send help when it is needed most."

He said goodbye. His powerful wings beat the air, taking him higher and farther away. Since I had nothing but time, I settled down to pray for freedom.

The first night at my new address, the cold mountain air sliced through my clothes. Frigid guest slipped through the gaps of my cloak, making my bones ache. While I tried to sleep, I shivered, prayed, and cursed the day Talus crossed my path.

Sometime before dawn, I drifted off. I woke from a hard kick to my side. A young woman wearing a ruby gown stood off to my right, the mid-morning sun backlighting her silhouette. I rolled out of the way, holding my bruised ribs.

She paced in front of me, her crimson gown swishing with each step. The elaborate gold sheath hanging from her belt caught the rays of the sun and blinded me.

"You are Brenna the Firebrand. I expected more." Her angular features were chipped from stone, bleached from the sun.

"Who are you?"

"Geyla, agent and chief diviner to Talus Trennen. I understand you are the fulfiller of the First Prophecy. Get up. It is shameful, you lying there like a worm."

I pulled my feet under me, my ribs still throbbing. "This cage is secure. How'd you get here?"

"Teleportation. You understand?"

"Um—"

"I did not think so. Weak *and* stupid. I will be doing the Linneans a favor."

"Excuse me?"

"My mission is to kill you. I was not permitted to kill the other prisoner, so forgive me if I choose to draw out the experience."

Other prisoner. Maybe she meant Mom. "Where's my mother?"

"She is with Talus, where she belongs."

Alive. I gave myself a moment with that information and almost smiled. One look at Geyla's glare, and I dug deep for my anger, pulling it around me like a cloak. I couldn't get out, couldn't reach my mom, couldn't find the Veil. Now I was stuck here with this psychopath. I clenched my fingers into fists, feeling power gather.

"You are impotent. A paltry human girl, an infant sent to a world you have little right to. Why would your mother choose you when she can be with her firstborn?" Geyla's lip curled into a mocking sneer.

"Firstborn? I'm her firstborn."

"You are mistaken. You are an unwanted female, a mistake, a second choice."

"Second choice?"

"Talus, your half-brother, is the chosen son."

My mind stuttered, went blank.

Her words pulled me out of my stupor. "So, I am going to kill you. You may fight back—if you wish."

I shot first, a flamer beam. The faster-than-light, micro-thin flame produced piercing pain wherever it landed. I'd mastered the technique during talent training. Landing on her forehead, the beam sent her stumbling back against the walls of the cage. I pulled my sword from its sheath. My stomach flipped, the nausea roaring into place. With a few shallow breaths, I calmed it to a shaky queasiness.

When she faced me again, suspicion carved her features even sharper. "A paltry sword?"

I ignored her question and clutched the hilt until my knuckles turned white.

She unsheathed her own sword and held it out in front. Opening her free hand, an unearthly blue light flowed from her palm. The brilliance slithered around the blade, coating it like oil.

Dread built in my stomach. My mouth took over. "You're using magic? Really? Hard to believe you can't handle me on your own." Sheesh. Shut. Up.

"You are finished." She slashed the azure blade of light toward my stomach.

Jumping back, I instinctively blocked her shot with a firewall. Her funky blue magic + my fire = massive explosion. The force knocked us both back and snapped several steel bars of the cage. Yikes. Too dangerous. I didn't want to do that again.

"You're destroying me because Talus told you to. Doesn't sound very powerful to me."

"You doubt my power?" She glared and swung again, sapphire blade flashing bright.

I parried her strike. The fury behind it caused my sword to wobble, and I staggered back. If I could get her to think about how Talus used her, maybe she wouldn't kill me. I tried again.

"You're powerful, but you don't make your own choices. You do what he tells you and not much else."

She stalked me in a circle, both of us moving opposite each other. I kept talking. "Is that power? Doing exactly what someone else tells you to do? Is it powerful to have your intelligence ignored, or to bend and scrape and serve while Talus collects the glory?"

Geyla squinted and stopped her pursuit. After a tense moment, she nodded. "You are right. That is why I will choose a more civilized method to kill you."

I closed my eyes, but only for a second. Stupid, stupid, stupid.

She opened her hand. The cobalt-blue magic flowed from the sword and back into her palm, then disappeared. "I will give you a fair sword fight, so you can have the useless opportunity to defend yourself." She ended her statement with a cut to my left arm.

White-hot pain arced from my elbow to shoulder. Blood welled, then trickled down my arm. Gritting my teeth, I stabbed at her once, twice, and parried her thrust to my other side. My sword drooped. I yanked it back up and blocked her next move. Keeping my sword pressed against hers, I maneuvered it off to the side, exposing her waist. My quick follow up ripped her gown, drawing a thin line of blood. I pressed forward, slashing at every opening. A sudden swell of nausea overwhelmed me, and I lost my momentum. Geyla knocked my sword aside with a smirk.

"You are good, Firebrand. But not good enough."

Lunging, she attacked with a flurry of strokes, leaving me desperate and stumbling. Landing on my backside, my head snapped back and hit the hard floor. I blinked, my vision fuzzy.

She glided forward, her sword pointed at my chest. "One thrust, and you would be dead. But I have not decided whether to let you bleed to death or to kill you quickly." She slashed my left arm again. "Get up."

Pain flashed. Struggling, I slipped on the bloody floor. My sword quivered in my weak grip.

Her dark eyes calculating, she attacked again. She pressed forward, her thrusts driving me back until I sidestepped. Her sword whistled through the air, the blade missing me by mere inches. I parried one thrust, two. My strength slipped away. This wouldn't end well. She was a better swordswoman than I was.

Big surprise there.

We circled each other. Snarling, she swung wide. The swords clashed. Pulling away, she lunged again. On impact, my sword snapped. The blade fell to the metal floor with a clang. Injured and dizzy, I clutched the bladeless grip. *Oh God, please help.*

Looking into her eyes, I dropped the hilt with a clatter. "I'm done here."

"You are weak, unworthy, and a coward."

"Probably." Opening both hands, I forced my gift out in a ball of flame.

Geyla's face filled with shock. The fireball hit her chest. Before she could retaliate, I flung another broad blast of fire. It exploded in her face, the flames flashing red and orange. I didn't want to watch, but it'd be suicide to turn my back on her. Screams filled my ears, her body consumed in the blaze. In seconds, she stumbled out of the hole in the cage and fell to the bottom of the crater. An eerie silence filled the sinkhole.

My legs crumpled. Laying a hand on the cuts on my arm, I mumbled a heartfelt prayer of thanks. Time slowed, and the hazy mist enveloped me. Warmth flowed through my fingers, clotting the blood, knitting the skin. The fog lifted, and my senses cleared. The urge to lie back and sleep almost overwhelmed me, but I refused to spend one more minute in this cage.

Geyla's sword lay at the edge of the cage where the bars had broken. Reaching out, I suddenly hesitated. I needed a weapon, but what if it were cursed? Or wouldn't respond to a different owner? With shaking hands, I gingerly picked it up. The floor tilted. I dropped the sword, the clatter making my head throb. Was the dizziness from fatigue? Blood loss? Or a weird sword? Trying again, I grabbed the handle and held my breath. When a few seconds passed and nothing happened, I slipped it into my scabbard. This one couldn't be much worse than the old one.

The steep bank ended in a cratered hollow about five feet down. Her burned body lay at the bottom in a crumpled heap. I tried not to look, but it was like a horrific car crash—impossible to ignore. With a running jump, I landed on the other side of the bank. Scrambling and scratching, I climbed out and lay facedown on the frosty ground. The world spun.

Dazed, I managed to get my legs under me and walk across the barren field that had once held a path, a village, houses—now all gone. I searched, but the sinkhole was invisible. The mirage still held. Crawling to the top of the rocky outcropping Arvandus had used, I collapsed. Everything, absolutely everything, had gone wrong. I never planned ahead, only this time, the result was an unmitigated disaster. My brain refused to accept what had happened. I'd sleep first, then handle whatever came next. Brushing off the snow, I covered myself with my cloak and fell asleep.

I woke to the icy darkness. My hands were stiff from the cold, and my stomach hollow with hunger. I flexed my fingers a few times, wincing at the pins-and-needles sensation. Gloves were something else I'd forgotten to pack. Drawing my cloak closer, I searched for my bag hidden in the cleft of the boulder. When I found it, I pulled out the stale roll stowed in there a lifetime ago. After several attempts, I gnawed through the hard exterior, then chewed slowly to make it last. My thoughts drifted, as substantial as cotton candy. Some of my mental numbness had dissipated during my nap, but I still didn't have a plan. Maron Cave was to my right, which was east. Maybe when the sun came up, I could hike my way there.

Arvandus? The fragile link joining us might not stretch very far. *Arvandus, I'm out of the cage. If you can hear me, come back. Please?*

Hot tears slipped down my cheek and dripped off my chin. I took inventory of my emotional truckload of garbage: my mother (still missing), a possible half-brother (blackmailed me, then tried to kill me), and a confrontation with a scary warrior chick (also tried to kill me). Now, I had the opportunity to hang out alone in a creepy foreign forest. Good times.

Why did I think a partnership with Talus would save my mom? The horrible choice hadn't brought me any closer to finding her. Clouds shifted in the night sky, hiding the crescent moon. Constellations littered the dark areas between the glittering Petrus Rings. Frigid wind smelling of fallen leaves dried my tears.

Across the dark field, several lights appeared. They bobbed closer. I moved back into the shadows. Grasses and leaves rustled. Animals? People? I couldn't tell. Large silhouettes shifted in the dark. Pressing against the rock, I squeezed my eyes shut. The creatures stopped under my hiding place. A growling snort pinned me in place, fear wiping my mind clean.

"Brenna the Firebrand, you may come down."

My heartbeat jackhammered.

"You have nothing to fear, Brenna."

"Who are you?" My voice was a squeak.

The rider lifted a lantern containing a helli plant to illuminate the group. "I am Emperor Rexson. This is Fadday and Saman." He nodded to the two hulking guardsmen with stern faces. Their embossed silver breastplates glinted in the lantern light. A large eight-pointed star, like the ones on the entrance passes, decorated the center of each one. All three rode broad, four-footed, hairy beasts with wide curling horns.

"Are you as lost as I am?" My voice wavered, and I bit my lip to prevent more stupid questions and tears from spilling out.

Emperor Rexson dismounted and climbed up the rocky outcropping. He sat next to me. The warm glow of the lantern between us lit his kind, rugged face.

"You have had a difficult few days."

"How do you know? Did Arvandus find you?"

"No. Before I left the city, I heard a rumor the fulfiller needed help."

"I don't need help *now*." Which was a lie.

One eyebrow lifted. "You must have everything you need then." He moved to leave.

"No, but—please don't go." Squeezing my eyes shut, I chose to confess. "You shouldn't help me. I messed up, big time."

"I would like to hear your story."

Sure, he said that now. He didn't know what I'd done. "I agreed to train with Talus and Rune. They have my mom. Rune promised to reunite us, but I failed their initiation. Talus trapped me in a cage, then sent his thug, Geyla, to kill me. I, uh, killed her." The utter horror of what I'd done swept over me. I shivered, tears spilling. I'd killed another human being. A spasm gripped my stomach. "I killed her. Just pushed out a wave of fire. Burned her to death. But her screams..." Leaning over the side of the rock, I threw up, dry heaves wracking my body. When I finished, I sat up, still trembling.

"Killing another is difficult for many. I hope you never need to experience it again." His low voice calmed me. "Fadday, pass me my water."

After one of the guardsmen gave him the container, Emperor Rexson handed it to me. "You need to drink."

"I can't. It's yours."

"I can get more later. You will become dehydrated." He pushed the container into my hands. "Drink, but slowly."

Several swallows later, I handed his water back. "Thank you. If you choose to have someone else find the Veil, I'll understand." A few tears leaked from my eyes, the cool wind turning them to icy trails down my cheeks.

He nodded. "What are your plans for morning?"

My shoulders drooped. In a split second, I lost the position of fulfiller. What had I hoped for? Complete forgiveness? "I don't know. I'll need to find the others. Maybe Baldwin could find the Veil."

"If you presented yourself to Rune, he would have you, no questions asked. Are you interested?"

The lying. The use of Shadow Power. The darkness. I shook my head. "No, I was only hoping to find my mother."

"Your heart was not committed to their cause. I would like you to continue the search for the Veil."

I shut my gaping mouth. "Aren't you going to yell at me for doing a lousy job? I don't even know if we're going to find it in time."

"Are you doing your best?" He sounded like Arvandus.

"Yes, but I keep screwing up."

"Elyon can make beautiful things from the ashes of mistakes. Especially when things do not proceed the way we expect. It is difficult to remember sometimes."

Ashes. Mistakes. Fire... "Emperor Rexson? I also injured Dirk, Renke's assistant. I used a spiegel globe and burned him. Talus said if I killed Dirk and joined Rune, he would release my mom." The memory weighed heavy, a painful ache in my chest.

"That is a classic ploy Rune uses to test loyalty. People are not valuable, merely pawns for his plans." His face turned earnest. "But your mistakes do not define you, Brenna. Nobody is ever beyond help or forgiveness. Continue to search for the Veil. There is still time. In addition, consider yourself a leader. Many are looking to you for guidance."

"What about my mom?"

"Talus and Rune lied. They will not reunite the two of you. If anything, they will thwart you at every turn because she is my ally."

"After we find the Veil, can I look for her?"

"We both will. It will be a priority. But other circumstances are involved that have made searching for her impossible. I can assure you she is alive."

My heart lightened. There was still hope.

He stood. "We must continue on. Remember who you are. It is easy to be misled when we desperately want to believe something."

"I'm so sorry about everything."

"You are forgiven. Be strong and courageous. You are capable of amazing things."

"Emperor Rexson?"

He waited, his face patient.

"Do you know if Talus is my half-brother?"

"I am not worried about your family connections, only about your connection to Elyon and Linneah. You have a devoted heart, Brenna. Sometimes you will have to make difficult decisions, but I trust you will do what is needed." He laid a long, thin package next to me. "This is for you, to help you during your journey. Use it well."

A gift? After everything I'd done? "Wow. Thank you."

He smiled, slipped off the rock, and climbed back onto his animal. "Sleep well. Morning is a long way off."

The three rode away, their soft conversation growing faint, the lantern's glow fading. I lay down, tired, but with a lighter heart. Closing my eyes, I let my thoughts wander.

Remember who you are.

So who was I? The small, sly hater in my head spoke. *Liar, traitor, murderer. That's who you are.* I pushed it away.

Yes, that part of me existed, and I'd never forget it. But there was another part.

Brenna James, Firebrand, fulfiller of the First Prophecy.

It was time to take ownership of my responsibilities, my choices, and my life. Being the fulfiller wasn't Baldwin's responsibility, but mine. It was a part of me, like being Sarah and Harrison James's daughter, or Tiny's friend. But was I also a half-sister? I didn't know. Emperor Rexson had never answered my question about Talus.

Chapter Nineteen

I WOKE TO THE sun shining full on my face, its warmth seeping through my cloak. An encounter with Emperor Rexson? Right. It was a dream. He was somewhere in the Steen Mountains.

Reaching for my bag, my hand closed around the long package wrapped in brown paper, sticking out of the top. That shot my just-a-dream theory to bits. My fingers itched to open the package, but I shoved the urge aside. I didn't have time. Everyone else should've reached Maron Cave hours ago. Would they wait for me? Why should they? Baldwin would be thrilled to find the Veil himself. I closed my eyes, pulling up a mental image of the map Grandma Helen had shown me. Gibor Mountain's northern face held Maron Cave. The sun, rising to my right, gave me my direction. I started walking east toward Gibor Mountain. If everyone else had left, I would try plan B.

Leaving the clearing behind me, I hiked into the trees. Tall spindly hardwoods blanketed with snow mingled with thick firs and pines. I gave the pines a wide berth. One run-in with a Blade Pine was enough, thank you very much. My feet crunched through the carpet of snow, stubby bushes, and dead leaves. I trekked over tangled vines and tree roots, slashing a path through the thick underbrush with my sword.

Hopefully I was going in the right direction, but no one had been this way for a long time. My stomach cramped. I picked up a large handful of snow, popped it in my mouth, then spent the next minute fighting brain freeze. Baldwin would've laughed himself silly if he'd been here.

Stepping over a large bank of snow, I slipped on damp rocks and tried not to think about my empty stomach. Reciting the times tables and the periodic table of elements helped a little.

Arvandus! I tried again to reach him. *You can come back now. I'm alone and would love to argue with you again.* Something whispered through my mind, but it disappeared. Still too far away.

After a half-hour of hiking, I stopped to rest. My head spun, and my legs trembled. A lack of blood and food seemed to do that. When the world steadied, I continued on, keeping the mountain on my right. Above the birdsong and rustling of tree leaves drifted a familiar sound. Voices?

Seconds later, Anna broke through the thick foliage. "Brenna!" She hurried over and gave me a tight hug. "Reefstars, I'm so glad to see you. Where's Arvandus?"

Baldwin came up behind Anna with Murray and the griffins following him. "Where have you been?"

"I've had a great time. Too bad you missed it." A sudden wave of weariness hit, and I slumped onto a nearby rock. The cold seeped through my pants, my skin going numb in seconds.

Murray knelt next to me. "You are not well."

"What is that on your shirt? Blood?" Baldwin dropped to a knee next to me. "Where are you injured?"

"I'm okay. I healed myself, but I lost some blood. I'm hungry. And if I ever see Talus again, I'll cut out his heart with my sword."

"He is not with you?" Baldwin's eyes narrowed.

"Well, he was earlier, but then he trapped me and sent his minion to kill me. After that, Arvandus said he headed north."

Baldwin handed me a roll and a canteen of water, then sat next to me. "Take a break."

Lev and Reina settled nearby. After I filled everyone in on my last twenty-four hours, I ate another roll. Nothing had ever tasted so good.

"Okay, to summarize, Talus is affiliated with Rune, who's holding my mother hostage. He knows where we are and what we're after, and when Geyla doesn't come back, he'll know I'm alive."

Baldwin frowned. "After we landed, Talus said he was going to search for Anna. Then Anna found us not long after he left but said she never saw him. When he did not return, we assumed he went looking for you."

I snorted. "Let's hope we never see him again. I'd love to see Arvandus, though. I wonder how far away he is."

"The Steen Mountain range is a day's journey," Murray said. "That is not too far. There are some amazing stories about the vinculus."

Yeah, but the mountains covered a broad expanse on the map. I turned to Baldwin. "Let me see those maps you and Murray study all the time."

"Why?"

"Because I asked nicely."

"You actually did not."

"Please let me see those maps." I gave him a fake smile.

"And again I will ask why."

I huffed out a breath. "We need to get to the lake fast. I'm all for safety, but we have less than a week left. Which reminds me, whose idea was it to go by foot for safety reasons?"

Baldwin dropped his head, while Murray studied the nearest tree.

"Talus? You listened to Talus?"

"He had all these different reasons—you were too weak to stay seated on your griffin during flight, the Dragon Demon attacks were rampant, if our griffins were injured, we would need to return empty handed." Baldwin shook his head. "He wanted to slow us down."

"Well, he did. But now we're doing this our way, and we're going to do it right."

In minutes, I spread the map in front of me, and all of us began to work on a faster route to the lake.

I looked up at the faces around me. "We're going to use the griffins to get there. If there are monsters in the air, we'll deal with them."

"Would you like to ride Reina? I can ride with Baldwin." Murray smiled kindly. "You will need to ask her, but she will most likely agree."

I walked over to the tan griffin. She had stretched out on a flat rock, her tail flicking, eyes closed. Although the massive rocks lay near the trees, they received the sun's full force. Tall saplings swayed in the light breeze behind her. "Excuse me. Would you allow me to ride you to the new lake? My bonded griffin, Arvandus, is away on business."

"Did you send him away? Or did he tire of you?" Her eyes drifted open.

I joined my hands together to keep from smacking her across her beak. "No, he left to get help when Talus trapped me."

"I will allow it—only until Arvandus returns."

"Thank you. I appreciate it."

"You should."

Off to my left, Baldwin smothered a grin. "Okay everyone, we need to load up and get in the air. We will ride hard today to make up time."

Baldwin and Murray rode Lev, while I rode Reina, Anna flying beside us. During a pit stop sometime in late afternoon, Anna tired of flying and joined me on Reina. We didn't stop again until darkness began to fall. By that time, all of us were frozen. My hands had iced into frosty little fists, and my thighs ached from being on Reina's back for so long.

I helped unload the griffins, then stretched my muscles in the clearing. After Murray found some kindling, I arranged the small bundle and tried to start a fire. Baldwin strode up. The tiny flames smoked, then guttered out. "What is wrong?"

"The wood's wet. This will take time."

While I generated heat to dry out the wood, Baldwin watched. His steady gaze made me jumpy, but I kept my mouth shut. After a long day of riding, my filter was nonexistent.

The wood caught fire, smoke curling. I dusted off my hands and stood while the flames hissed. His eyes gleamed black in the twilight, the growing flames contouring his jaw with a red glow.

What was he thinking? "Is everything okay?"

"Yeah, now. When you went missing..." He shook his head. "I didn't know how we'd find you. I, uh, I missed you."

My gaze met his, and something gleamed in the depths. Oh. "I missed you, too."

"What happened to you?" he asked. He traced the tear in my tunic.

"Flying lizards."

"What?"

"The Dragon Demons. You know, the creatures that almost knocked you off Lev?"

He shook his head. "Not much scares me, but I hope I never see those things again."

"I could get you one—a pet of your very own."

"No, thanks. I have enough excitement in my life."

"Yeah? Like what?"

"There is this distracting girl I met. She is opinionated, stubborn, accident prone, and really dangerous to be around."

My cheeks heated. "I think you're safe."

"I do not feel safe around her." His gaze dropped to my mouth. My stomach dipped.

"Excuse me, you two." Anna stopped next to us. "Lev is back with dinner." She pointed at Baldwin. "Your griffin, your turn to get supper ready."

After he walked away, she linked her arm with mine. "So you're interested in Baldwin, huh? He's shell fine."

"He's just a good friend."

She wrinkled her nose. "Brenna, none of my friends look at me the way he looks at you. No drift about it."

I shrugged but said nothing.

"You don't care? Can I go after him?"

Her pants and trendy fleece coat were clean. Her glossy hair curled over a shoulder. It even looked like she had makeup on. "Whatever."

She shook her head. "Classic reef logic. Even if you won't admit it, you like him. I'm not moving in."

I turned away. Things were messed up enough. Did I have the energy for one more problem, even if it was as good looking as Baldwin?

The next day, we woke to a dusting of snow. My cloak hadn't kept me warm enough during the cold night, and I hadn't slept well. We repeated the day before—get up, fly all day, and land when the light faded. During supper, it became apparent I didn't have to worry about a new problem. I must've imagined the moment between us yesterday. Baldwin snapped at everyone, brooded while he was alone, and was a general pain in the butt. We couldn't find the new lake soon enough.

On the morning of the third day, we rose and ate a quick breakfast. While we packed, a heavy snow began to fall.

Baldwin studied the sky. "We cannot fly in this. There is no visibility."

I was beyond ready to get to the new lake. "What if we get above the cloud cover?"

He shook his head. "This is going to last awhile."

The snow squall grounded us until mid-morning. I huddled with Anna and glared at Baldwin. It felt like his fault, though a small part of me knew I was being unfair. We needed good news—all of us were cranky, sleep-deprived, and cold.

Watching the snow fall was as exciting as watching paint dry. My thoughts drifted to what lay ahead. Where was that stupid lake, anyway? It couldn't be much farther.

Anna sat next to me, eyes closed. How could she sleep in this cold? I shifted my numb feet, tucking them under the blanket that sheltered us. Near the griffins, Baldwin and Murray sat across the clearing under a small makeshift awning made from someone's cloak. They spoke in low tones, the murmur of their conversation hushed in the snowfall.

By the time the snow lessened, the covering on the ground was ankle-deep. A light sprinkling continued, but the clouds shifted, revealing a clearer sky and better visibility. The griffins shook off the snow, their wings throwing the flakes high. We wiped down our saddles and mounted.

After several hours in the air, a massive body of water came into view. Finally! I grinned, relief making me a little giddy. The lake's watery borders stretched in all directions until it met land far in the distance. An island dotted with palm trees lay not too far from shore. A long, sandy land bridge on the left connected it to the mainland.

"Reina, what is that?"

"It is a peninsula in a body of water."

She was often less than helpful like this, and I wished harder for Arvandus to return.

We landed not far from the lake's edge. After a short discussion, Baldwin asked Lev to drop the two of us on the island. He would call for the griffin if we ran into trouble.

Stuffing my bag behind some brush, I covered it with dried weeds, making sure the brown paper package sticking out of the top was well-hidden, too. I hated to leave it behind, but it would only slow me down. I'd get it when we returned.

Anna walked up, her hand outstretched. "Here." She handed me what looked like a silver wire bracelet. "I don't know what it does, but I know you need it."

"For what?"

"I don't know, but I know it's yours. That's all I can tell you."

"Where'd you get it?"

"When I was in Wildamek a few times ago, I traded for it. I wore it for a while, then stashed it in my bag. It's been there ever since, waiting for a new owner."

"Thanks." I slipped it on my wrist. The gorgeous silver filigree cuff held a clear, faceted stone set between spirals of silver. Two smaller stones sat on either side and glimmered in the light.

"Be careful," she said when I turned to go.

I glanced back. "I'm always careful."

"Said the girl who was poisoned, trapped, then almost killed by Talus."

"Now I know, okay?"

Anna raised her eyebrows but said nothing.

Baldwin and I rode Lev the short distance to the island. After we dismounted, Baldwin turned to his griffin. "If you do not hear from us by nightfall, come find us." Lev nodded, then flew back to shore.

I stretched, arching my back, and took in our surroundings. In the middle of the island, a large volcano protruded. Inland, the fine-grained sand transitioned to dark, rich soil. Exotic plants with waxy green leaves and lush flowers blossomed everywhere. In other words, a tropical dream. A light breeze blew, the air humid. I frowned. Despite the gorgeous summer atmosphere, it was all wrong this far north. On shore, it'd been chilly, almost frigid. Snow and frost had covered most surfaces. Here, warm sun shone overhead, punctuated by a beautiful cerulean sky. And there was a certain smell...

Wrinkling my nose, I turned to Baldwin. "It stinks here."

"I do not smell anything. We should head for the mountain."

"That thing? That's not a mountain. It's a volcano. Don't you have those here?"

He gave me a blank stare.

"You know, plates under the ground shift, gases build up, molten rock explodes out of the top..." I gave up. "It's unpleasant. Let's check the perimeter of the 'mountain' first. Then if we don't find anything, we can talk about our next step."

"Fine. You make the decisions." A muscle twitched in his tight jaw.

"Is this the way it's going to be? Because I really don't need a three-year-old along for the trip."

"Whatever. I am a mere bodyguard for the great Firebrand." Ouch. "What is with you?"

He shrugged and walked away.

Following Baldwin, I hiked in silence toward the volcano's base, searching for people or a dwelling.

I jumped when a coal-black ball of fur scurried across my feet. The size of a mouse, its chocolate eyes shimmered. A razor-sharp pointed nose wiggled, sniffing the air. Rather than running when it saw me, it stopped before inching closer, its big eyes unblinking.

I knelt, stretching out a hand. It darted onto my palm, its tiny claws scraping the tender skin of my inner wrist.

Baldwin walked back to me. "What are you doing?"

"Look! Isn't he cute?"

"Stop!" The terrible look in his eyes froze me in place. "Put it down, slowly, and walk away."

I moved to do so, but the creature jumped from my hand and scrambled up my arm.

"Get it off!" His hoarse shout filled me with panic. After I flailed my arms and executed a wild spin, the creature fell off and ran for cover.

Baldwin checked my arms and back, even lifting my hair. "That 'cute' creature is a Bragnaborn, a parasite. They tunnel into the back of your neck and take over motor functions. Most people do not live more than a few months after being infected."

I shuddered. "Ugh. That's disgusting."

"If we sleep in the open, we will have to cinch the hoods of our cloaks tight. The Bragnaborns will burrow anywhere in the hope of getting to your neck."

I swallowed hard and resumed walking. After a few minutes, voices filtered through the trees. Tiptoeing closer, I motioned Baldwin over. We found dense foliage nearby, crouched down to hide, and peered through the leaves.

Off to the left stood a long, two-story stone building with four imposing columns. It nestled against the base of the "mountain," a tangle of vines and mixed greenery gracing the top. A short set of stairs rose from the ground and led to a pair of rough-hewn doors. While we watched, a man exited the building and stood on the steps. I resisted the urge to get up, even though my foot tingled with pins and needles. I braced my hand on the moist earth and sunk lower behind the overgrown fern.

The man's strong, straight nose, heavy brows, and dark complexion made up a forbidding face. His temple had been tattooed with a sword curving down onto his cheekbone while marks, trails like Talus's, branched across his face. An etched brass breastplate covered his muscled chest, and a sheathed sword glinted at his side. Seriously scary-looking dude. His expensive clothes were trimmed with leather and gold studs along the cuffs and neckline. Hundreds of thin, black braids streamed down his back, his copper hairstreak prominent. Brass beads and feathers decorated the ends. Despite my effort to remain calm, my pulse pounded in my head.

"This is the beginning of what I have promised you." Tattooed Dude's powerful voice carried to our hiding place. "Prince Rune promised this path leads to greatness, to power, to ruling what is ours. We will claim the victory!"

A mix of shouts, shrieks, and roars followed, swelling into an earth-shaking din. Curious, I peeked around Baldwin.

He leaned back so I could see better, his brow furrowed. In the clearing, a motley assortment of men, women, and beasts gathered. They raised their weapons, cheering, their armor shining in the sun. And there were thousands of them.

CHAPTER TWENTY

THE MAN'S MALICIOUS SMILE grew. "Today, we begin our march on Linneah. We will lay waste to the land and crush the enemy beneath our feet. We will not stop until we are the highest power!"

Again, hisses and shouts responded to his words. The mass of people surged forward, thrusting spears and swords in the air. When the man snapped his fingers, two men scrambled to bring forth a strangely familiar creature.

The serpent we had tracked through the village of Linneah writhed, its tail thrashing. Despite the elegant saddle on its back, the two men struggled to control it, muscles straining as they fought to keep a hold on the reins. Baldwin's accurate thrust had rendered its one eye scabbed and useless, and other wounds scarred its long body. The serpent snapped at the man, its yellow fangs dripping saliva.

"He is angry, Lord Trennen."

Laughing, Tattooed Dude grabbed the reins. "Talus, bring me my shield."

Talus walked into view. "Here, Father."

"Now, you are clear on your responsibility?" The older man narrowed his dark eyes.

"Yes." Talus scanned his surroundings, his gaze lingering near our hiding place. I held my breath. After a moment's hesitation, he faced his father. "I will bring the Veil after I have fulfilled your request. It will not take long."

"Do well, and you will finally receive the prized Trennen mark." Lord Trennen pointed to the tattoo on his temple. Turning to the assembled people, he raised one muscled arm. "For Prince Rune!"

He straddled the serpent and rode to a path opposite our hiding place. Cheers and shouts of "For Prince Rune" followed him. Under the noise of marching feet and clanking metal, I leaned close to Baldwin. "Contact Lev to prepare those on shore. They need to hide so they won't be seen from the land bridge."

"Already done."

The assembled army contained Largamants, griffins, and unrecognizable large beasts. Camlos and Weldens mingled with Kells. A few Linneans were sprinkled in the mix. All of them were taller, broader, and bigger than any person I'd ever seen.

I peered through the leaves again, my stomach jittery. "After they leave, I'll distract Talus while you come from behind and tie him up."

"Tie him up?"

"A soldier wouldn't hesitate."

"A soldier would kill him, Brenna."

Sheesh. "Um—"

"And that soldier would have failed because the Veil would still be hidden. Talus will lead us to it. Be patient."

Like I'd told Arvandus, I wasn't good with patient.

The last of the crowd followed Lord Trennen toward the clearing leading to a sandy trail. Talus had disappeared, which wasn't a good thing. I edged closer to the ferns. I wanted to get in and get out, but we had to wait until everyone left.

"Our group's going to have to split up," I said.

"No. That is a bad idea."

"We have to send someone ahead to warn Linneah so they're ready. Tell Lev to send Reina and Murray."

"Anna will be left behind."

"She's a shape-shifter. She can either go with them or wait with Lev. She'll be fine."

Baldwin crossed his arms, his expression pensive.

"It's the only way we can help Linneah."

With a reluctant nod, he focused on a distant point while he relayed the message to Lev.

Once I saw the clearing was empty, I edged out. No stragglers, but Talus lurked somewhere. But I had to focus. Find Talus—find the Veil.

I jogged toward the steps of the building, Baldwin behind me. He pulled out his sword, a reminder to draw my own.

Yanking open the door, I crept into the room, my sword ready. I scanned my surroundings, then blew out a long breath mixed with nerves. No Talus waiting inside.

The enormous chamber had gray stone walls and a dark wooden floor. A few small windows let in sunlight. Grisly paintings of war and bloody battles hung on the wall. Opposite the entrance, a doorway led to a narrow, ascending staircase. We searched for a clue, but all that remained was a long wooden table, two-dozen matching chairs, and the fading smell of rancid spices. I turned to Baldwin.

"I've got nothing." My quiet voice echoed. "By the way, what does the Veil look like?"

"White, as long as a man is tall, fancy purple stitching at both ends."

He pointed his sword at the staircase. We tiptoed up the stairs and spent fifteen minutes searching numerous bedrooms and closets, all in various states of disarray. But no Veil and no Talus.

My nerves fraying, I met Baldwin at the top of the stairs. "It's not here."

"You need to find Talus first. Can you think like him?"

I closed my eyes. Talus loved to boast and show off, so he wouldn't leave without the chance to brag about what he'd done. His devious side would require a hiding place. I swallowed against the dread clogging my throat. This had the makings of a trap.

"Does this place have a basement?"

At Baldwin's blank look, I said, "The lowest level on a building, like the castle's storeroom?"

"Maybe, but I do not see any other staircases."

Another search downstairs turned up nothing, until I found an O-ring bolted to a large floor panel in the corner of the room.

"Hey, I got something here." When I pulled the ring, the panel lifted without a sound. A wide set of stairs disappeared into a walled staircase of stone.

"You stay here. I will make sure it is safe to proceed." He stepped forward.

"Baldwin, this isn't working."

"Fine." He backed away from the opening and crossed his arms, his eyes shuttered.

"Which means it's anything but," I said under my breath. "Why am I the bad guy all of a sudden?"

"Am I doing an acceptable job leading the expedition?"

"Yes, of course."

"Then why are you taking over?"

"I'm not taking over."

"You are," he said. "Do you know that in one time I will join Emperor Rexson's men? I will be an adult, permitted to fight against Rune and his army. I could do so now if ability was the sole criteria. Yet you do not trust me to keep you and the others safe."

"That's not it."

"It *is* it. If I had not been here, could you have led the group all the way from Linneah?"

"No—"

"Could you have escaped the Blood Spinners on your own?"
His cheekbones flushed.

I shook my head, my words shriveling in the face of his anger.

"You should not attempt this alone. You are younger—"

"Only by a year!"

"—and inexperienced. What will happen if your decisions
put you in danger?"

"I'll be fine."

"You cannot know that. I do not want you to get hurt."

"Yeah, I know. My dad wanted you—"

"No." He moved closer, his warm breath brushing my cheek.
"This has nothing to do with your father. And everything to do
with you and me."

I tried to take a deep breath. Why wasn't there enough air?

His green eyes glittered. "Yet you keep pushing me aside. And
I am supposed to be okay with that."

"You have to be okay with it, Baldwin. The prophecy implies
this is a job for the fulfiller."

"But I cannot stand by—" His voice faded, and he swallowed.
"I care about you. So what am I supposed to do?"

I took his hand, his fingers strong in mine. "Trust Elyon. And
me. You can't march forward, find the Veil, then hand it over
to me." A small part of me wished that scenario would work,
but I hadn't forgotten my midnight leadership meeting with
Emperor Rexson. "I couldn't have gotten this far without you.
And I'd like to work as a team, which means I need your help,
but also your trust. Can you do that?"

"Can I offer advice?"

"Sure. But I may not take it." I gave him a small smile, our hands
linked, the truth lying between us. "I can't think of anyone I'd
rather do this with. Please say you'll work with me." The alternative made my stomach drop to my knees. Baldwin saying forget it,

I was on my own, and how stupid I was for attempting a death mission here in the Northern—

"Okay." He tucked a lock of hair behind my ear.

"Oh. Good." I grinned, relief flooding my heart. I squeezed his hand before letting go. The staircase waited.

He followed me down the stairs, both of us keeping our footfalls quiet. The flight of steps went on forever, the stone walls closing in. At the bottom, a tunnel stretched into the distance. It had been carved from rock, and helli lights lit the path at intervals. The stench of Shadow Power intensified, and the air grew colder. I shivered, goosebumps breaking out on my arms. After following the tunnel for about twenty minutes, a bluish glow appeared ahead. I hurried on. Fear and worry stirred low in my stomach. This trap would give us a single exit with nowhere to hide.

Clearing the tunnel, I stumbled to a stop. The ceiling soared high above. Helli lights, arrayed in rows, graced the walls. Glittering crystalline shards grew between the lights and hung from the cave walls, throwing sharp blue light in my eyes. We stood on the outer cusp of an ice-rimmed, rocky lip about fifteen feet wide. The edge bordered a slush-filled lake, the wavelets *shushing* on its frozen shore.

To the right, a massive stone platform hung from the ceiling by four thin columns of ice. In its center, a giant set of justice scales gleamed. The golden cups wobbled, a captive on one side, struggling. In the other cup, a sheet draped between two chains.

"Baldwin." I tugged his sleeve, my voice dying in my throat. "It's my mom." Even at this distance, I could identify her. And I would've gambled my next year's allowance the sheet on the other side was the Veil. I hurried toward the scales, staying close to the wall. Several archways around the cave's perimeter showed more tunnels leading in different directions. Hope threatened. More escape routes? I couldn't be certain.

Still no Talus.

I studied the cavern wall closest to the platform. No steps, ladders, or any other way of reaching the top. My fingers curled into the crevices in the wall's rough, cold surface.

"I'm going up. Hold my sword." I thrust the weapon at Baldwin.

"You cannot be unarmed."

"It'll slow me down, banging against my leg the whole way up."

"Welcome to hell!" The loud voice boomed in the cavern, mocking and too familiar. Talus entered the cavern from one of the side tunnels, his arms spread wide in welcome.

Baldwin pushed the sword into my hands. "Hand over the Veil," he answered, his voice authoritative.

Talus stalked closer, his wild eyes glittering like the crystal slivers on the walls. "Go ahead and take it. No one is stopping you. Perhaps you are afraid?"

"I am not afraid. You are the coward, stealing and hiding like a child."

"Liar. You are afraid to die. That is what will happen to both of you today. You first." He pointed at Baldwin. "Then the fulfiller of the First Prophecy, the great Firebrand."

Blah, blah, blah. I resisted the urge to roll my eyes. We didn't have time for his villain monologue. "Talus, don't you think everyone will know what you've done when we don't return? You'll become Linneah's Most Wanted. And they already don't like you."

He took a step forward. The dashed lines of his addiction came into vivid focus, tracking over his cheeks and chin. His voice lowered, vibrating with fury. "You minuscule piece of garbage. You have no idea of the extent of my power. I could crush you like a bug." He snapped his fingers, and a blue spark flared, then died. "In fact, *our* mother should see her precious chosen daughter die before she follows you."

"Is that what this is all about? You have abandonment issues?" I chanced a quick look at Baldwin. His eyes shone black in his flushed face.

"Her lawful place is at the right hand of my father, Taurin Trennen. Did you know she ran away like a coward and left him?"

"Doesn't surprise me. She probably couldn't get away fast enough." As soon as I said the words, I wanted to grab them and stuff them back in my mouth.

Talus's eyes blazed cobalt, a sword materializing in his hand. "You will not mock Lord Taurin Trennen!"

I raised my sword to block his heated first thrust. The second and third were harder, faster. Baldwin charged from the side, his sword a glittering blur. Gritting my teeth, I clenched my sword tighter. Talus's onslaught gave me no time to recover, and his strikes reverberated up my arms. With my limited skills, I was outclassed, and everyone knew it. He drew close, then slipped to my left side. With a lunge, he forced me back toward the subzero lake. An arctic breeze slipped down my neck, icing my bones.

In a desperate move, I parried his vicious thrust to my chest. He laughed, the evil sound echoing in the cavern. "Time to say goodbye, Brenna." He knocked the sword out of my hand.

I took a step backward, my foot finding only air. Baldwin saw me tip, and his shocked face turned white. My arms pinwheeled. I gasped. "Baldwin!"

Game over.

Chapter Twenty-One

"No!" As BALDWIN GRABBED my hand, a blue flash filled the cave. He jerked me from the edge and into the safe haven of his arms. Talus stood frozen, his laugh fading with an eerie echo. Baldwin's heart pounded against mine. I rested my forehead against his shoulder, keeping one eye on Talus.

"Thank you."

"No problem." He stroked my cheek before pulling away.

"What happened?" Silence filled the cave. The waves no longer lapped at the lake's rim, and Talus remained statue still.

"No idea."

I pointed out the obvious. "He's not moving."

Talus stared at a distant spot in the cavern. Tugging on his sword, I slid it from his grasp, then tossed it into the still, slushy water. A shower of white sparks escaped in a cloud, and the sword sank from sight.

Baldwin scrutinized the silent Talus. His immobile form still glowed with a blue tinge.

"Come on." I picked up my sword and shoved it into his hand. "We'll figure it out later."

Running my hand along the wall, I found a good niche and grabbed hold. He stopped me with a hand on my shoulder. "You need a weapon." He unbuckled his belt and slid off his knife's sheath. "Here."

"No, I can't take that." It was the knife I'd seen him study on the balcony so many weeks ago, the one his father had given him before he left.

He gave me a half-smile. "Use it if you need it. We can swap when you come back down." He pressed it into my hands.

Fumbling with the sheath, I tried to slide it on my belt. He pushed my shaking hands aside to finish the job. His hands grazed my waist, the heat from his fingers stealing through my tunic. Feeling my cheeks flush, I looked up to thank him. The warm look in his eyes made the words stick to my tongue like peanut butter.

Turning back to the wall, I hauled myself up, my hands and feet searching for holds. "Follow if you want, Baldwin."

"No, thanks."

"You afraid of heights?"

"No, a little dizzy. I will guard Talus."

In minutes, I reached a small ledge big enough for my size-seven feet. I scrambled onto it. All that remained was a gap. A three-foot gap. It wasn't a big deal—unless I counted the long drop to the rock floor.

Taking a deep breath, I jumped. When I landed with a bone-jarring *thump*, I caught a glimpse of the icy cavern floor. Vertigo kicked in, and I looked away. The giant scales loomed above me, the cups inches beyond my reach. Several boulders lay scattered on the platform. I stacked a couple next to Mom's cup and stood on top of them to reach her.

She struggled against her ties, tears running down her face.

"Hi, Mom." I gave her a shaky grin. "Don't move."

She held still while I severed her bindings. She undid her gag herself, then grabbed my arm. "I can't leave."

"What?"

"This whole thing is booby trapped. The balance is calibrated. If the weight changes, the platform will crumble."

Leaning forward, she gave me a hug, the scales tipping and an ominous *creak* echoing in the cave. She looked me over, a smile flickering across her face. "You are so beautiful, so grown up. Brenna, I want you to take the Veil and run, okay?"

"No, that's not happening." Leaving my mom *or* the Veil behind wasn't an option. I didn't have a plan, but time ticked on.

"We need to leave. I am beginning to see movement," Baldwin said from below.

"I'm working on a strategy. Give me a minute."

Several minutes later, Mom and I had discussed and discarded several ideas. I reached over to scratch my wrist and bumped the filigreed bracelet. The faceted center stone flashed a circle of light on the ceiling for several seconds before going dark.

My mom gasped. "A replicator!"

"What?"

"It's a replicator. It clones objects. I used one a long time ago. Where'd you get it?"

"My friend, Anna, gave it to me. Do you know how to use this one?"

"It's not difficult. They all use the same principle. Pressing the center stone gives you light like a flashlight. But to copy, you center the beam of light on the object. Then press both stones on either side."

"Where does the object end up?"

"Wherever you put it. When you first press the stones, it replicates. Then when you let go, the object's released."

"Can you replicate people?"

She furrowed her brow. "It replicates form, but not souls or life."

I took a deep breath. "One Mom Number Two, coming up."

"Oh, sweetie. That's a bad idea."

"It's all I've got. Unless you can think of something else?"

Mom said nothing, her face filled with distress. I had to admit—the idea creeped me out, too.

"Okay, when I place You Number Two in the cup, jump out." I placed the beam on her, pushed the two silver buttons, and waited. After a pulse of shimmering light, a hazy image appeared and intensified. In seconds, Mom Number Two hung suspended above the scale platform.

"On the count of three . . . one, two, three!" I placed Mom Number Two in the cup as Mom jumped. She landed with a relieved grin, which vanished when one of the columns disintegrated with a dreadful *crack*. Ice and rubble crashed to the floor in a spray of debris. Mom Number Two lay still, crumpled in the cup.

We hurried to the other side. My pulse thundered in my ears. I centered the bracelet's light beam on the Veil. "I'll replicate it, then we can get out of here."

"You can't." Mom's voice echoed. "Replicators won't reproduce sacred objects."

"What?" Worst news ever.

Creaks and groans split the silence while I tried to smooth out this newest wrinkle in my plan. The whole setup was going to go. "Okay, okay, okay." The chant helped me think. But nothing was okay.

"We need to go. Now." Baldwin's voice was strained.

Pulling off the bracelet, I compared it to the Veil. Metal wire versus a large sheet? My single chance for survival was a long shot. "Mom, jump for the ledge. I'll be right behind you."

She shook her head, her eyes fixed on me.

"Please? There's not enough room for two people. Start climbing down."

After a slight hesitation, she leaped off the edge of the rock platform, landing on the ledge. With a quick glance back at me, she began to climb down.

I eyed the Veil again. The bracelet was crafted of thick, solid wire. The Veil wasn't sheer, and it had a neat, close weave. Were they close to the same weight? If I tried to switch them, and it didn't work, I'd ride a slab of rock a long way down. But the switch could buy me a happy ending.

I yanked the Veil from the cup, dropped in the bracelet, and sprinted for the ledge. Before I reached it, the columns splintered. Explosive *pops* filled the cave with noise and ice. The platform tipped and broke in two, snapping free of its last frozen link.

Epic fail. My eyes connected with Baldwin's, his emerald gaze fixed on me with laser focus. The deafening fall of rock crashed behind me, and the floor rushed up to meet me.

My rock chariot began to glow neon blue.

It jerked, stopped, and I fell to my knees. The blue slab drifted, swaying back and forth, then plunged to the floor, now only a short distance away, where it broke into smaller pieces.

Mom grabbed me in a quick, tight hug. "Nice. Where'd you learn that?"

Pulling away, I rubbed my sore knees and poked the rock. The blue glow faded, the stone unremarkable with its dull-gray hue. "No clue. Was that me?"

"I did it," Baldwin said. "You can thank me later. Here, take your sword."

"Give it to my mom." I handed over Baldwin's knife. Talus's arms trembled. Muffled grunts came from his twitching form. "Let's move."

We all headed for the tunnel, but Baldwin stopped and looked back into the cave. "You go ahead."

"Why?"

"Because. I have something to do." He swayed.

I reached out a hand to steady him. "Are you okay?"

He shook his head and blinked a few times. "Yes. Go. I will catch up."

"No. We all go. Now." I waited for him to step ahead of me in the tunnel.

Frowning, he hurried forward with Mom. Maybe I was an idiot for leaving Talus behind and alive, but I couldn't stomach the thought of more killing.

While we ran, I made puffing introductions. "Mom." *Pant, pant.* "Meet Baldwin." *Gasp.* "Baldwin, meet my mom." *Wheeze.* Sheesh.

In minutes, an angry yell echoed from the cavern.

"Is he moving now?" I asked.

Baldwin ran faster. "Probably."

Despite the stitch in my side, I lengthened my stride, following my mom and Baldwin through the tunnel. We reached the steps leading to the trapdoor. Light streamed from the opening at the top.

Once we cleared the door, I dropped it shut. Of course there was no lock. I sighed and turned to leave. Mom pulled some dirt from her pocket and scattered it around the door.

"What're you doing?"

"Can I borrow your canteen, Baldwin?"

He handed it to her, and she sprinkled water on the dirt. "It's locking powder, but it must be activated with water." The brown powder swelled like a loaf of bread baking. "I had some in my pocket Talus never found. They confiscated my sword and dagger but thought the powder was dirt."

"How long will it hold?"

"Long enough for us to get away. I hope. We need to move quickly."

All of us ran for the coast where Lev had dropped us off. At a roar from above, I checked the sky.

"Arvandus!" The mighty griffin tilted his wings, his silver-tipped feathers catching the light, before he flew around again and landed in front of us. "Mom, meet Arvandus, my griffin."

He lowered his head in a courtly bow. "A pleasure to meet you, Lady James."

She smiled. "Likewise, Arvandus."

Baldwin shielded his eyes. "Do you see Reina?"

"Why do you need Reina?" The blue sky remained clear.

"Lev said to trust her, but I cannot call her because we are not bonded. And Lev is not responding."

I turned to my griffin. "Can you carry the three of us off the island?"

"It will be a slow flight, but it is not far."

A sudden tremor rippled under our feet, the rumble coming from deep underground. I pushed Baldwin toward Arvandus. "Get on. You too, Mom."

I climbed on behind them, keeping one eye on the volcano. With a detonating bang, a cloud of white ice crystals ballooned into the air, glittering. Gray slush and rock spewed into the sky and began racing down the volcano's sides.

Arvandus took flight, his powerful wings straining under the heavy load. Wavelets lapped below. The volcano continued to spew snow, ice, and gravel. Despite all the destruction, a small kernel of worry settled in my chest. What if Talus managed to escape?

When we reached the opposite shore, Arvandus landed and allowed us to dismount. I spun around when another thunderous explosion rocked the shore. Back on the island, the deep green foliage curled and crumbled into brown dust. Trees withered, and sand transformed into snow. Missiles of slush and ice landed in the tossing waves.

"Thank you." I burrowed my fingers into the fur at Arvandus's neck. "I've missed you."

"And I you, Raven." He hung his head. "I did not come back in time to help you. Please accept my sincere apology."

"Actually, you did help. Rumors of my capture reached Emperor Rexson."

"Capture?" Mom grabbed my arm. "When?"

"It's a long story. I'll tell you later." I squeezed her hands and turned back to Arvandus. "What happened in the Steen Mountains?"

"I was detained in Syeira. The city was busy and hurried, and rumors of an uprising are widespread. Their army is gathering. No one knew Emperor Rexson's location, only that he had left the Steen Mountains shortly after my arrival. When I received your message to come back, I came."

"You heard me?"

"Yes, although it was faint. And I would prefer not to argue with you."

I stroked the ruff of his neck and smiled.

Baldwin began searching for Lev, when the tree in front of him warped. He stumbled back. With a yelp, it fell behind some heavy brush. In seconds, Anna emerged, rubbing her hip, bits of bark stuck in her hair.

"Shells and shimmer, I'm glad you guys are back." She grinned at my mom. "You have to be Brenna's mom. I'm Anna."

"It's nice to meet another friend of Brenna's."

Anna tapped Baldwin's shoulder. "Reina will be back from feeding soon."

"What about Lev?"

"Skimmed the blue to Linneah. He and Murray left already."

He rubbed his forehead. "Why?"

"Reina said he should go because he was the faster griffin. They had a big discussion about it. Then she left to hunt."

A nervous wave washed over me. "We don't have time to wait. If Talus escaped, he won't be far behind."

"Whose fault is that?" Baldwin glared at me, his mouth set.

"I wasn't going to kill him just because he took the Veil."

"Maybe you should have!"

"He's my half-brother, okay?"

"Reefstars," Anna said under her breath.

"Even so, if you do not kill him, he will never stop." Baldwin sat on a nearby log.

"Talus has made some very bad choices," my mom said. "But he is still my son."

Baldwin flushed. "Uh, Lady James, I am sorry—"

"I understand your animosity. Nevertheless, he's my son, and I love him. Despite his bad choices, he does not deserve death. That's not who he is..." Her voice trailed off. I'd never seen her look so sad. "He's still young."

"But...he's working with Prince Rune." I tried to make the words more a statement and less an accusation. They hung in the air between us.

"I know." Mom sighed. "His father's been very influential. One of my many mistakes."

Before I could ask what she meant, Reina flew in, touching down next to Arvandus with a ruffle of light brown feathers.

"So, you have finally arrived. I am ready to leave," she said.

Baldwin opened his mouth to argue, but I caught his eye and shook my head. It wouldn't do any good. Reina made her own rules.

Chapter Twenty-Two

I FOUND MY BAG where I'd hid it, safe and undisturbed in its grassy nest. Running my hand over the mysterious package from Emperor Rexson, I thought about what it might be. A yardstick? A rectangular picture frame? A family-size package of Belgian waffles? Again, there was no time to find out. After a quick discussion, we decided to ride for a few hours to gain ground on the army. Mom and I rode Arvandus, while Baldwin followed on Reina. Once we were in the air, Anna swooped and darted around us in crazy patterns. It wouldn't be long before she'd tire out.

Mom and I talked about everything that'd happened since she'd left, especially the events that'd occurred when we arrived in Linneah. I didn't mention my title of Fulfiller of the First Prophecy. Although I believed it now, I wasn't sure Mom would. After she finished asking all the questions I expected (What's your talent? Who trained you? For how long? How's Dad? Where's Grandma Helen?), I asked her one.

"What happened with Talus? I mean, when you were young?"

She hung her head, her long, red hairstreak hiding her expression. When she looked up, lines had settled into her face. "I was eighteen when Taurin and I met. He was different then, charming, powerful, romantic, and very persistent. We married, moved to Ginselwyn, and I became pregnant with Talus. A few years after Talus's birth, Taurin met Prince Rune. Rune promised him all sorts of things, but mostly more power, which he'd always craved. I objected. At that point, things became—difficult."

"What do you mean?"

"He said Rune would give us everything we wanted, or rather, what *he* wanted. When I complained, he became angry. We'd argue, but things never changed. Over time, our arguments escalated, and he became violent." Her eyes gazed back into the old memory, her voice quiet. "One afternoon, Rune came to visit me. Taurin was in town with Talus, and I was alone. He had heard about our arguments, but he wanted to ensure Taurin's involvement. He told me I needed to learn my place. My husband was lord, and I had shamed the family." Her lip curled.

"I bet that went well."

She shook her head. "When that failed, he began to issue threats. He told me to stop resisting, or my son Talus would have a fatal accident. In order to guarantee my cooperation, that monster arranged to have Talus stay with him for a 'long vacation.' I was powerless to stop him. That night, Taurin came home alone with a container of Shadow Power. What that drug did to him…" She shuddered. "If I hadn't left, he would've killed me. So I escaped with Grandma Helen. It broke my heart, leaving behind my son. He was only four." She wiped her eyes with a trembling hand. "I built a life in Pennsylvania, but I never forgot Talus."

"Did Taurin ever come after you?"

"I don't know. Your grandmother had stockpiled enough locking powder to cover the portal for a year. Maybe after a while, he gave up. He had what he wanted most, his son." She attempted a smile. "I always hoped someday Talus and I would reunite."

"So why did you go back?"

"The rumors of a war had grown, and Linneah needed my help. I am one of the most powerful Sensitives they know, and they were trying to secure peace in the Northern Provinces. I've been back before, for a day or two. This time my assignment took a little longer. I focused on completing my mission and coming home. But Taurin has never forgiven me. He waited for the right time, abducted me, and introduced me to the son I left behind."

"How long did they have you?"

"A little over a month." She exhaled a shaky sigh. "They hid some Truthteller Lily serum in my water about four weeks ago. They found out about you and your dad. I'm so sorry. Did they cause problems for you at the portal?"

"It's okay. They weren't expecting Grandma Helen." Mom felt bad enough. No way was I mentioning Dad's injury. He could share that particular story.

When we stopped for the night in a valley hidden from the main path, darkness blanketed the landscape. This mountainous area with its valleys and rocky hillsides provided plenty of hiding places. In an effort to avoid the Trennens and their army, our route took us toward Linneah on the other side of the river. According to Arvandus, we would pass over Wildamek, then fly home.

To keep our location hidden, we went without a fire. Anna and I handed out bread, dried meat, and fruit. The two helli lanterns we had kept us from running into each other at the campsite but wouldn't keep predators away. Still, we couldn't risk being spotted. After our lackluster supper, everyone bedded down, flanked by the griffins. I took the first watch until midnight.

After an uneventful shift, I made myself comfortable on my thin bedroll. Mom had started her shift several minutes ago, Baldwin would be next, and Anna would take the early-morning watch. I rolled over to look at my friends, fast asleep. A dim helli lantern illuminated our sleeping area. Curled into a ball, Anna slept nearby, while Baldwin sprawled a short distance away, closer to the griffins. The clear night sky sparkled with stars, the Petrus Rings glowing. A cool breeze blew, and I pulled my cloak tighter around me. With a final turn on my pad, I relaxed, lulled by the wind rustling through the leaves.

After a few minutes, twigs snapped and my eyes sprang open. Geyla stood a few feet away, carrying a helli lantern. Her face and body were horribly altered, disfigured by the fire.

"Remember me?" She grinned, the skin of her face twisting.

I scrambled back. "You—you're dead. I saw you fall."

She stalked toward me, charred locks of hair breaking off and drifting away in the wind. "What follower of Elyon kills another? Did you enjoy watching me burn, Firebrand?" Her eyes glowed red.

Grabbing for my sword, I clutched air, the space next to me empty.

"Looking for this?" She raised the sword, the blade glinting in the moonlight. "This is mine, murderer. My mission is not finished. I will use the blade to carve you open." She snarled, the scars near her mouth splitting.

With a cry of rage, she lunged. The sword arced wide, its silver edge racing toward me. I bolted up, a scream lodged in my mouth. A quick scan of the sleeping area revealed the truth. Empty. Tears tracked down my face. I shoved a fist against my mouth to stifle my whimpers. Grabbing my canteen, I stumbled a short distance away so I didn't wake the others. My hands trembled when I opened the container, water spilling down my front. Sheer terror had settled deep in my abdomen. Why wouldn't the tears stop?

"Brenna?"

I squeaked, spinning around to confront my attacker.

Baldwin stood in the shadows, barely visible. "What is wrong?"

"Geyla—here—I—alive..." The words poured out in an incoherent rush.

"Come here." He walked close and pulled me into an embrace, the solid strength of his arms reassuring. "Take a breath."

I tried and hiccupped.

His calloused hand brushed my cheek, his thumb lingering near my mouth. "It was a bad dream, nothing more. Take another breath."

This attempt shuddered, gathering oxygen in fits and starts.

"Good job." His soothing voice calmed my nerves. "Do you want to talk about it?"

I gave him an overview, my tears drying while we talked. "It was so real."

"I have had dreams like that."

"About what?" He was quiet for so long, embarrassment washed over me. "That's okay. Forget it."

"I am in a room made of gray stone. There are no windows and no door. I am trapped, and I cannot get out. Usually, I feel an urgency. There is a reason I have to get out, someone needs me or something like that, but I cannot find an exit. The longer I search, the smaller the room becomes." He shrugged. "Not as scary as someone trying to kill me."

"But if it feels real, then it'd be terrifying."

"Well, there is that."

"When do you wake up?"

He cleared his throat. "Right before the walls suffocate me."

I nestled into his embrace and laid my head on his shoulder. It fit perfectly. "I'm glad it's only a dream."

"Yeah, me too." He brushed a kiss on my forehead. After a moment, he pulled away and chuckled. "You make it very difficult to go back to my position."

In the light of my nightmare, I'd forgotten he was on watch. "Sorry." I moved away.

He caught my hands. "Do not be. If I had the time..." He let the sentence lay unfinished. "I do not want to go, but I have to. Do you think you can fall back asleep now?"

"I think so." I let go of his hands, my palms now cold and empty. "Thanks for talking with me."

"Anytime. Sleep well, Brenna." His soft voice wrapped around me, melting the cold spots of terror. I fell asleep with no trouble.

Early the next morning, after a quick breakfast, we mounted in the predawn darkness. Baldwin and I rode Arvandus while Mom and Anna rode Reina. Despite the griffin's unhappiness with two riders, Anna wasn't used to flying such long distances. She promised Reina she'd fly on her own after lunch.

Baldwin leaned close, his hands warm on my waist. "Were you able to fall asleep last night?"

I nodded. "Talking about it helped."

"That usually works. Do you know when I went back to bed I dreamed of Lev? He walked up to me and accused me of preferring Reina over him."

I snorted. "Fat chance of that."

"Right. She should never have sent Lev ahead without me."

"What if he really is faster than she is? Wouldn't that make sense to have him go so they can warn Linneah earlier?"

"Hmm, that is a tough decision. We are separated, and the vinculus does us no good. He is without his bonded rider in a dangerous situation."

A dangerous situation. Much like what was happening right here with the warmth from Baldwin's chest penetrating my cloak and warming my back. I wanted to lean back in his arms, rest my head on his shoulder. Maybe a different topic was in order.

"When we were in the cave, did you notice any weird flashes of light or glowing rocks?"

He leaned closer to hear me over the wind. Early morning light touched his profile, highlighting his chin, the curve of his jaw, the thick green strands at his temple.

"Your hair!" I pointed to the lock of hair.

"What about it?"

"You've got a hairstreak, a green one. Nice."

"Thanks." His pleased grin was understated, but excitement simmered underneath the smile.

"You discovered your talent!" I shot him a mock glare. "So you're holding out on me? Great."

He leaned back, one eyebrow raised. Model material, right here. "When should I have shared this with you? When we were running out of the tunnel? How about when the mountain top exploded?"

"You found out yesterday?" I hadn't noticed. Of course, we'd flown out on separate griffins.

"You could not see it in the dark last night. I did not notice until this morning."

"So what's your talent?"

"A Time Reeler. It is the ability to warp, stall, and adjust time for either one individual or a group. Those flashes of light? That was me. I altered time for Talus and slowed your landing in the cave."

"How did you figure it out?"

"It was an accident. When you almost fell into the lake during your battle with Talus?" He gave me a stern look. "Do not do that again. Ever. My emotion took over. Sometimes gifts are discovered that way. So slowing Talus to an immobile state was an accidental overcompensation." He grinned. "Not a completely bad thing, of course. I had time to think about it while you were on the rock platform. And when it broke loose, I did the only thing I could. I focused on altering the time it took for the rock to drop. Sorry about the landing. I need to work on my control."

"Amazing. Thanks for the help."

"Anytime." His gorgeous smile sent my heart spinning.

I turned and faced forward. My feelings for Baldwin had changed so fast. Our friendship had grown, and now I'd fallen for him—hard. What would happen once we arrived in Linneah? Or when I left for Pennsylvania? Dating someone from another alternity didn't seem like a good idea.

I pulled my thoughts to the present. "We need a plan. I'm not sure we're going to get to Linneah much sooner than Taurin's army."

"Lev and Murray will make good time. But I am uncertain if we have prepared enough."

Dread settled low. "Are you saying Linneah's going to lose?"

"No, but I am saying you cannot underestimate Prince Rune. He is a master strategist—sneaky, manipulative, and vengeful. Add the force of Taurin's army, and Linneah will need to be careful."

"Will Emperor Rexson fight?"

"If he is there. If he is not there yet, he will be soon."

That gave me a measure of comfort. A strong and powerful ruler like Emperor Rexson made our odds better. That had to count for something.

Do not borrow trouble, Raven, Arvandus said. *The men and women of Linneah have been expecting this. We will be ready for Taurin's army.*

I hope you're right.

The rest of the day, the griffins poured on the speed, trying to arrive in Linneah before Taurin's army. We didn't know what kind of pace they were achieving, especially if Shadow Power was involved.

When the sun began to set, darkness gathered in the mountains. "We should land," I said to Arvandus.

After a few minutes of looking for a place, we found a hollow and dropped into it. Our uninspiring supplies had dwindled to scarce amounts. We unpacked and ate another light meal of dried meat and hard biscuits. While we cleaned up, Baldwin did a double take, then dashed into the underbrush. In a few moments, he returned with his sword drawn and a small dead animal in his hand.

"Bragnaborns. Everyone cover up."

Mom gasped.

"Use my cloak." I pulled it out of my bag.

"What will you use?"

I handed it to her. "I have a few extra things in my bag. After my watch is over, I'll put something on." The only "extra things in my bag" were the veil and the red dress I'd bought in the Linnean market. That's what I got for packing at the last minute.

Everyone settled down for the night. Minus Anna. In a clearing of helli plants, I found her appearing and disappearing over and over again. "What're you doing?"

She grinned, her smile appearing first like the Cheshire cat. "I'm shape shifting into wind."

"Can you do that?"

"I'm working on it. See?" Her form misted over and disappeared. A gust ruffled my hair. The gust giggled, then she reappeared.

"I'm surprised you're letting me watch. What about the feeling-naked-in-public thing?"

"That's drift talk. Since I'm disappearing, you can't see anything." She did it again.

Creepy. "Cool. Everyone else is in bed. We'll head out early."

"Fun. Can I have first watch?"

"I've got it. I'm not that tired anyway. We signed you up for the second shift."

A knowing smile lifted her lips. Unraveling the gray scarf from around her cloak collar, she looped it around my neck. "It'll help with the Bragnaborns when you bed down. I've got another one."

I shot her a thankful smile and walked away.

My worry gone regarding the Bragnaborns, I pulled the still-wrapped package out of my bag. I'd never forgotten it. Its three-foot length stuck out of the top of my bag, teasing me with possibilities. Now that I had the time to open it, I moved closer to a helli lantern and tore off the brown paper.

Savoring the moment, I let the awesomeness drift over me.

Emperor Rexson had given me a new sword.

I grasped the scabbard and waited. Something was different. No nausea. No dizziness or clamminess. I gave a half-smile. Weird. I'd come to expect it.

A work of art, the scabbard had been crafted in silver. The flames etched on the metal glittered in the low light. I pulled out the sword, a faint ringing shimmering through the dark. Slender like a silver ribbon, its rigid length sliced the air when I took a practice swing. Flame-like cutwork decorated the blade, and inlaid, sparkling-red stones adorned the top of the silver hilt. Aside from its physical beauty, this sword fit my hand perfectly.

Remembering my responsibility, I studied the surrounding shadows. The evening birds called back and forth, saying goodnight through the trees. No bushes transformed into menacing trolls, and no little Bragnaborns crossed my path.

After a minute or two, I relaxed a little. A cool breeze whispered through the leaves. Low clouds scudded across the sky, hiding the moon and parts of the Petrus Rings.

I glanced down and spied a piece of paper on the ground filled with a powerful handwritten script. At the bottom was an embossed seal, the eight-pointed star of Linneah. I picked it up and opened it.

Brenna, I believe this sword will rectify any problems you have been having. Although Adrik is an excellent blacksmith, he is unaware of a Firebrand's singular weakness. Never use a vladlen-steel blade. It will make you feeble, and your swordsmanship will be clumsy. Vladlen steel wounds will also need to be treated with extra care. Aideen Siriol, a great Firebrand warrior from nearly four hundred times ago, used this sword. It is made of zoharet silver, one of Linneah's most precious metals. The stones set in the hilt are rare Fire Diamonds of the deepest red, found during Aideen's greatest adventure. Use it well.

Emperor Rexson

I smiled and tucked the note in my bag for safekeeping, right next to the Veil. Swinging the sword in a practice arc, I attacked a few imaginary opponents. Aideen Siriol's sword was wicked fast. I transferred it to my side, confident.

Nothing would harm us tonight.

Chapter Twenty-three

With two days of flying behind us, I was tired, on edge, and ready to arrive in Linneah. Bad dreams had followed me home. Last night, I'd had another. Geyla had chased me through my REM cycle, her sword nicking my spine repeatedly. I woke up sweaty and discovered sharp pebbles had slipped into my bedroll.

We arrived late and camped across the river from the city. From the edge of the woods, the castle rose into the sky, still and silent in the moonlight. Even now, the delay didn't feel right. What if the city was fighting now and here we sat, waiting for daylight? For some reason, my mother and Baldwin wanted to wait. Anna refused to vote on the situation, which left me in the minority. I took the downtime to practice using my new sword. Despite the weird quirks of Adrik's vladlen-steel weapon, I'd adjusted. Learning to use my new sword was like swimming in a pool after training in the ocean.

Baldwin pulled me aside before everyone turned in for the evening. "There is something you should know. About the First Prophecy."

"Oh, goody, more surprises. What? More snakes?"

"No, something else my mom told me about the prophecy. You need to prepare to fight your enemy one on one."

"I already did that. It was a complete failure, one I barely escaped. Thanks for the reminder." I grinned to soften my sarcasm.

"Talus is not the main threat. There are other more powerful enemies. Like Taurin or Rune."

"Does the First Prophecy say that?"

"No, but she had a vision of an armed female, facing an enemy. And—" His voice broke.

"What? I die?"

"All I can tell you is, she felt an immense sacrifice was made."

My stomach plummeted. "Okay. Thanks for the info." I turned away.

"Brenna?"

I didn't answer. *Go, just go.* I began to practice again, hoping he would take the hint and leave. After a long moment, he walked away. Heaving out a breath, I sheathed my sword.

It would be better to get the confrontation out of the way. Waiting always made me nervous. Nerves made me make bad decisions. And bad decisions were always, well, bad. For all I knew, Talus had escaped. Maybe at this moment he'd joined Taurin to hunt the Veil. Which lay in my bag.

The thought followed me all through my shift. After Anna and I switched, I grabbed a couple of good-sized stones and headed back to wait in my sleeping area. Lying down, I didn't bother to take off my sword. My bag was within arm's reach, the rocks conveniently resting on top. The camp quieted. Still, I waited, listening to the silent camp. Tree frogs croaked, bushes rustled with nocturnal creatures, and the wind's sigh barely moved the leaves. Anna walked the perimeter of the site, varying her pattern as Baldwin had taught us at the start of our trip. When she turned to walk to the other side of the camp, I grabbed the stones and heaved them into the forest. The rocks landed, leaves and underbrush crunched, and she moved away to investigate. I seized my bag and crept from the sleeping camp.

The spotty moonlight illuminated trees in stark relief one minute and plunged me into complete darkness the next. Squinting in the inky shadows, I picked around rocks and boulders, using them for cover in case I was followed. The sound of rushing water met my ears, and I wilted. The river. I'd forgotten all about it. It ran fast and deep. The sudden moonlight revealed a fallen shield tree spanning the river. Judging from the path worn in the grass, others had used it as a bridge. I held my breath and stepped onto the branches. They bent, the limbs cracking. The bark broke off, and I stumbled. Gritting my teeth, I continued toward the opposite bank.

Halfway across the river, Arvandus's dark form flew above. A flying shadow, he spread his disapproval like fertilizer from a crop duster. He landed on the grassy bank, his back to the forest. By the time I reached the riverbank, I'd prepared for an argument.

His first words surprised me. "This is not wise, but in the future I would like to be notified of your plans."

"If this isn't wise, why are you here?"

"The vinculus. We succeed or die trying—together."

"I'm gonna die, Arvandus. Baldwin's mom said there'd be a great sacrifice." Fear dried out my mouth, my tongue thick.

"You are not dead yet. What is your plan?"

"I can't wait until morning. I should be there. Either I find the army waiting for daylight, or I find them fighting."

"How much are you willing to sacrifice for Linneah?"

"Everything." Despite my short time here, I'd grown to love this paradise. "I need to get into the city."

His head shot up, and he stood, the silver tips of his wings glittering with small sparklers. His glowing, golden eyes focused over my shoulder. "Raven?"

At the familiar whisper behind me, my flesh crawled. "Allow me to take you into Linneah."

Before I could turn, a hand clamped onto my shoulder, the forceful fingers digging into my neck. "Shut up, and do not move. If you disobey either command, I will kill your griffin." Talus chuckled, and the stink of Shadow Power wafted over me. "Not that it would be any great loss, since he obviously did not sense me stalking you. Invisibility has its benefits." He squeezed, pain streaking up my neck. "King Donalt's blood is a strong elixir."

My stomach flipped. "You drank it?"

"Not all of it, of course. After Hedeon bled him dry, it was divided among my father, his soldiers, and me."

"That's disgusting."

He squeezed my neck harder. "That, dear sister, is power. Something you could have had, but perhaps your loyalty satisfies you enough." With his other hand, he grabbed my bag and opened it. "Ah, the Veil." His smug voice held a touch of glee. I followed his movements, twisting my neck around under his painful grip. He arranged the Veil so it hung around his invisible neck, suspended in the darkness. The material glowed, a beacon in the night.

"Mm." He gave a hum of satisfaction. "The power is indescribable. And to think my dear sister is responsible."

I bit my lip, swallowing against the bile in my throat.

After one more cruel squeeze, he released me. "All the same, be an obedient little half-breed and do not cause trouble. Head for the city."

"Why should I?"

A shocked beat of silence followed. "What did you say?"

"Why should I obey any of your orders?"

"Because I will kill you if you do not."

"You're going to kill me anyway. I can hear it in your voice. You have no intention of letting me live."

Arvandus's low growl comforted me in the darkness.

"Listen, Princess." Talus's sour breath blew hot against my face. "I am taking you and your griffin into Linneah. That is all you need to know."

"How are you planning to move a griffin the size of a bus?"

A bolt of white light blazed from the spot next to me. The beam hit the griffin's flank with a sizzle. Arvandus snarled, his wingtips flashing brighter sparks. Horrified guilt flooded my stomach.

"Now move." Talus gave me a hard shove. I stumbled forward and kept walking. It never occurred to me to argue. He had it all—me, Arvandus, and worst of all, the Veil.

Herded in front of him like sheep, we walked toward Linneah. He demanded silence. I couldn't have said a word anyway. Despair built a dam in my throat. Faking a misstep, I placed my hand on Arvandus's wound as if to steady myself. Darkness lurked there, a heavy evil in the injury. I pushed heat into it, flushing out the poison Talus had unleashed. By the time we reached the city gate, the griffin's skin had knit together.

"Halt!" A guard materialized from the shadows. "State your business!"

Talus's bolt of light tunneled into the guard's exposed throat. The man dropped to his knees. He gasped once, before Talus shot a killing beam between the guard's eyes. He collapsed without a sound.

Before we could walk any further, another guard came running toward us. Could I stop this horrific scene from playing out? "Don't—"

Talus flung a broad beam in the guard's direction which exploded in the man's face, dropping him where he stood.

Talus pushed us forward through the gate. When we arrived at the Linnean Garden at the base of the castle, Talus stopped, his grip firm on my arm. His murky outline and features faded in and out like smoke. Apparently, he couldn't stay invisible forever.

"You have not met my father. I will make introductions. After all, he will want to watch while I kill you."

"I don't think so, Talus." My mother's voice rang out. She strode toward us, her eyes glittering with anger. "Let Brenna go. Now."

In Talus's misty face was a glimpse of a hurt little boy. "You are in no position to make demands, Mother."

"Don't do this. You don't need Rune's corrupt power. Use the natural gift you have. I saw it when you were small."

"Yet you left anyway."

"That decision was the most—"

"I. Do. Not. Care. You are selfish. You make promises, then leave when you accomplish your goals. You care little for anyone else. You left your first husband, your first child, and now your second child. I see a pattern here."

"Not true, Talus. I love you and have always loved you."

For a moment, his hazy features brightened with hope. I blinked, and it vanished. "Father will be pleased to have you come home, where you belong."

Mom's face blanched, but she gripped Geyla's sword tighter. I'd never been so thankful I'd given it to her. "Brenna and Arvandus, come with me."

"Nobody is going anywhere," Talus said.

When I unsheathed my sword, he laughed. "Ah, yes, Princess. I remember how well you handled yourself last time. Too bad your little soldier is not here to help you."

A blinding beam of white light shot from his fingers. I reacted and slashed left and right, my sword flashing when it cut through the bright bolts. Hope flared brighter than the beams. Unbeliev-able—a sword that sliced and diced magic!

Mom was wicked fast with her sword, managing better than I ever had. Despite her skill, a few beams tore through her sleeve. In the next instant, she cried out and dropped the sword with a clatter. She gathered her tunic's hem to staunch the blood welling up on her wrist. In seconds, it soaked through, staining the soft fabric.

At some point, Arvandus had disappeared into the shadows. I couldn't protect him right now. Despite my struggle to defend myself, I backed up to be a human shield between my mom and Talus. He took a step toward me. His face came into focus, the marked lines tracking across his face clear.

He sneered. "And then there was one."

His fingers were more effective than any sword. I parried the bolts, my sword a silver blur. In a sudden movement from the shadows, Arvandus pounced and attacked the nape of Talus's neck with his powerful jaws. His mighty wings flapped, the silver feathers casting hundreds of brilliant sparks in the shadows.

Talus screamed, the bolts of white light going wide. When Arvandus lifted him, the Veil slipped off his shoulders and puddled on the ground.

My mother stood silent, her face agonized, blood dripping from her cradled wrist.

"Put me down." Talus's face blanched, his hands grabbing the air.

Arvandus gave me a warning look, his leonine features grim.

"No," I said. "If we let you go, you'll kill every one of us."

Talus's eyes narrowed. His hands came together, and a wide ray of white light exploded toward me. Turning the flat of my sword toward him, I blocked most of it. The edge of the beam slipped past the sharp edge, scorching my tunic and skin. The largest part of the ray reflected off my blade and returned, finding its mark in his abdomen. Talus gasped, his eyes glazing as the blinding light cut off.

My hands numbed, and I dropped my sword. When I glanced at my mother, guilt flooded me. Tears streaked her face. Taking a step forward, she reached out as Talus's eyes lost focus and he went still. She slumped to her knees and buried her face in her hands.

Arvandus turned, dropping Talus in the shadows before moving to block our view of the body. "Gather the Veil and put it in your bag. Then please see to your mother's wrist. She has lost too much blood. You will need attention as well."

Now that he mentioned it, my upper right arm burned, the pain deep. I lifted my sleeve—one of Talus's beams had left a bloody gash. Huh. I'd been so hyperfocused, I hadn't even noticed the pain.

After storing the Veil in my bag, I had Mom rest against one of the large tree trunks that supported the castle. While I concentrated on healing her wrist, silent tears ran down her face. Guilt, helplessness, and frustration weighted my shoulders. An incessant voice in my head whispered names and accusations—*murderer, traitor, killer*. I pushed it aside and sank into the timeless fog of healing. When the only sign of her injury was a pale line, I healed my own wound.

No magic words could make everything better, but I had to try. "I'm so sorry."

Her arms came around me, and her soft sobs carried away on the breeze.

After removing Talus's body, Arvandus returned some time later. We were all quiet while we rested at the castle supports.

My mom's ashy face had aged, the lines settling deep. "I don't blame you, Brenna."

Liar, backstabber, deceiver, murderer. The lump in my throat grew. "It's my fault. I did it."

"No, you saved us. He would've killed us all. I miss the child he used to be, honey. But it's not your fault. Talus made his choices."

Her tight hug washed away some of my guilt. Maybe time would banish the voice, too. I turned to Arvandus. "We're heading for the castle. Please guard this entrance until you hear from me. If fighting breaks out, contact me and find cover."

He settled his bulky form in front of one of the arched stone doorways. Before I passed through the archway and out of his sight, his voice stopped me. "I will not cower from combat, Raven."

"I'm not asking you to, but I just—stay safe, okay?"

He nodded, his expression watchful. Mom and I walked through the archway and climbed the staircase leading to the castle entrance.

CHAPTER TWENTY-FOUR

IN THE SILENT CASTLE, our footsteps echoed in the empty hallways. A quick inspection confirmed what I already knew in my gut. "Where is everybody?"

"They must be operating on a skeleton crew. A few may be hiding in the lowest level of the castle. The rest are with family members or friends." Determination gleamed in my mom's eyes. "I'm going to call Campion. The archers will need help."

"What?"

"I'm pretty good with a bow and arrow, sweetheart."

"But what if you—"

She put her hand over my mouth, stopping my words. "Trust Elyon. Okay?"

Dread blanketed my stomach, but I nodded anyway.

Mom gave me a tight smile, her eyes serious. "Go hide with the others down in the storeroom until the battle's over."

"No."

"Young lady, you will—"

"Linneah needs me. The Prophecy says the Raven can save the land."

She shook her head. "That prophecy can be interpreted a hundred different ways. You'd be safer if—"

I gave her a big hug to cut off the lecture. "Don't worry. I'll hang with Arvandus. When this is over, I'll find you. Right now, I need to find a safe place for the Veil."

A muffled shriek came from outside. Mom gave me a quick kiss on the forehead. "Campion is here. Stay safe. I've got to go. I love you, sweetie."

"Love you too, Mom." My throat swelled with a golf ball-sized lump. I couldn't watch her walk away.

Fears swirled through my mind. I wouldn't think about her dying, never coming back. Instead, I'd focus on the newest dilemma of the day—where to hide the Veil. An image of the enemy storming the castle and burning the Veil drifted through my mind. To my right, an open doorway led to the Gathering Room. I wandered in, my boot heels clicking across the wooden floor. The carved chairs had been pushed against the walls, waiting like middle-school kids at the beginning of a school dance. I walked toward the front of the room where a waist-high table stood. Its wooden surface reflected a muted mosaic of color from the moonshine filtering through the stained glass.

Although I'd never been big on church, things were different here. Supernatural things were visible. I'd experienced divine protection, seen evil in physical form. God had kept me alive and protected my family and friends through chaos and near-death experiences. There was more to come, too. But this moment of calm in the midst of the crazy was a good place to say thanks.

Dropping to my knees, I pulled the Veil out of my bag. The soft fabric was wrinkled, crushed in my bag for so long. I folded it, smoothing out the creases. "Elyon, thank you for, uh, everything." That was me, Ms. Smooth. Overwhelmed by too many words, I paused and let the quiet sink deep.

The moonshine coming through the Vision Window made the glass glow with a muted light. The pieces shifted, twisting and turning like a kaleidoscope. Murray's words drifted through my mind while the pieces settled in place. *Whatever your question, the answer will be shown in that window...* The image showed the table in front of me with an open drawer on the side. I blinked and jumped to my feet, searching for a latch, handle, pull-tab, anything. But the table was a simple wooden affair with no obvious grooves or handles, only an engraved poem that circled the edge. Reading the words out loud, my voice rang in the empty room. "Under wood and in between, Linneah's secrets lie unseen. With a gem of love unsealed, Linneah's secrets are revealed." I glared at the table, wishing the words were a magic spell. Reading them again, I swallowed a sigh. At the moment, riddles sucked.

Since I thought better while moving, I began to pace the length of the room. The first and second line could refer to the hidden side drawer. What about the last two lines? Gem of love meant what? Rubies, sapphires, diamonds? Maybe a crown or jewelry had been hidden somewhere in the room. Walking around the room's edges, I checked shelves, nooks, and drawers for anything that resembled a gem of love. That search came up empty, but I continued to search under chairs and at the base of the floorboards. When I finished, I'd scored two hairclips and a dust bunny.

Maybe the poem referred to something else. I picked up my pace, walking back and forth. Diamonds were usually used in wedding rings, and weddings were all about love. I studied the fire diamonds set into the handle of my sword. Could they be pried out? Grasping the hilt, I picked at the gem's edges with a fingernail. My nail split to a ragged edge. Great. I hurried out to the cobblestone hallway and banged the handle against the stone. Nothing came loose.

Back to pacing. The room echoed with my footsteps. What other gems were available? Maybe it was something everyone owned.

No matter who showed up, the table would open. My steps slowed, stopped. Blinking once, I touched my jasper. A gem given by the Most High King—to any child of the Jasper Territory. Because I was valuable, important, loved. Pulling it off, I held the silver chain so the red stone hung suspended. Its facets glittered, on fire in the low light. I stepped up to the table and placed my jasper on the surface. Nothing happened. Several excruciating seconds passed. I spun away from the table, blinking back tears of frustration. Impossible. I'd hide the Veil somewhere in my room.

When I turned around to pick up my necklace, I gasped. A red flame danced from the gem's center. The table didn't burn, its wooden surface undamaged beneath the fire. From the side came a soft *snick*, and a drawer slid out. Its depth and width would hold the Veil, if I folded it two more times. Slipping the cloth inside, I pushed the drawer closed. The necklace's flame winked out. When I picked it up, the sparkling jasper lay cool in my palm.

Hurrying outside and back down the staircase, I slipped through the Linnean Gardens. In our absence, the workers had made great strides improving its appearance. Helli plants bloomed, their glow illuminating cleared walkways laid with clean stones. A lime fringe of new grass pushed up through the soil, and the moonflowers near the stone archways closed their blooms as night ended. If Taurin and his soldiers gained the castle, they would destroy all of this again.

I joined Arvandus. Reina had arrived with Anna and a furious Baldwin. The green of his eyes glittering, Baldwin strode up to me and gripped my upper arms. "What is wrong with you? Are you trying to get killed?"

"It's going to happen anyway."

Arvandus stood and stretched his legs, his tail flicking. "Not yet, Raven. The great sacrifice Mariel saw was Lady James's sacrifice. She gave up her son."

Baldwin's mouth dropped open. "She killed Talus?"

"No, I did. Sort of." I turned away, afraid to say aloud what had happened, afraid it'd make it real and worse. My dreams at night were bad enough with Geyla haunting me. If Talus joined her, I'd never sleep again.

He clasped my hand, his fingers strong yet gentle. "Hey. Are you okay?"

"I will be."

His eyes softened, and he squeezed my hand before releasing it.

Arvandus glanced at the sky. "Lev is here."

"Yes!" Baldwin did a modern fist pump.

We mounted the griffins and flew for the far northern city gates. Once in the air, I scanned the horizon for Taurin's army. Erhardt had manned each city gate with several guards and two scouts. When we reached the city's outer limits, I spotted a shadowy, lone figure slipping through the gate.

Arvandus, can we follow that person?

In answer, he swooped lower. We tracked the figure through the thick forest.

Oh, hey! That's Rosamunde. Let's land.

In a nearby clearing, we slid off our griffins. Anna turned to me. "What now?"

I kept my voice low. "Rosamunde's headed for Rune's army. We need to warn her."

Baldwin strained to see into the darkness. "She is getting too far ahead. We are wasting time. Lev, follow me."

Anna raised her eyebrows. "You won't catch her on a griffin. They'll slow you down. Skim the blue, and I'll hang with them until you get back."

He tilted his head. "Half the time, I have no idea what you are saying. Skim the blue?"

I grabbed his hand. "Never mind. Come on." Shooting a thankful smile at Anna, we sprinted in the direction I last saw

Rosamunde. After a few minutes, we spotted her shadowy figure moving north.

When we got close enough, he called out to her. "Rosamunde!"

She spun around, a hand pressed to her chest. "Oh, Baldwin! And Brenna! You have both returned unharmed. Praise Elyon." She swept us both into a hug.

The odor of Shadow Power laced the air. Unease slipped through me. I wrinkled my nose and glanced at Baldwin.

He studied her, his brow furrowed. "Why are you leaving the city?"

"I was out for a walk."

"Before dawn? While we prepare for war?" he asked.

"I needed to clear my head." Her forced smile fell away.

"The enemy army's headed this way," I said.

Her lips twitched, but she said nothing.

Oh, no. My heart sinking, I made a calculated guess. "But you knew that. That's why you're out here, because you're going to meet them. Who're you meeting? Talus?"

"That is preposterous."

"And true." Hurt flashed in Baldwin's wide eyes. "I cannot believe you are working with him. He promised you more knowledge, more power, and you could not resist. Did you kill Uncle Donalt, too?"

She shook her head. "I could never hurt him."

"I'm guessing you helped Hedeon and Talus break in. You didn't expect them to kill him, though," I said. "That was a surprise. Did you help Talus steal the Veil?"

"No! He did not steal the Veil or kill King Donalt. Together, we will find the king's murderer and bring healing and closure to grieving Linneans. Talus cares about Linneah." She lifted her head, her eyes filled with desperate hope. "And me."

"Man, are you delusional." I drew away, the smell of burnt spices turning my stomach. "Talus cares about Talus, period. Everything he did—killing King Donalt, stealing the Veil—was for Rune. But it doesn't matter. Because—" Guilt clogged my throat, my voice dying. I couldn't say it.

Baldwin stepped forward, his lip curled. "Because Talus is dead."

She gasped, her face going pale. Then she bolted.

I darted after her, Baldwin close behind, jumping rocks and downed trees. Yet thick underbrush and dark shadows fooled my eyes. Her body blended with the predawn gloom. I stopped, scanning the forest, while Baldwin continued to search.

He finally returned, panting. "I cannot believe she would betray us like this. What could she gain by working with the enemy?"

"More knowledge? I don't know. We should go back. I'm betting Taurin and his army aren't far away."

When we arrived at the edge of the city, we learned Erhardt and the army had headed off to meet Taurin in a preemptive strike. On a little rise, Mom and Murray were deep in conversation while she filled a quiver with arrows. Small torches and helli lanterns flickered nearby. Armored guards put on helmets and picked up shields. Nearby, four-footed, horned beasts pulled a catapult into position, their shaggy hair covering every inch of their bodies. They were identical to Emperor Rexson's ride through Silvastamen.

I nudged Baldwin. "What are those animals with the horns?"

"A wood rason. We use them for farming and travel, although compared to a griffin, they are sluggish animals." He didn't look at me, his focus on the military activity.

"Maybe we should catch up with the army." We needed to find Erhardt. He'd want to know we were back. Maybe he could put us in a place where we could help.

"Lev and I could go look for Erhardt and the army," Baldwin said.

Anna spoke up. "Well, I'm not staying here."

"All right," he said. "All of us will find him, then make a decision."

The Linnean army gathered in a clearing between the city gates and the woods. The forest loomed ahead, dense and impenetrable. All of the soldiers wore black metal helmets and breastplates embossed with the eight-pointed Linnean star. A platoon of men sat astride griffins, the animals' modified armor shining in the lantern light. Other armies from the Jasper Territory were there, too. A battalion of Camlos dug a trench spanning the path into the woods, while Kell soldiers angled spears in the trough. A squad of Linnean archers shouldered large quivers full of arrows. They settled into position with satyrs and centaurs on a nearby rise.

Erhardt stood at the front, double checking the troops and giving last-minute orders. I almost didn't recognize him in full-Warrior mode. A bronze and silver breastplate spanned his chest, and streaks of red paint slashed across his forehead and high cheekbones.

Anna giggled and turned to me. "He's a definite surge boss."

"Baldwin, Brenna, you are back!" One of his blond eyebrows rose. "And were you successful in your quest?"

I resisted the urge to click my heels together and salute. "Yes. And Talus is no longer an issue."

"Taurin will want revenge. The two of you are to go to the castle."

"What?" Baldwin's mouth fell open. "Nothing is going to happen there."

"Exactly. All civilians must evacuate to a safe place. Go to the castle." He turned to Anna. "And you are?"

She performed a low curtsy with precision. "Annalise Annalice, ready to join your forces against the army of Taurin."

"Your offer is appreciated. Stay with Brenna and Baldwin."

When he turned away, Anna tugged on my arm. "He noticed me. He noticed me! Is he married?"

"Don't ask me. Ask his cousin." I nodded at Baldwin.

While she pestered Baldwin with questions, I walked over to Arvandus. "Something doesn't feel right."

"Combat makes people nervous."

"No, that's not it." I leaned against his warm side, studying shadows in the near-dawn light. "Taurin's army should be here by now. They were stronger, faster than we were. What slowed them down?"

"What if they were not slowed down? What if the city of Linneah was not their first target?"

"But there isn't anything between us and the army. Taurin said they were marching on Linneah." I turned to him. "Let's get in the air. Maybe we'll see something."

"Erhardt ordered us to the castle."

"Yeah. Not happening. I'm not going underground like a coward."

Arvandus chuckled.

Once in the air, I studied the ground. Spread around the city were hundreds of Kells, Camlos, and Merripens from Matana Island. The colored flags identifying each army whipped in the breeze coming off the ocean. A large detachment of Welden soldiers marched in from Ginselwyn. They traveled toward Linneah, their banner flying.

More reinforcements. Emperor Rexson is stationed near the southern gate. Linneah has done all it can.

Arvandus? One question wouldn't leave me alone. *What if we don't win?*

I cannot answer that, Raven. We can only defend our home. Which reminds me, we both need armor. We will go to the armory for you, then we can return to the griffin house for my breastplate.

The armory was long and narrow, a one-storied building constructed next to the blacksmith's shop on the castle grounds. When we arrived, a short, old man was locking the front door of the building. His orange hairstreak offered a striking contrast to his bushy, white hair. He pocketed the key in a leather pouch and wiped his hands on his gray pants.

I slid off Arvandus and hurried over to him. "Hi. Do you happen to have a shield?"

He waved me away. "I am on a breakfast break. Come back later."

"It's kind of an emergency."

Stopping, he turned and threw up his hands. "Where were you two days ago?"

"I got back today. I was traveling."

"Oh, off on a fancy trip, were you? And you dance into town before daybreak and expect a nice shield with matching bracers?"

"Ooh. Do you have that available?"

"No."

Then why'd he bring it up? "Look, this is my first battle. I've trained, but—"

He cut me off. "Saints and sinners! What makes you think you have any right to be on the battlefield then?"

Pushing down a flare of anger, I produced a small fireball and shot it toward a bare patch of dirt. It exploded on impact, spraying a wide circle of dirt and pebbles. "I thought I could help."

His bushy eyebrows rose. "Come in then. Maybe something is left."

The armory wasn't large, maybe the size of two or three castle bedrooms combined. It had a cobblestone exterior but wooden walls inside. At the back of the room was a large table cluttered with sheets of metal and blocks of wood. Wide storage closets stood side by side on the right wall. Dozens of hooks, all empty, hung from the walls. The thin old man propped his hands on his hips. "As you can see, I have been picked clean. You do not need a weapon, correct?"

"No, just a shield."

"Hmm. You will need bracers, as well." He opened a few closet doors before pulling out a round shield. It was a dented piece of silver craftsmanship, but at this point, I didn't care. It was protection.

"Thank you. It's perfect."

He raised an eyebrow. "Perfect is an overstatement. Put these on." He slapped a heavy pair of leather bracers into my hands and leaned the shield against the wall. They laced up the inside of my forearm, and after struggling with them for several minutes, the old man heaved a sigh. Rolling his eyes, he pushed my hands aside. "Let me do it. It is painful to watch you struggle with something so simple."

When they were laced, I picked up the shield and gave him a thankful smile. "You're awesome. Thanks. How much do I owe you?"

He waved away my question. "I heard of your search. Did you retrieve the Veil?"

"Yes, it's safe and back where it belongs."

Opening the door, he herded me outside. "That is enough payment for me. Now, I need breakfast." He locked the door again and began walking toward the residential area of Linneah. "Fight well."

"Thank you." *Not enough. Couldn't I fight well* and *come back alive? He was helpful, not super nice, but helpful.* I climbed onto Arvandus's back.

Beetle gave you what you needed. That is sufficient. He launched into the sky with a burst of power.

Beetle? Really? I laughed, the sound carried away by the wind. *No wonder he was grumpy.*

We arrived at the griffin house in minutes and saw nothing out of the ordinary on the way. What piece of the puzzle was I missing?

The front door of the griffin house hung slightly ajar. Inside, most of the dim stalls stood empty. A few pregnant griffins slept while an older griffin remained on guard inside the door. He was a winged cat like Arvandus but with the massive mane of a lion. His feline face held a long scar across one eye, and his opposite ear was torn. I followed Arvandus back to his sleeping area and pulled the protective shield from its hook.

"There is also a piece that covers my flanks. I will need that."

I attached the pieces together, my hands trembling. "Arvandus, I need to say something before this all gets crazy. I may not have the chance later."

"Raven, there is no need—"

"Let me finish. I'm so grateful we're bonded. You're the truest friend." My eyes stung, and I swallowed hard. "I haven't been the easiest person to be bonded with. So thank you for putting up with me."

His low chuckle was gravel wrapped in velvet. "I am not an easy griffin to deal with, either. We are a perfect match."

I gave him a quick hug before we walked back outside. Dawn had arrived, holding hands with a vivid orange-streaked sky. The elderly griffin still kept watch inside the door.

Arvandus turned to him. "Has it been quiet?"

The griffin nodded, his keen eyes scrutinizing the area. "Yes, but the scent of Shadow Power rides the breeze. It will not be long." His eyes met Arvandus's. "May Elyon bless you. Fly true."

Arvandus knelt for me to climb into the saddle. When I grabbed the leather edge, the puzzle pieces clicked into place as if a light bulb flared to life. I gripped the saddle, my knuckles turning white. "Arvandus, I know why we couldn't see the army. They're invisible. Remember, Talus said the king's blood made him invisible. So, if everybody in Taurin's army drank it, we won't see them coming. We need to tell Erhardt. Now."

A blood-curdling scream seized my heart like a giant fist. It came from the battlefield. A series of eagle screeches followed. Lev? Reina?

Arvandus's low voice was filled with warning. "They have arrived. And Lev says they are attacking our soldiers from behind."

Chapter Twenty-Five

"Let's go." I jumped onto his back. The scarlet sun had ushered in a brilliant vermillion sunrise. It wouldn't last long. A few clouds drifted in, their ominous darker cousins following from the west.

"Where would you like to go?" He rose in the air, his powerful wings carrying us higher.

Good question. "I have no idea. The First Prophecy never mentioned war strategy."

"Its meaning is not always obvious."

"'The Raven's share can save the land.' Which means...?"

"Your share is your assets or your portion. Gifts at your disposal, perhaps."

"Emperor Rexson gave me a new sword." Dread weighed sick and heavy. The emperor's message had been simple. *Use it well.* "Okay. Get me to the front of the army." Yes, please. A super-sized order of homicidal warriors, coming up.

"Raven, are you sure this is how you want to proceed?"

No. My mind raced ahead to what waited for me. Despite the superiority of this sword compared to that steel stick Adrik had made, I wasn't good enough. Especially not against all the trained warriors of Rune.

Raven?

This won't work, Arvandus. Even if I use my talent. My sword skills aren't good enough to defeat trained warriors. Something tells me I'd be more use to Emperor Rexson alive than dead.

Before Arvandus could reply, a low whizz sliced the air near my ear.

"What was that?" I leaned closer to his neck, the fur warm against my cheek.

Archers. Hold on tight. Arvandus rolled to the left.

In my ears, the wind whistled, and my eyes watered from the icy blast. Curl, roll, dip—my stomach lagged behind. He gathered speed, then shot through a cluster of clouds. A fine mist collected on my cloak. Nerves jittered under my skin.

When someone hollered my name, I yelped. Baldwin pulled even with me, riding Lev. Behind him, Anna rode Reina. She'd confided in me yesterday that Reina had agreed to carry her into battle, if needed. I grimaced, shaking my head. She was welcome to the grumpy griffin.

"Land over there." Baldwin gestured to a large copse of trees away from the fighting.

We landed. Immediate relief flooded my system, followed by a healthy dose of guilt.

"Brenna, if you go in there with your sword flying, they will kill you," Baldwin said.

"Thanks a bunch."

"It is the truth, and you know it. Anna and I are willing to fight with you."

"And then the three of us will die instead of just me. Tons better. No, thanks." A tree in the next field over exploded in flames, and I winced.

Taurin's soldiers were ghosts, faint visions of mist and light. Jeering shrieks rent the air. The next line of Linnean soldiers fell. The horrific chaos continued all around, and I fought the urge to

curl into a ball until it was all over. Although the enemy hadn't
breached the city walls yet, it wouldn't be long.

"Think, Raven." Arvandus's voice took on a determined note.
"What other options do you have?"

Desperation seeped into my pores. "I don't have any."

"What makes you special? What are your assets?"

"Average sword skills, fire starting, a great family." I ticked them
off one by one on my fingers. "Really cool friends." A plan flashed
through my head. "Wait. You guys are the 'Raven's share'!"

Baldwin cocked his head. "What?"

"Okay, here's the plan. Me swinging a sword around is a stupid
idea. But this? This could work." And I laid it out for all of them.
When I finished, Anna and Baldwin grinned.

Grabbing Anna's arm, I looked into her gray eyes. "You've got
to be careful. I don't want you to get burned."

"I'll be slick as a reef eel. No problem."

"Arvandus, can you get me to Erhardt at the front of the army?"

Baldwin interrupted me. "Erhardt doesn't lead from the front.
He will be at the back of the line."

"Well, I'll start there and work my way forward. The fire should
be blown away from the residential area. There are too many
people and too many homes." I gave the griffins an encouraging
smile. "Can you get help?"

"Why would we need it?" Reina looked down her beak at me.
"Are we not ferocious enough?"

"Yes, you're very ferocious." It was like placating a
three-year-old diva. "But we're dealing with thousands of soldiers.
I want them kept out of the residential area. With several more
griffins, you'll be able to herd the soldiers toward the cliffs. They'll
be hemmed in with Linnean soldiers in front and Linnean griffins
on either side."

Arvandus's eyes glowed with a wild light. "We will get the
others."

After a quick flyover, we located Erhardt near the back, away from the bloody front line. We alighted, then the griffins flew off to get reinforcements.

Erhardt barked orders to harried messengers. When he saw the three of us, he stomped over. His already-dark frown grew thunderous. Maybe today would be the day I'd see the inside of a Linnean prison.

"Why are you here? I ordered you to the castle. This is not a game for children." His cheeks flushed.

"Linneah needs to attack from the sides," I said.

Erhardt looked at me, his eyes wide. "And now you are an expert? I do not have time for this. Go back to the castle."

Baldwin stepped closer, his chin set at a stubborn angle. "It is a good plan. At least listen to her explanation."

"Sir." A young soldier pushed in front of us, his scrawny arms clutching a wooden shield. How old was this kid? Eight? "The enemy is forcing a large detachment toward the residential area."

"The griffins are coming," I said. "If you let the griffins do their work, they'll force the soldiers toward the cliffs and stop them from heading toward the residents. Order your soldiers to herd the enemy in the same direction. At that point, Baldwin, Anna, and I can handle it."

Erhardt paused, giving me a long, searching look. "How?"

"My lord." Another messenger hurried over, this one an overweight teenaged boy. "The front line is collapsing. We need a new formation."

"Argh! I have no time for explanations." Erhardt clenched his large hands into fists. He glared at each of us before turning to both runners. "Hold Taurin's army until the griffins arrive."

"Already here, sir," the second boy said.

"Good." Erhardt gave a brisk nod. "Have the men attack from the sides. Herd the enemy into the Funnel."

"Sir?" The first boy hesitated.

"Now!"

Both boys scurried back toward the fighting to deliver the orders.

Erhardt picked up a helmet and shoved it on his blond head. "I will direct the men. This plan must work in a short amount of time. The three of you are in charge of the next phase. If it fails, I will take over, and you will live to regret it." He grabbed his shield and stalked away.

"Show time," I said to Anna and Baldwin. Their fierce expressions firmed my resolve. I wouldn't let my friends die.

Pulling my sword from its sheath, I psyched myself up to hack my way forward. With a combination of Baldwin's sword skills and my firepower, we fought off the few enemy soldiers who had slipped through the griffin's formidable line. The elixir the enemy had drunk began to wear off, leaving some fully formed men, while others were ghosts wielding swords. Anna, a lone dagger clutched in her fist, was boxed in by Baldwin and me while we advanced. Before I knew it, the three of us had reached the griffins.

Metal clashed, men grunted. A Largamant keeled over, and the griffins screeched in triumph.

Baldwin stepped in front of me and blocked an enemy's sword. "Hurry. The griffins will get hurt, and the men can only hold the enemy in this formation for a short time."

I blocked a thrust from a gruesome horned creature with my sword. A puff of fire, and it fell back.

"Catch the shimmer." Anna faded. A cool rush of air brushed against my cheeks.

Baldwin squinted, and the Linnean soldiers closest to us began to glow with a red shine. Their weapons blurred, their strikes faster and lethal. A few of the enemy soldiers cursed, swinging wildly. They were dispatched, cut down with a single stroke.

I muttered a quick prayer under my breath, the power gathering in my arms. Heat rushed through my wrists. My hands prickling,

I pushed. Fire burst from my palms in a wave. The blustering wind that was Anna blew the flames over the attacking army. Their horrified screams rose in the air. The remaining soldiers struggled to defend themselves against a squadron of the red glowing, 100% faster Linnean army.

The enemy turned to run, but along the sides stood more griffins and a few rare talents. Firebrands, Weatherbrands, Waterbrands, even some Merripen shapeshifters stood scattered among the griffins and Linnean soldiers. Baldwin altered time for a different set of Linnean soldiers. They began to glow, their movements quicker. Taurin's frightened soldiers tangled together, their planned strike disintegrating. The wind gusted again, and I pushed out wave after wave of fire. A small detachment of Linnean soldiers engaged the enemy that slipped through the fiery onslaught.

Arvandus contacted me. *Raven, pace yourself.*

I've got help. Don't worry. I jogged after the now-retreating enemy. They rushed toward the Galt Cliffs, a red glimmer surrounding the soldiers. In the chaos, Taurin's army would be over the cliffs before they realized they'd run out of real estate. I released another blast of fire and wiped the sweat off my forehead with a shaking hand.

You are overdoing it. Stop.

Just a little more, Arvandus. I discharged two more waves of fire, Anna's wind rolling the flames toward the sea. The enemy soldiers rushed away, their backs to me. When the earth tilted, my world shrank to a tiny pinhole of light. Then everything went black.

I opened my eyes to Tiny's cornflower blue ones two inches away. Whoa. Way too close. Squinting, I moaned and turned my face to the side.

"Geez Louise, you took a long time to wake up. Watching you sleep was totally boring." She gave me a bright smile and sat back.

My despair over being home in Pennsylvania swelled—until I took in my environment. The stone walls of the castle infirmary surrounded me. Renke bustled by in the background, and one of the male orderlies kept checking out Tiny. Who shouldn't be here. What was going on?

Covering my face with my hands, I groaned. "What're you doing here?"

"I love you, too. You look horrible. Massive bed head. I came through the portal when I heard you were sick."

"I'm not sick. And you shouldn't have come. The portal could've killed you."

"Actually, anyone from the Jasper Territory can use it. So that includes yours truly since I'm a Welden. My hometown is Ginselwyn." Tiny smiled. "Surprise."

"But you've got legs. I've seen them."

"Stellar cloaking techniques, sweetheart. And long skirts and boots work well."

"Huh. Did you know I was from Linneah? You know, before I left?"

"I guessed. After all, your mom and gram look like typical Linneans. And most people don't go around shooting fire from their hands."

"Tell me about it." I sank against the pillow, exhaustion pulling me down, down, down. One thought pushed through. "Is everyone okay?"

"They're all fine," she said.

I smiled. The world closed in on me again.

The next day, Renke moved me into an overflow room. Several of the empty rooms near the infirmary had become sick bays. He reserved the infirmary for the most severe injuries. With minimal help from a nurse, I ate breakfast and dressed, then wandered downstairs. Murray shuffled around the Gathering Room, putting chairs in order.

"Hi, Murray."

He turned and gave me a bright smile. "Brenna. You are awake. Praise Elyon. I visited yesterday morning, but you were still asleep."

"Aw, thanks. That was sweet. Did I have a lot of visitors?"

"I suppose Renke did not tell you. They allowed you a few visitors, your family and friends. Then Erhardt had to station guards outside the infirmary to keep out the crush of well-wishers. When the townspeople learned you were ill, many prayers were sent up for your healing. I believe numerous gifts were also put into your room."

"Gifts? Why?"

"You are a—what is the term? Uh, riprider." He smiled. "Anna taught me that word."

Of course she did. "But everyone helped."

"And Anna and Baldwin are ripriders, as well. But you were hospitalized, and the citizens were concerned." He patted my arm. "The Vision Window showed your recovery."

"Oh. Well, good. That reminds me, Murray. I wanted to let you know where the Sacred Veil is."

"Oh yes, we found it in the side drawer of the table. Did Erhardt share that hiding place with you?"

"No, after we got back, I started looking for one. I stepped in here for a quiet moment, and a picture of it appeared in the Vision Window."

"Elyon's provision. He sometimes uses it to answer our prayers."

I nodded. "I'm heading outside. Want to come?"

"Thank you, but no. Maybe later."

The fresh air beckoned. Once outside, I sat on the castle steps. Across the lawn, the portal's curtain of water fell in an endless cascade. Dark clouds threatening rain drifted overhead. A moist sea breeze blew, playing with my loose hair. I smiled. Today would be a good day. Beyond the portal, a dark form approached. Arvandus. My good mood vanished, blowing away in the breeze. He stalked forward and settled next to me, his dark frown giving him a sinister edge.

The silence stretched thin between us. I waited him out. Fidgeted. And sighed. "Okay, you were right. I overdid it. I'm sorry."

"You never listen, Raven." He shook his head.

"So, now what? You're ditching me?"

"The vinculus is forever, no matter how difficult the rider."

"Excuse me? I'm sure there have been more difficult riders than me."

He sniffed. "Not many. What is your plan now?"

"I don't know. Grandma Helen, Mom, and Dad want to stay for the Shaverim Festival. I'm not sure what happens after." My sadness grew. They'd visited me this morning, but we hadn't talked about it. I didn't feel like going back. Life in Pennsylvania seemed like a long time ago. "Do we stay bonded even if I have to go back?"

Arvandus nodded. "Your mother is still bonded to Campion."

"I haven't seen Baldwin and Anna yet. Are they okay?"

"Yes, tired but fine. *They* did not overextend themselves."

"Okay, I get it. You were right, I was wrong. Can we move on?"

With a sideways glance, he changed the subject. "There will be a special presentation the first night of the festival. Each of you will receive the Linnean Star of Bravery."

I grinned. "Crazy." My wild idea had defeated Taurin's army. During their visit, my family had shared how many enemy soldiers plunged over the cliffs. In the chaos, Taurin escaped and even now remained at large. Despite that piece of bad news, residents had begun to plan for the Shaverim Festival. Many employed in the castle discussed in low tones who would be crowned king. I glanced at Arvandus. "Can a griffin be crowned king?"

"No. It is not done."

"You're smart enough."

"Yes, of course. Thank you." He stood. "I must go, but I will come see you tomorrow. Maybe you will be well enough for an afternoon ride."

"I'd like that."

He nodded once, then took a running leap, his powerful wings lifting him into the air. Although the few pedestrians didn't seem to notice, he was an impressive sight.

Tiny spoke from behind me. "Wow. He's gorgeous."

"Yeah, he knows it, too. Are you bonded?"

"No, we don't have griffins in Ginselwyn." She sat next to me, her hips and legs an indistinct, shining blur of white light under her thin skirt. Under the hem of the gauzy fabric glowed more light, but no feet.

I gave her a long look before shaking my head. "This is going to take some getting used to."

"Yeah, it's okay. You'll adjust. Here." She handed me a box wrapped in shiny green paper.

"What's this?"

"A get-better present."

"I am better, almost normal."

"See, it worked. Go ahead, open it."

After unwrapping the cardboard box, I peeked inside and grinned. "A Belgian waffle!"

"My mom made a batch before I left, so I brought you one. Maybe you could give it to the castle cook to duplicate it."

"Sweet." I gave her a one-armed hug.

In a casual tone, she said, "I met Anna and Baldwin. They seem nice." She leaned toward me, her voice a whisper. "What's the deal with Baldwin? You guys have a thing or what?"

"I don't know. Maybe. Probably. My goal was to find the Veil and my mom. Now I'm just happy to be alive."

"Well, I think he thinks you guys have a thing."

Butterflies fluttered in my stomach. "Why? Did he say something?"

"He wanted to know if you were 'paired.'" She air-quoted the word, grinning.

I started to freak out. "What does that even mean?"

"Relax. It's like dating. Just talk to him."

Nerves jostled for space in my stomach. "Maybe I'll do that."

After lunch, I searched the castle for Dirk. Even though I dreaded this meeting, it had to be done.

At the open door of his room, I knocked and peered around the edge of the wooden door. "Up for a visit?"

He rested in his bed, reading. His bandaged feet stuck out from under the covers. "I am not going anywhere. Some company will keep the boredom at bay."

After slipping into the room, I perched on the edge of a chair near his bed. My awkwardness spread until I didn't know what to do with my hands or feet. "How're you feeling?"

He glowered, the weight of his stare an anvil of guilt. "My burns keep me mostly in bed, and I have trouble walking."

"That sucks. I'm sorry."

"Why do people say that? It does not make sense. Is the situation your fault?"

And there was my opening. I scrounged deep for a drop of courage. "Yes. That's why I'm here. To apologize."

"The fire—but you were not here."

"Ever heard of spiegel globes?"

Apparently, he had. His brown eyes blazed. "Were you trying to kill me?"

"No, no, it was an accident. I never meant to hurt you. I'm so sorry."

"Get out."

"Please listen. I've learned to heal. I could undo some of the damage."

"Undo? You are here to finish what you started. Why should I trust you?" His sharp eyes bored into me.

"Because what I did was wrong. I want to make amends, to help."

"Do you always get what you want?"

"No, not usually." The situation had spiraled out of control. "But maybe I could help you heal faster."

"Maybe?" Dirk pointed to his door. "Leave. I am not interested in the help of someone like you."

"But—"

"The Great Firebrand, eh? Linneah was safe before you shoved your way in. Now nobody knows how to tell you that you are no longer wanted."

"I—what?"

"People are uncomfortable around you. They whisper, stare, do not visit long." He leaned forward with a condescending sneer. "It is time for you to leave us in peace."

Realization spread through me. He was right. The visitors who'd stopped by yesterday hadn't stayed long. Today, the whispers and stares followed me into rooms and down hallways. I'd ignored the attention, assuming it would die down after a few days.

"You are a menace, clumsily wielding your power. Although King Donalt suffered, your plan to kill the innocents of Linneah has been foiled. Who was your next target? The elderly? The children?" Red spots mottled his pale cheeks.

"I'd never—"

"Lies. We see you for what you are. A half-breed traitor. Filthy murderer. Get out of my room. Now!" His voice had risen, and his hand shook as he pointed at the door.

I stood, my breath coming fast and my heart pounding. Turning, I ran into the hallway and bumped into Baldwin.

"Brenna, hi. Are you okay?" He put a hand on my elbow to steady me, his eyes narrowed in concern.

Hot tears dripped off my chin. "No. Yes. I have to go."

"No." His grip on my arm was firm. "What is wrong?"

He led me to a bench in an alcove farther down the hallway. I wiped my tears with the edge of my sleeve.

"What happened?"

"Things didn't go so well with Dirk."

Baldwin's eyes turned fierce. "Did he hurt you?"

"No. No, he didn't touch me. We only argued." But the words still hurt, the accusations crowding my mind.

Relief flashed across his face, and he nodded. "Go on."

He had no idea what I was talking about. Great. I'd have to admit my mistake again, this time to someone I really liked. "When I met with Talus, he gave me an assignment. To prove my loyalty, he wanted me to use a spiegel globe to kill someone. I didn't plan to kill Dirk, but I thought I could discover my mom's location by doing what Talus asked. I miscalculated, and Dirk was almost killed."

Swallowing hard, I chanced a glance at Baldwin. He had leaned forward, bracing his elbows on his knees while he listened. "His burns are my fault. So today, I asked for his forgiveness and offered to heal him. Instead, he accused me of killing King Donalt and called me a murderer." My voice quavered on the last word.

Baldwin leaned back but remained quiet. He studied the worn cobblestones beneath his feet.

Well, that was it. And I couldn't blame him for being disgusted. Dirk had been right. Linneah and Baldwin no longer wanted me around. I'd served my purpose.

His voice broke through my dark thoughts. "Talus was a great manipulator. He damaged all of us, bringing out our worst. Maybe in time, Dirk will change his mind and forgive you."

I'd seen his face. That wouldn't happen anytime soon. "Maybe. What kind of person does what I did on purpose?"

He reached out and took my hand. "Someone put into an impossible situation. If it makes you feel better, I would have done the same in your position. Brenna, if you have asked forgiveness from Elyon and Dirk, you should forgive yourself next. Otherwise, the guilt will crush you. Do not think about his accusations." He shifted closer. "They are not true. You care about others. I have seen it."

The question lurking deep inside broke free. "Is everyone waiting for me to leave?"

"No. Why would anyone want you to leave?"

A weight lifted off my shoulders, and I shrugged.

"Just because someone says it, does not make it true. You are a kind, brave, beautiful person."

"Thanks. But you don't have to say that to make me feel better."

A tender expression played at the corners of his mouth. "I am not. It is the truth."

My answering smile fragile, I said nothing.

He stood and squeezed my hand. "And I will keep repeating it until you believe it. Okay? Now walk me to the dining room. I missed lunch."

"Sheesh. Guys always think about food."

"What else is there?" His playful expression lifted my mood, and he tugged on my hand. "Come on."

CHAPTER TWENTY-SIX

WHEN WORD SPREAD THAT I'd recovered, Renke pressed me into service in the infirmary. Dirk hadn't shared his accusations, or I never would've been allowed within ten feet of the vulnerable wounded.

Renke and I worked in tandem. He nursed the soldiers with medicine, then had me follow up with my healing talent. This time, I kept it in check so I didn't burn out. The soldiers I couldn't help broke my heart. Some hovered near death with critical injuries, while a few were in a coma, the severity of their wounds unknown. Others would improve with long-term physical therapy. Those men were the real ripriders.

The days unspooled in a misty fog of healing, and each night I slept an exhausted, dreamless sleep. When the Shaverim Festival rolled around three days later, many of the soldiers had improved enough to be moved to regular rooms. The more serious injuries stayed in the infirmary under Renke's watchful eyes. There'd been too many funerals earlier in the week, beachside services held one after the other.

The first evening of the festival, Anna and Tiny descended on my room with makeup, shoes, and accessories. I dressed for the special occasion in the red dress I'd purchased in the Linnean market a couple of weeks ago. It'd been badly wrinkled from being stored in my bag, but I'd hung it in my closet. A few days later, the wrinkles had fallen out of the soft, red material.

I pulled the rag curlers out of my hair and finger combed the waves. My stick-straight hair never curled, so I was left with the wavy look. "When does the Crowning Ceremony take place?"

"My mom said tonight." Tiny handed over her copper eyeliner. Her parents, both from Ginselwyn, were staying in Linneah with Tiny's younger siblings. Her two older brothers and one older sister were away and wouldn't be at the festival.

After carefully applying a thin line of eyeliner, I then smudged it, shooting for a smoky look. Tonight was also the ceremony for the Linnean Star of Bravery. The thought of being on stage in front of the entire city made my hands shake. I waited a little before I finished my eye makeup.

"What do you think?" Anna did a slow spin to show off her light-blue hair, tied in an elaborate up do.

Tiny wrinkled her nose. "I liked your other hairstyle better."

She allowed it to tumble down around her shoulders, the color morphing from blue to brown.

Thirty minutes later, Tiny and I stood near the doorway, ready to go. Anna, intent on impressing Erhardt, changed her hair, outfit, and shoes while we walked down the castle steps. I finally told her to knock it off, or I'd tell Erhardt she was planning their wedding.

The festival took place under the castle in the Linnean Garden. Helli lanterns of all sizes hung around the perimeter, lending a soft glow to the area. A raised platform with a set of attached stairs had been erected in the center of the lighted area where the Crowning Ceremony would take place. The curved wooden backdrop would project the speaker's voice, while its height would give the crowds overflowing into nearby areas a good view of the new ruler.

Soldiers from other regions of the Jasper Territory had agreed to help Linneah with crowd control. Families of Camlos, Kells, and Weldens mingled with Merripens. Anna's family wouldn't arrive until tomorrow. Griffins roamed the outside of the gathering, policing the crowds in shifts. Or so Arvandus had told me.

A tangible excitement filled the air. Colorful tents filled the normally empty fields surrounding the Linnean Garden. There were storytelling booths, magicians, and games of chance. Several men and centaurs set up in a nearby field for tomorrow's archery trials. While their parents talked, a bunch of kids ran around in a clearing, playing games. Their laughter floated on the breeze.

I scanned the crowd and saw Mom, Dad, and Grandma Helen talking with some other people near the platform. Mom stood tucked against Dad's side, his arm around her shoulders as she laughed at something he'd said. Catching her eye, I smiled and offered a wave.

She grinned at me. I thought she was going to walk toward me, but one of the people pulled her back into the conversation.

Upbeat music drifted through the air from a band playing in the corner of the garden. Some of the instruments were unfamiliar, but there were also drums, a guitar, and something like a fiddle. Tables piled high with delectable food and colorful drinks ringed the lighted area, too. After weeks of crisis after crisis, I inhaled deeply, taking in the scent of sea and smoke.

"Hey."

I jumped and turned toward the voice. Baldwin stood behind me. He wore black pants and an emerald-green shirt that matched his eyes.

"We'll go get something to drink." Tiny winked, pulling Anna in her wake.

"You look fantastic."

Warmth curled through my stomach. I flushed and gave him a shy smile. "Thanks. You too."

"Do you feel better?" His brow furrowed. "No more encounters with Dirk?"

"No, not lately." Dumb conversation starters piled up in my throat. Why couldn't I think of anything else to say?

We stood swamped in the awkward silence until Baldwin turned to me. "Can I ask you something? During the end of the battle, why did you push yourself so hard?"

"I guess I wanted to finish the job, to get rid of them, so they never came back to my home."

"Really? Linneah is your home?"

"What?" Did I say that?

"You have not been here that long."

Fire lit my veins. I set my chin. "Are you saying I don't belong here?

He stepped closer and covered my mouth with his fingers, stealing my voice. "Why are you trying to start an argument?"

Grabbing his wrist, I pulled his hand away. His pulse beat steadily under my thumb. "You said I didn't belong. Rude and incorrect, by the way."

"I did not say that. I did not think it, either."

"Well, what did you think?"

"That I cannot imagine Linneah without you."

My cheeks warmed, my heart melting in my chest.

Erhardt strode up, wearing a uniform of creased black pants and a black shirt. Maybe he was trying to look like a ninja. "You are both needed on the platform now. The Linnean Star ceremony is about to start."

With a quick, shared glance, Baldwin and I followed him through the crowds of people. Three beefy men and a solemn older couple stood waiting to the side of the platform. All of us climbed the wooden steps. Two Linnean soldiers wearing black uniforms similar to Erhardt's waited on the platform.

Erhardt lined us up at the back of the stage in a single file. "When I call your name, step forward. Jedreks or Sigurd will step forward to give you your award. You will shake our hands, one at a time, bow to the audience, and then step back into position. After everyone has received their award, you will vacate the stage so the Crowning Ceremony may take place."

He walked toward the front of the platform and faced the crowd. People gathered in large groups and small clusters, talking, dancing, and eating. The celebratory mood spilled over, laughter filling the cracks in the buzz of conversation.

I caught my breath at the throng assembled in the garden. So. Many. People. Off to the right of the stage, a young boy hefted a bright-silver horn as long as his arm. Placing it to his lips, he blew. A powerful, low note rolled out and quieted the crowd.

"Tonight," Erhardt called, his voice carrying. "We have two ceremonies that must take place."

A few enthusiastic members of the audience clapped.

He held up his hand and waited for them to quiet. "We will begin with the presentation of the Linnean Star of Courage. Six esteemed Linneans will receive the Star for their bravery during battle. When I read their names, they will come forward."

The three hulking generals waiting with us had served under Erhardt. One was on crutches, a pant leg hanging empty. When his name was called, he maneuvered to the front of the stage, the crutches thumping out a hollow rhythm. The two other generals also bore injuries. One supported his left arm in a sling. The last general carried a bandaged right hand like a club, his movements awkward when he shook hands. Next, the man and woman received a star for their son who'd died from his injuries five days before. After they received their award in a wooden box, they returned to their place in line. The woman wiped at the tears streaming from her eyes while the stoic man clutched the box, a reminder of his dead son's sacrifice.

"Baldwin Marek." Pulling my attention away from the grieving couple, I straightened my spine. Now was not a good time to zone out. Baldwin took the box, shook hands, bowed to the crowd, then walked back to his place, reserving a flirty wink for me.

I bit my lip to control my answering grin.

"Brenna James." My name rang out, loud in my ears. Mom, Dad, and Grandma Helen's proud smiles pulled me from my spot. My knees wobbled. *Don't fall, don't trip, easy now, almost there.* Jedreks handed me the box, his face impassive. I shook hands all around, reserving Erhardt for last. His face held no smile, but approval flickered in his expression.

"Good job, Lady James. Well done," he said under the clapping of the crowd.

I bowed, my cheeks growing warmer, then followed the others off the stage.

"And now, we crown the new ruler of Linneah. Many of you have not seen a crowning before. It is a miraculous event blessed by Elyon. After the terrible murder of our beloved King Donalt, a thief stole the Sacred Veil. It has been recovered for our ceremony."

Despite his simple words, the people applauded, and those nearby turned to look at Baldwin and me with beaming smiles. The story had traveled the Linnean grapevine and, in its retelling, had reached epic proportions.

"Sheesh," I said under my breath.

"Keep smiling." Baldwin tucked his hands behind his back, posture perfect, head up. His royal upbringing was evident in his every move.

Erhardt turned to accept a gold box from a man behind him. Opening it, he pulled out the Sacred Veil. The white cloth and purple stitching shimmered in the flickering glow of the lanterns. "This is the Sacred Veil. Elyon will place it on the individual He has chosen. The purple threads will brand His servant. Although it will not be painful, it is binding." Erhardt held it above his head, an offering. "Our Most High King, please choose Your servant."

In seconds, the Veil slipped from Erhardt's hands and began to ascend, its silken ends fluttering in the air. A few in the crowd gasped and drew away from the platform, their eyes wide. The length of fabric began to glow, its white material radiant. It cleared the platform and dropped. Winding its way through the crowd, its glow illuminated faces as it passed.

The material wove around my family, and my breath stalled in my throat. I moved closer to get a better view. Slowly, the Veil dropped until it draped across my mother's shoulders like an embrace, its ends covering her arms. The purple thread lengthened, swirling around her wrists, marking her as Elyon's choice.

Erhardt smiled and gestured for her to come to the platform. My mother stepped up and looked out at her new kingdom, her face pale and her blue eyes wide.

"May I present to you all, Queen Sarah James of Linneah!"

The crowd roared its approval. While Dad and Grandma Helen grinned and clapped, Mom motioned for Dad to come up on the stage with her.

"Thank you," she said to the crowd. "I will do my best to serve Elyon and all of you."

The crowd cheered again, and the band struck up a celebratory melody. Erhardt removed the Sacred Veil from my mother and put it back in the gold box. My mother gave my dad a hug, the dark-purple, swirled tattoos vibrant on each wrist.

When the ground tilted, Baldwin caught me and carried me to an area away from the crowd.

"Too much excitement?" He sat next to me on the grass, his arm strong around my shoulder.

"My mother is the Queen," I said, trying to take it in.

"Yes, she is. That makes you a princess." He grinned.

"I hate that term. Talus used to call me that, and it always made me mad."

"Really? Hmm, I could call you Your High and Mighty-ness? Your Royalship? Your Excellent Excellency?"

"You stink at this."

Pushing a lock of black hair behind my shoulder, he took my hand in his. The butterflies in my stomach dive-bombed when he laced his strong fingers through mine. "I have to call you some-thing."

"How about just Brenna?" I looked up to find his face closer than I had expected.

"Okay, 'just Brenna.'" He closed the distance between us.

When his warm lips touched mine, my mind went delicious-ly blank. And when he pulled away, I somehow remembered to breathe.

While we grinned at each other like idiots, Tiny and Anna chose that moment to find us.

"Saints and sinners!" Tiny said. "Your mom is the Queen!"

"What does that make your dad?" Anna wrinkled her forehead.

"No idea." I stood, Baldwin's hand holding mine in a firm grip.

Anna nudged Tiny when she noticed our joined hands.

I rolled my eyes. "Let's go find my mom, guys."

"Reefstars," Anna said under her breath. "Time to meet the Queen."

In a crowd that large, I didn't reach her until about a half-hour later. Somehow, I became separated from Baldwin, Tiny, and Anna. Dozens of people I didn't know wanted to shake my hand and talk about the Veil. After facing another thankful citizen, I turned around to find Mom, Dad, and Grandma Helen behind me. With a grin, I threw myself at them for a group hug.

"Congrats, Mom. The Queen, huh? I guess we won't need to move out of the castle."

She smiled, and Dad gave her shoulder a small squeeze.

I traced the swirling purple tattoo at her wrist. "They don't hurt?"

"No. They tingle a little. And it's strange to see them there."

"I like them." Grandma Helen pushed up Mom's sleeve for a better look and smiled. "They look amazing."

"One question," I said. "We're staying in Linneah, right?"

Mom and Dad shared a look, but said nothing.

Panic clawed at my throat. "We have to stay, because of your new job."

She gave me a gentle smile. "I am staying. You and Dad will have to return to Pennsylvania for school."

"What? You'll be here, far away. Again."

"I know. It's not ideal. But it is what it is, sweetie. At least for now. You and Dad can visit often, because I'll miss you. And you can spend the summers here."

Just the summers? So, I'd get Mom for three months out of the year. What a lousy deal. Judging from the expressions on both of their faces, their decision was final.

Baldwin stood on the far side of the garden, talking to Murray. Anna drank punch and flirted with Erhardt, while Tiny chased her little sisters in a game of tag. Leaving this place and these new friends behind was unfair. At least Tiny would go back with me.

I escaped when more people came up to meet the Queen. My skin itched from all the attention, so I left to get some punch.

Later that evening, I found Baldwin after supper. The amount of delicious food at the feast had been overwhelming. Thousands of sweet Kunkelsteuchen rolls, hundreds of ripe, juicy melons, sugar-squash casseroles by the dozens sparkling with golden caramelized syrup, and platter after platter of delicious roasted meats and herbed cheeses I never learned the name of graced the tables. The Kunkelsteuchen rolls were my new favorite. I had eaten a little too much of everything, so Baldwin agreed to help me walk off the calories.

His face fell when I told him I had to go back. "Are you sure they will not change their minds?"

"No, they want me to stay in school."

The music from the band drifted over the clearing. People talked and snacked on seconds and thirds from the dessert table.

"I will miss you." His low voice was quiet.

"Me, too. But I'll visit—weekends, most holidays, summer vacation."

"It is not the same, but I will take it." He took my hand as we walked the perimeter of the festival. "Because of our trip, you missed a lot of normal Linnean life."

"Like what?"

"You have not seen the conservatory."

"The conservatory? Like a school?"

He nodded. "This year is my last."

"I still have another year left."

"Baby."

"Old man," I teased with a grin.

A guy with bright-red hair and a white hairstreak interrupted our teasing. "Baldwin!" His smile was wide as he walked up to us. Several hard slaps to Baldwin's back and solid slugs to his shoulder followed. "I cannot believe you left to be a hero and did not tell me."

"You were in Wildamek."

"So?"

Baldwin turned to me. "Brenna, meet Kersen, my best friend since we were little. Kersen, this is Brenna."

"Hey." I gave him a little smile.

The redhead blushed, a pink stain mottling his fair cheeks. "Wow."

"Nice." Baldwin nodded. "Very smooth."

"Shut up," Kersen said. "Gorgeous *and* the fulfiller of the First Prophecy."

Pleased embarrassment shriveled to discomfort. How did you avoid fame? "No, no." I waved away his statement. "Just Brenna, okay?"

"Okay. But your mom is the Queen."

"Yeah. So what?"

Baldwin chuckled. I looked at him. "What?"

"It is not easy to be a part of the royal family. You will have to adjust."

I didn't know what kind of adjustment I'd have to make, but I had a feeling I wouldn't like it. Our conversation stalled when half a dozen of Baldwin's friends arrived. They were nice, but Baldwin introduced them to me all at once. Their names tangled in my head.

"Baldwin!"

Before I could blink, a petite, curvy blonde threw her arms around Baldwin, her body pressed against his. "Hail the hero!" She leaned back with a flirtatious smile, her green laser-like eyes focused on him. "Imagine my fascination when I learned you ventured through Silvastamen and back."

Laughing, he extricated himself from her embrace. "Not alone, Gari." He turned to me and held out his hand. "I was with Brenna, too. Brenna, meet Gari."

I slipped my hand into his, trying to pull comfort from its strength. "Hi. Nice to meet you."

She gave me a smirking once over and tucked her chin-length hair behind one ear. Her purple hairstreak seemed to glow against her porcelain skin. "I have heard stories about you."

"Don't believe everything you hear." I mentally cringed. Wow. So awkward.

"I do not." She turned her back on me.

Dismissed.

A half-hour later, while I talked to Tiny, Anna, and Kersen, Baldwin sidled up to me and pulled me close. "You are a hard person to find."

His lips tickled my ear, and I shivered. "What do you mean?"

"I turned around, and you were gone."

"I've been here, talking with everyone. You were busy talking with Gari." Oops, jealousy in all its ugly greenness.

"Sorry. She is a bit clingy." He grimaced.

"And rude." A thought occurred to me. "Were you two ever together?"

"Long ago."

"How long?"

He gave me an awkward grin. "A time ago. But it is over and has been for a long time. What about you? Tiny said you were not paired."

"I've dated. Some." In ninth grade, I'd dated Jack Harris for a few months. And school dances, if they counted. They weren't memorable, and at this point, I couldn't remember who'd asked me.

His smile sent my heart tumbling. "You call it dating? Would you be willing to date me?"

I nodded, finally allowing my beaming smile to break through. "Yeah, that's a good idea."

"I probably should have asked earlier. Everyone can see we are together."

"Right." Everyone except Gari. I avoided mentioning her, knowing I'd need to get a handle on my jealousy. I trusted him, but I didn't trust her.

CHAPTER TWENTY-SEVEN

THE REST OF THE night passed in a blur. Anna's laugh, Tiny's bad jokes, and the warmth in Baldwin's smile were memories I pressed in the pages of my mind's scrapbook. The kiss Baldwin stole before he said goodnight received a special page of its own.

The next day turned out to be my first full day as The Person Who Brought Back the Veil and Fulfilled the First Prophecy. Friendly villagers I didn't know wanted to talk about my trip through Silvastamen. Complete strangers asked me to demonstrate the firewall technique I used during the battle. One young mother brought her toddler to the castle court, determined to see the fulfiller bless her young son.

By lunchtime, my patience had run out. While I ate lunch, I sat in a corner and fiddled with my silverware. I refused to meet anyone's eyes or engage in conversation.

Afterward, I met my mom in her private rooms.

"Nice place," I said when I walked in.

Wall hangings in calm tones of blue and cream graced the walls, and a deep-blue rug lay in front of a grouping of chairs. A door on my right opened to a bedroom. Dad's worktable in the corner of the sitting room was cluttered with grid paper and books, though he'd left earlier to watch the preliminary archery trials.

"I have a beautiful view of the ocean." She settled across from me in a blue wing chair. "How're you holding up?"

"I should ask you that. You're the one ruling a kingdom."

"Well, I don't think it has sunk in yet. After the festival, I'll select a few advisers. That might make it seem more real."

"Was Rosamunde ever found?"

Mom pursed her lips. "I'm not sure what happened to her. I don't know if she survived or if she defected to the Kasek Territory. I'll have to put out some feelers and pick an advisor to replace her." She studied me. "Is everything going okay?"

I tried to nod but failed. "No, not really. There are all these people, and I don't know any of them, but they all act like they know me and want something from me. I had ten people stare at me during lunch. It's like living in a fishbowl."

"I'm sorry, sweetie. It'll get better. However, that's part of being the royal family. And fulfilling a prophecy." She paused a moment, then asked, "Do you have a solution?"

"Can I go back early? To Pennsylvania?"

She thought for a moment, then nodded. "That might be for the best. Don't you want to see the rest of the festival?"

"Yes, but I can't do this. If I go back now, maybe when I come back to visit, things will have died down a bit."

"Your father might go back with you, too. He's used up a lot of vacation time and needs to get back to his classes."

"I have to say goodbye to Arvandus."

"Nobody else?"

"Well, yeah. Anna. And Baldwin."

"Let me know when you're ready to leave. I'll come see you off."

She pulled me into a hug, and I allowed myself to sink into it as I used to when I was little. Although I already missed her, underneath the missing lay relief. She was here in Linneah, not a captive in another territory.

I hurried toward the griffin house. Arvandus met me outside. "You are leaving."

"How can you tell? Do I smell different?"

"Your impertinence is not appreciated."

I grinned. "But won't you miss me?"

"Of course. You will be careful and study hard while you are gone?"

"Yes, I promise." Throwing my arms around his neck, I buried my face in his fur when my eyes started to sting.

"Come, Raven. I will walk with you to the castle."

"If I message you from Pennsylvania, can you hear me?"

"Hmm. I do not know. We will have to try it."

When we reached the courtyard, I turned to him. "I'll really miss you."

"And I, you. But you will be back. So I will not say goodbye." He nodded once. "May Elyon bless you. Fly true."

"Fly true, Arvandus." I swallowed the lump in my throat and left to search for my other friends.

Tiny and Anna stood in line at the storyteller's tent. Their choice made sense when I saw the ticket seller wink at Tiny.

"Hey, you two. I'm leaving."

"Shells and shimmer!" Anna's mouth fell open. "But the festival isn't over.

"I need to go home. Things are crazy here."

A young boy I didn't know walked over to us and tugged on my sleeve, his eyes wide. "Hey, I know who you are. You are the fulfiller of the First Prophecy. Wow, let me get my friends. They will never believe this. You can show us your firewall. Stay right there!"

I forced a smile before turning back to Anna and Tiny. They wore identical looks of surprise.

Tiny tilted her head. "Is that your definition of crazy?"

"Yeah. I need a break."

Anna gave me a fist bump. "Girl, let the waves carry you back soon."

"Absolutely," I said.

"See you in a couple." Tiny waved before turning her attention back to the guy selling tickets.

I walked away before that kid returned with his friends. And I still had to say goodbye to one more person.

After searching for half an hour, I gave up. I couldn't look for Baldwin forever. I debated leaving a note, but what would I say? *Thanks for the great times through the Dark Woods.* The thoughts whirling through my head were much more personal. *I'm falling for you, so please don't break my heart.* That thought would never see the light of day. Instead, I'd just apologize for not leaving a note the next time I saw him.

After packing, I slung my bag over my shoulders and cast a quick look around my room. Mom and Dad waited near the portal fountain, but I took my time walking the halls, memorizing every detail.

Striding through the double doors, I stepped into the bright day accented by a fresh blue sky and fluffy clouds. At the portal, the water sparkled in the sun, the crisp air icing the drops flung from the fountain.

Dad enveloped Mom in a hug, then touched her cheek before reaching for his bag. "Next weekend."

She nodded, then gathered me close. "I love you. Be good. Get your homework done so you can visit with your father."

"I promise." Inhaling, I caught her scent of lily of the valley and vanilla.

She gave us a small smile, her eyes bright with unshed tears. With a wave of her hand, she cleared a path through the fountain to the center of the portal. "Brenna, don't let go of Dad's hand. He needs your protection through the portal."

"Brenna!"

My head jerked toward the voice. His voice.

Baldwin sprinted toward me. He lurched to a stop next to the fountain, panting. "Anna told me you were leaving, so I ran all the way from the beach." His bright eyes flashed with hurt. "Were you going to leave without saying goodbye?"

"Nobody knew where you were. I looked everywhere."

"I was competing. Down on the beach." His brow furrowed. "Why are you leaving now? The festival runs for another day and a half."

"I can't stay. All the people—" I stopped. He wouldn't get it. He had grown up as part of the royal family, so all the attention didn't bother him. I tried again. "That adjustment you mentioned about being part of the royal family?"

Understanding flooded his face. "Right now, you are a novelty, a new individual to study. It does get better."

"Good, because I'm struggling with it." I shrugged.

Disappointment darkened his eyes. He held out a gilt-edged sapphire ribbon. "I won the first round of trials."

"For what?"

"Swordsmanship."

I smiled. "Congratulations. I knew you were good."

Taking my hand, he curled my fingers around the ribbon. "For you."

"But it's yours."

"It is a way for you to remember me."

"Baldwin, I don't need a ribbon for that."

"Keep it anyway. It matches your eyes." Drawing me into his arms, his lips brushed my cheek before he pulled away. He smiled, his eyes sparkling. "If you want, you can return the ribbon the next time you visit."

I nodded and tried to ignore the lump in my throat. After stepping onto the portal circle, my mom waved her hand to turn on the fountain spray again. I grabbed Dad's hand. My view of Linneah disappeared.

The journey back through the portal went much better than our initial trip. Although my vision fogged, the temperature swings were mild. When the earth fell away beneath me, I locked my legs.

Big mistake.

The hard cobblestone of the spillway shoved up under my feet, and I fell from the impact. Chilly water soaked through my pants in seconds. Next time, I'd keep my knees soft.

We'd left Pennsylvania at the peak of fall. Signs of winter had edged in during our absence. Clouds scudded across the sky, the puffy white forms pushed by the chilly breeze. Naked trees shoved their spindly branches to the sky, their leaves browning on the forest floor. The crisp snap of late autumn filled my nostrils, a faint imitation of Linneah's scent. Glad no Largamants waited to greet us, I hurdled the stone wall. I offered Dad a hand, but he didn't need it. His recovery complete, I'd overheard him tell Mom his scar had become almost invisible.

"Ready?" He pointed toward Grandma Helen's house.

"You go on ahead. I need a minute."

Tears still pushed at my lids. My heart ached, cold and incomplete. Pieces were missing—Mom, Baldwin, Arvandus, Anna. Although I'd see them again, it still hurt to leave.

He nodded. "I want to call the school before it closes for the day. I'll get the work you missed."

"What're you going to tell them? We skipped off to another dimension for a vacation?" I smirked.

"This past month, you've had a very educational trip out west."

"Dad! That's a lie."

"Do you want to tell them the truth?"

I grinned but said nothing.

"The truth has to be our secret. So you can study up on the western United States on the internet." He pressed his lips together. "I don't like it, but there it is. No other excuses, just hard work."

Ugh. My life was going to become one massive homework binge.

He shifted his bag. "How's pizza sound for supper?"

"From Antonio's?" The local pizza shop *might* make this day better.

"Sure. Hawaiian, if you want."

Ham, pineapple, and lots of melty cheese.

"Absolutely."

He grinned. "Don't be too long."

"Love you, Dad."

Since our adventure, I'd been saying it more. I'd never take another day for granted, especially since I'd almost died a few times in the last few weeks.

"You too, Brenna." He walked toward the path leading to Grandma Helen's house.

I dropped onto the cobblestone wall and tried to reason my way through the sadness hanging over me like my personal rain cloud.

The portal was conveniently located. It'd be easy to pop in for a day or a weekend visit—if I ever gained traction through the mountain of homework waiting for me. Mom ruled a city in relative safety with guards stationed around her to keep the crazies out. In a few days, my best friend Tiny would return. My gorgeous boyfriend missed me and looked forward to my next visit. The same went for my griffin.

I waited for a minute, expecting the sadness to lift.

Nothing.

My heart still cold, I stood to leave. Hopefully, after a long shower and some fantastic pizza, I'd be able to put things in a better perspective.

"Brenna?"

The voice made my heart leap in my chest. I turned.

Baldwin stood in the middle of the spillway.

"What're you doing here?"

Hesitation settled in his eyes. "Coming to see you. Is that okay?"

"Yes, totally okay. But I just left."

"Right, about that." His face grew serious. "When you left, you took something of mine with you."

"Oh, sorry. I thought you were giving the ribbon to me. Did I miss something?"

"No, that was a gift." He vaulted the stone wall easily. "Something else."

I frowned. "Is there something in my bag that's yours?"

"No." He took my hands, his touch chasing away the cold in my chest. "When you left, you took my heart."

Best. Line. Ever.

One look into his green eyes, and I was drowning.

He arched one eyebrow. "All things considered, I will not ask for it back. I want you only to promise me you will take care of it."

Nodding, I attempted his mock-serious manner and failed miserably. "I promise."

He slipped his arms around me and pulled me close. "Glad we settled that." His lips were warm against mine.

After a few blissful moments, I pulled away. "How do you feel about pizza?"

He tilted his head. "Who is he?"

"It's not a who, but a what. A delicious hand-held food made with bread, cheese, tomato sauce, and other toppings." I gave him a sideways glance. "Are you sure you've never had it?"

"Positive."

"It's unbelievable. You live on the other side of that portal."

"Believe it." He gave a half shrug. "When I said I had not traveled much, I meant anywhere."

"Right. Well, if you have the time, you're invited for pizza."

"I would love to stay, even if we had Mud Rat stew."

"Well, this is loads better." I took his hand and started toward Grandma Helen's house, barely visible through the trees. "You know, if you've never traveled beyond the portal, things here will really blow your mind."

"Too late, Brenna. You already did that."

Blushing, I gave him a sideways glance. "That's sweet, but it sounds like another line. I don't know whether to be flattered or annoyed."

He cocked his head. "Maybe it is a line. Do you like it?"

"I don't want lines. I'd rather have your honesty."

He stopped in the middle of the path, his slow grin curling my toes. "Something can be a line and still be true. You are an amazing person, and I enjoy spending time with you. There is a spark of...something between us. I want to be here, with you."

My heart fluttered. "I'll take it. But it still sounds like a line." I grinned and nudged him with my shoulder.

Laughing, we continued on the path through the woods, adventure a tantalizing promise on the horizon.

Epilogue

Tiny was late.

Surprising, considering I was usually the one running behind. Maybe I was managing my time better. Yay, me.

Early evening light slanted through the trees, dappling leaves with a fading glow. We'd finished our last exam today, and Tiny had suggested a trip to Linneah to celebrate. Since it'd been a few weekends since I'd seen Mom, I'd bolted a quick supper and had packed a bag. Dad had to stay behind and revise the summer syllabus for the college quantum physics class he was teaching.

On my way to the low stone wall ringing the reservoir, I jumped puddles caused by the rain last night. The natural spring gurgled with extra water before it careened over the cobblestone spillway. The forest path leading to Tiny's house remained clear, so I hefted my bag higher on my shoulder and waited. Grass grew up through the mud in dark green bursts, and the candy-sweet scent of butterfly weed floated on the breeze. A sudden chill froze my chest, and I pulled my jasper from under my T-shirt. The pendant bit ice-cold into my fingers.

A twig cracked, and I jerked my head up. An older man stood on the other side of the spillway, wearing shiny black boots and a dark, tailored trench coat.

"Hello. Did I frighten you?" Whoa, Mr. DJ could work at a radio station with a voice like that. Despite his honey-smooth voice, something about him made my skin crawl.

"Uh, no, I'm fine." I swallowed, my pulse a jackhammer.

Where'd he come from? The portal? That meant he'd come from Linneah. But he didn't have a hairstreak. Shivers skittered up my neck. His salt and pepper hair combed straight back revealed a high forehead. A close-cropped gray beard covered his chin and some of his scarred, weathered face. But I couldn't pull my attention from his eyes. They glowed a pale glacial blue.

"Are you lost? If you follow the path, you'll end up downtown. You know, in Cloverdale. If that's where you want to go. Not that you have to." I mentally cringed. When nervous, I usually blurted out whatever floated through my mind. No filter, just right past the brain and onto my lips.

He gave me what I assumed was a smile. He needed to work on it, because it was terrifying. "No, I am enjoying a walk."

Right. "Nice day for it."

His face wavered, shadow and light shifting. "Do you come here often?"

Something about the way he said it...was he trying to pick me up? Gross. So, so gross. This wasn't a club, he was too old, and the guy needed to leave. "Sometimes, but I've never seen you around here." So go away.

His eyes narrowed, his strong shoulders blurring before coming into focus again. "This is not my usual path. But I think I might explore it more. It is a beautiful place."

Great. Creepers in the woods. I forced a smile and tried to think of a way to end the awkward exchange. Before I could come up with anything, Tiny's blonde head bobbed into view. Walking up

the path, she sang a bad rendition of the title song from the spring
school musical.

The man jerked, then gave me another menacing smile. "A sincere pleasure. Good day." And disappeared.

My mouth dropping open, I scanned the area. People didn't just
vanish, no matter what alternity they were from. He hadn't even
been standing on the portal.

Tiny strolled up to me. My mouth still gaped. She frowned.
"What's wrong?"

"There was this guy…"

"Where?"

"Right on the other bank."

She wrinkled her nose. "When?"

"Just as you came up the path." I rubbed the headache building
at my temples. "I was waiting for you. I heard something, turned,
and there he was." I gave her a brief rundown of the conversation.
"Then he—poof—disappeared. Just gone."

"Are you sure he didn't step onto the portal?"

"Well, yeah. He was standing on the other side of the spillway."

As she hurried to the other side, her lower limbs became a lighted
blur. She stopped and examined the ground.

I rolled my eyes. "He's not hiding in the grass."

"You need to see this." Her voice came out strangled and small.

"What?" I was at her side in seconds.

She pointed. "Was he standing here?"

On the ground lay a scorched circle the size of a kiddie pool, the
once-bright grass charred. A burned odor drifted on the breeze.

"What in all of Linneah is that?"

She bit her lip. "Maybe it's from a pesticide?"

"But it's the only dark spot." I scanned the area. "And what
about that guy?"

Tiny grimaced. "It was probably just a harmless person passing
through."

Sure, people did that all the time, appearing and disappearing all over Cloverdale, charred circles left in their wake.

I shook my head. "I don't think so. I'll mention it to Mom when we arrive. Maybe the guards will know what's going on."

As I approached the spillway with Tiny, the memory of the encounter lingered. In the last several months, I'd seen lots of strange things in Linneah. So, I wasn't sure why this one bothered me so much. I shook my head. Mom, or perhaps one of the guards, would have a simple explanation.

That's all I needed—a simple explanation.

THE END

Every prophecy begins with a spark... but the fire is only rising. Continue the fight in *Flare*, Book Two of The Firebrand Chronicles.

Turn the page to enjoy a short story of Brenna and Baldwin's celebration of Sonatalis in "The Peddler."

The Peddler

Part I

Closing my eyes, I stood beyond the cobblestone wall of the reservoir. *Arvandus, if you can hear me, say something.* Only silence followed.

Maybe if I moved closer to the portal. After jumping the stone wall, I waited at the edge of the spillway. *Arvandus? Can you hear me?* Still nothing. I swallowed a sigh. Every time I used the portal, I tried to contact Arvandus. Admittedly, I hadn't had the chance very often. After my return from Linneah, an avalanche of homework had buried me. I'd had a handful of free weekends to visit Mom and Baldwin, and then I didn't see daylight until early December. It was time to admit the hard truth—there was no way to communicate with my griffin from this side of the portal.

Tiny's voice broke through my disappointment. "Can we go now?" She hitched her bag higher on her shoulder.

"Tell me again why you're using this portal and not one connected to Ginselwyn?"

She shrugged, avoiding my pointed glance. "I have gifts for people in Linneah."

Sure, she did. But that wasn't all of it. Tiny had voted to stay with me at the castle until her mother arrived for the Christmas holiday tomorrow. "Gifts? For people?" I grinned. "Would one of those be a cutie people?"

Her fair cheeks flushed a deep rose. "I don't know what you're talking about."

Tiny always managed to run into Flynn, one of Baldwin's friends, whenever she came with me to Linneah. They'd struck up a *friendship*, as she called it, but kept the details to herself. It drove me crazy.

Christmas was two days away. I'd bought gifts for Mom, Dad, and Grandma Helen. Tiny and I'd exchanged gifts yesterday at school. But I had one person left to buy for, and I was out of ideas.

"Still waiting to get Baldwin's gift?"

"Yeah, I think he might like something from the market." Which was a lie. Hollowness settled in my stomach.

We'd been dating, very happily, for three months. The gift had to be personal, but not so personal that it bordered on creepy, like a girl who gave her boyfriend monogrammed underwear. Although Baldwin was fascinated with electronic gadgets, he couldn't use them in Linneah. Same with music files, or anything that required batteries. I'd purchased a nice pair of sunglasses for him, but he wouldn't use those until spring. Winters weren't very sunny in Linneah, at least not from what I'd seen so far. Maybe I could save them for his birthday.

Avoiding the icy patches, we stepped onto the cobblestone spill-way. I fingered my jasper as the earth fell away. My legs wanted to lock, but if I did that, I'd fall, so I kept my knees loose. A short blast of heat enveloped me, followed by a slap of subzero wind. In seconds, we were through, standing on the cobblestone fountain in Linneah. Wearing my jasper made all the difference.

Finding one of the four silver bars laid into the round stone circle, I stepped in front of it and waved my hand at the spray, like moving aside a curtain. The fountain parted, allowing us a dry passage and a view of the stone Linnean castle. My second home.

Waning late afternoon sunlight couldn't dispel the bite in the air. The Silent Season wasn't until a month from now, and the usually beautiful landscape was colored with grays and browns. The sea was a flat, dark gray, and I took a chill.

"My ladies." A guard stepped forward with a bow. "May I help you?"

"Um, here to see the Queen." Also known as Mom.

He squinted with a furrowed brow before recognition brightened his expression. "Shaynedel Lee and Brenna James." He stepped back with squared shoulders.

There were still castle employees I hadn't met. "I'm sorry. I don't think I know you."

"Terribly sorry, my lady. I am Reginald Price. You may call me Reggie." He held out a hand.

"Nice to meet you." I grasped his forearm and shook, using the traditional welcome in Linneah. Tiny did too, offering him a pretty smile.

Reggie blinked and then blushed before recovering. "Lady James, your mother said you would arrive today and to bring you along as soon as you appeared."

Mom had become very interested in my comings and goings. Some would call it motherly concern—I called it paranoia. "I need to finish my holiday shopping."

He shook his head. "I am sorry, but the Queen ordered."

Of course. Just like I was three years old. "Okay, but you don't have to escort us." I glanced at Tiny. "You coming? Or do you want to search for Flynn?"

With a glare, she matched her pace to mine. "Nobody said I was coming to see Flynn."

I almost snorted. "Nobody had to."

"What's that supposed to mean?"

Suppressing a grin, I shrugged. "Nothing. Just that it's amazing how often we see him whenever we visit."

As we climbed the castle steps, she smirked then changed the subject. "We should see if Anna's available."

"Ooh, good idea. Can you get a message to Matana Island to tell her we're here? Let's hope she's not grounded. Again." It'd be great to touch base with my shape-shifting friend.

Inside the castle, holiday decorations filled every alcove and hallway. Strings of tiny stained-glass lanterns glowed, illuminating the entire hallway with different shades of light. Garlands of ivy with clusters of miniature oranges nestled in window nooks. Large candles in white stands adorned the tables in the dining room. I inhaled, the scent of citrus and candle wax lacing the air. From what Mom had told me last weekend, Linneans celebrated Elyon's Son's birth, calling it Sonatalis. It was all about the nativity and the birth of the baby Jesus, but with different songs and traditions. They gave three gifts to each person to mimic the gifts from the wise men, and a grand feast was planned for the special day.

Mom met us at the bottom of the stairs in the wide hallway. "Hi, sweetie. Happy Sonatalis! And Shaynedel, you too. Glad you could visit us." She smiled, the action illuminating her face. "Grandma Helen and Dad came earlier. We didn't expect you to arrive so late."

"I was shopping." And getting distracted with packing and wrapping presents and, and, and... Typical ADHD behavior.

"Well, I'm glad you're here now." She gave me a hug. "Are you hungry?"

"I grabbed a sandwich before I left, but I need to hit the market."

"Oh, you better get going then. It closes in two hours."

I nodded and gave her another hug, just enjoying the ability to do so. Living away from her most of the year wasn't my idea of a good time. "I'll be back in time for supper." No way was I missing a meal, especially if they served my favorite Linnean specialty, Kunkelsteuchen rolls.

She frowned, her blue eyes narrowing. "Maybe you should take a guard."

Yet another thing Mom had decided was necessary during my visits—constant supervision. "No, I'm good."

"Jace is around here somewhere." She scanned the hallway.

"Tiny will be with me." I looked at her, standing silently next to me. "You're going shopping too, right?"

She bit her lip, her eyes rounding. "Um, well..."

My hope for Tiny's support scattered, but I continued. "See? She's going, too. I'll be fine." Grabbing my friend's arm, I headed for the double doors. "Love you, Mom. I'll see you for supper."

As we escaped, the carved wooden doors closed behind us with a heavy slam. I maintained my brisk pace in case Mom found a guard and chased after me.

I shot Tiny a glare. "Thanks for the support back there."

"I didn't want to lie to the Queen."

I rolled my eyes. "You weren't lying. But I'm sure you'll ditch me if you see Flynn."

She shrugged. "Not necessarily." But the dreamy smile on her face said otherwise.

The main road leading into the heart of Linneah's business district bustled with people. Shops lined the roads, their colorful signs declaring the businesses' intent, like "Glassware" or "Fresh Eggs." In a spare lot where the two main roads intersected, the outdoor market stood, banners of pale blue and silver lining the entrance. Next door, a line of customers snaked out the door of the Golden Pickle, Linneah's best-known restaurant and pub.

A guy our age called Tiny's name from his place in line, his deep brown eyes sparkling.

Her face lit up. "Oh, there he is."

Mock-sighing, I waved her on. "See you back at the castle."

With a distracted smile, she hurried toward him.

I entered the market. Stall after stall stood, many decorated with the traditional pale blue and silver bunting. Several vendors sold food, and the smells of fried dough and roasted meat mingled in the air, making my mouth water. While negotiations between customers and sellers rose and fell, I fought to quell the desperate dread creeping over me. I perused the contents of each table and waited for inspiration to strike. Would Baldwin like a warm sweater? Or a new leather wallet? Or maybe a pretty, handwoven basket? No, no, and no.

My shoulders slumped. I was so dead. A wooden table loaded with what looked like junk stretched before me. Pans spotted with rust, cracked wooden spoons, wobbly glasses, along with other mismatched items lay along its rough surface. Near the end, a thin, dusty box caught my eye. I brushed off the wooden top and opened it. Two diaries lay inside, the leather covers worn. I leafed through one. Empty.

It was nothing special, but wouldn't it be better than a pair of sunglasses?

Releasing the top of the box, I let it close with a snap. It was a dumb idea. I turned to leave.

"I am surprised you are letting that treasure go." A voice pulled me back to the table.

An older man I hadn't noticed stood behind the table. He shifted his weight off his wooden leg and braced a hand on the tabletop. His dark hair was liberally sprinkled with gray. His light brown hairstreak matched his unusual amber eyes.

I gave him a blank stare. "Sorry?"

He grinned, the expression revealing a charming dimple in one cheek. "All of these items are treasures."

Right.

My expression must have shown my skepticism because he continued. "Looks are often deceiving." He pointed to several items.

"This glass will never empty. The contents of this pan will never burn."

And maybe he had some magic beans or golden eggs hidden somewhere. "What about this box?"

"Ah, it is more about the books than the box."

Opening the box again, I studied the unremarkable notebooks. Maybe Baldwin could use one.

I ran a finger over one of the soft covers. "What do they do?"

"Now, I would remove all your enjoyment if I told you. The joy is found in the journey. How much do you have?"

It was a common opening for bartering, trading, and all market transactions. I shook my head. "No goods, just zoharet nomas." I fingered the coins tucked in my pocket.

"No worries, I can use both. How about twenty nomas?"

"Twenty?" Sheesh. "I think nine is fair." Not. But to arrive at what I was willing to spend, I'd start low.

"Nine?" His eyebrows climbed toward his hairline. "That is your definition of fair? I will lower my price to eighteen."

With the solid wooden box, the two journals were probably worth fifteen. I mentally winced. That's all I had. I shook my head. "Eighteen is still too high. I'll give you twelve."

His eyes glittered with excitement. This guy clearly loved negotiating. "Twelve? Ah, I will spend Sonatalis in the poorhouse. The box is solid wood, the journals covered in fine rason leather. Sixteen."

"Fourteen. My final offer." I gave him my best don't-mess-with-me stare.

"*My* final offer is fifteen, but I will add this useful pen. Guaranteed to never run out of ink." He pulled a pen from a clutter of items.

I blinked. It had a fancy golden tip and a wooden barrel. I could've sworn that hadn't been there earlier. "Hmm. Okay, fifteen." The pen, plus the box, plus the journal equaled three gifts. Blessed relief filled my chest. Shopping for Baldwin's gift was done.

The vendor plucked the box off the table and wrapped it in brown paper.

Fishing the coins out of my pocket, I placed the filigree discs on the table. After taking my money, he placed the package in a sturdy paper bag. "It is going to rain, so the bag will keep it dry."

The grayish-blue sky was cloudless, the Petrus Rings becoming more visible as the sun descended toward the horizon. "Um, okay." Whatever.

He handed me the bag, his expression serious. "You are fortunate. This treasure will serve you well. After all, not everyone can find such a rare connection across alternities."

"Thank—, what?"

His amber eyes glowed, a small smile gracing his lips. "Special relationships are rare. Yours is deep and true. Nurture it." He stepped back, the intense moment dissipating like fine snow. "Happy Sonatalis!"

"H-happy Sonatalis." As I walked away, my mind reeled. Was it obvious I wasn't a native? And how did he know about Baldwin? I shrugged. It was probably just a lucky guess. After all, I didn't sound like a Linnean.

I exited the market, past the fluttering banners, and headed down the road toward home. Although our relationship was going well, I held things back, not being completely honest, just to ensure smooth sailing. Baldwin didn't need to know what a screwup I was. But everyone did that in a new relationship.

My mind continued to whirl, sifting through the encounter. When the castle came into view, a cold drop landed on my nose. In seconds, a light rain began to fall, the mist wetting my shoulders.

Sonatalis morning dawned bright and clear, the ground dusted with a light icing of snow. It was enough to remind me of Christmases at home in Pennsylvania. Christmas without snow just didn't seem right.

After breakfast, I headed to the griffin house. I'd messaged Arvandus a few times since my arrival but wanted to wish him a Happy Sonatalis in person and give him his gift.

I approached the griffin house with care, the light snow making the ground slick.

He appeared outside the door. "Happy Sonatalis, Brenna."

"Arvandus, Happy Sonatalis! I've got a gift for you."

He settled in front of me, his tail flicking as a few silver sparks drifted into the air. "Raven, it was my understanding we had mutually decided against gift-giving."

"Technically, yes, we did. But I didn't get you three. I only got you one because, well, because I'm fond of you, big guy."

He growled, but affection gleamed in his golden eyes. "I did not get you anything."

"That's okay. That's not what Sonatalis is about." When he said nothing, I pressed, "Right?"

He shook his head. "One of these days, your penchant for rule-breaking will cause trouble."

"Yeah, but that's why I have you." I smiled and held out a gray blanket.

"What is this?"

"Your gift. I didn't wrap it, but I thought you'd appreciate a warm blanket for your room." The last time I'd been in his sleeping area, a worn, scruffy blanket had been his only barrier from the scratchy straw.

He drew close and sniffed it. "Thank you. That is a very thoughtful gift."

"Can I put it in your sleeping area?"

"Yes, please do."

I followed him into the griffin house. Many of the griffins loitered inside, where it was warmer. Arvandus's stall had been cleaned with fresh straw. I moved the older blanket aside and laid out the new one.

After walking around once on the blanket, he folded his wings and settled into its softness. "Very comfortable."

I sat next to him. "Although I tried, I think it's safe to say we can't communicate when I'm in Pennsylvania."

He nodded. "I expected as much. The barrier between our alternities is thin, but not thin enough."

We talked and visited a little longer before I walked back to the castle. The early coating of snow had already melted, leaving the path to the castle sticky with mud. There were just too many people in different places for this holiday. Tiny had discovered Anna was grounded—again—so a visit with her would have to wait. But my family was together for the first time in a long while. If I could catch some quality time with Baldwin today, I'd consider this visit a success. Before entering the castle, I scraped the soles of my boots on the edges of the stone steps then escaped to the warmth inside.

Although Baldwin had sent me a brief message asking to get together, family time and other activities kept interfering. Sonatalis was busy for everybody. He caught me in the hallway before lunch. "Hey, you." He grabbed my hand and planted a sweet kiss on my cheek. "You are a hard person to find."

"So are you. Happy Sonatalis."

"The same to you. We should meet after the feast."

"Sure. But you'll have to roll me out the door. They're serving Kunkelsteuchen rolls." My mouth watered as I remembered the flaky dough, the cinnamon and sugar topping, and the buttery sweetness of each pastry.

He grinned. "Yeah, those are delicious. Would you like to meet afterward in the library?"

"Sure." I gave him a wink and a quick kiss before escaping into the dining room.

At the Sonatalis meal, massive platters and bowls covered the table—large cuts of meat cooked with glazed vegetables, something that looked (and tasted) like roasted turkey, and several species of fish. A massive gilded tray held a spicy herb dip surrounded by a spiral of raw veggies. Exotic cheese and crackers, meat and raisin-stuffed pastries, and bowls of a pretty fruit soup decorated with cream were served. My mouth watering, I kept eyeing the fragrant basket of Kunkelsteuchen rolls near my seat.

During the meal, I sat with my parents and Grandma and watched a children's choir perform after dinner while I nibbled on my second Kunkelsteuchen roll. Delicious.

My attention wandered, and I scanned the dinner guests as the children began another song. Everyone wanted an invitation to the palace dinner—the full seats proved it. Near the far wall, Baldwin sat with his parents and—my mouth twisted. Gari, his ex-girlfriend, sat on his other side. How did she get here? She leaned close and whispered something in his ear. Baldwin gave her a polite smile, nodded, and leaned back. Her gaze lingered on him before she turned to watch the performance.

I sighed. He wasn't doing anything wrong, but I really hated seeing them sitting together. I knew they were friends, had been since they were little. It didn't mean I had to like it. And despite several friendly overtures on my part during past visits, Gari was *not* interested in a friendship with me. Like ever.

When the choir was done, I clapped, snatched a third roll, and then excused myself from the table before I embarrassed myself. Hurrying up to my room, I grabbed the brown bag and pulled out the package. I'd already removed one journal for myself and rewrapped the three gifts. But it needed a bow. Or a ribbon. Or something. After scrounging in my desk, I found a pretty dark blue ribbon stowed in the drawer. I tied it around the package and finished it in a simple bow—good enough.

I hurried back down the stairs, hoping Baldwin wouldn't be waiting too long for me in the library.

As I approached the library, voices drifted down the hall—Baldwin's lower baritone and a feminine voice. I wasn't surprised when I reached the doorway and saw Gari and Baldwin alone in a comfy seating area.

Awkward.

Neither of them noticed my arrival, and I watched them from the doorway. Although I felt like a stalker, I couldn't muster up the confidence to interrupt them.

Gari pouted with finesse. She'd obviously done this before with success. "I just wanted to wish you a Happy Sonatalis."

"And Happy Sonatalis to you. But I did not get you a gift."

She gave him a coy smile. "I do not expect one. I just wanted you to know I was thinking of you. Here." She placed a box on his lap.

Baldwin shook his head and opened his mouth. But Gari wasn't done. She placed her hand on his. "Please? I enjoy giving my friends gifts."

I just bet she did. When Baldwin sat back, my stomach clenched. With a Herculean effort, I unstuck my feet and hurried back to my room.

Once inside my sanctuary, I dropped Baldwin's gift on my bed and sighed. I should've interrupted the cozy meeting, but I didn't have the strength to deal with Gari right now. My relationship with Baldwin was still new, while his history with her went back years. Or times. I plopped down on my bed. Whatever they called it, they'd known each other forever.

Fiddling with the blue ribbon on the package, my thoughts followed depressing little rabbit holes. What had she bought for him? Probably something better than a simple wooden box.

I jerked at the knock on my bedroom door.

"Brenna?"

Baldwin stood in the doorway, a bag in hand. I stood and brushed at my shirt to avoid looking at him. "Sorry. I got sidetracked." Or rather, my doubt had sidetracked me right back to my bedroom.

He flushed. "Unwanted company delayed me. I guessed you would be here."

"Unwanted company?"

He sighed. "Gari followed me to the library, intent on giving me a Sonatalis present."

I decided to fess up. "Well, yeah. I kinda saw that part. What did she get you?"

Ignoring my question, he stepped forward. "But why would you leave? I would have welcomed the interruption."

"She makes me uncomfortable." I gave a half-hearted shrug and looked away.

"Hey." His fingers were gentle on my chin as he turned my face to meet his earnest gaze. "I turned her present, and her, down. She has nothing I want."

A liquid glow filled my chest, and I offered a teasing response. "Yeah? You're just saying that so you get your presents."

"No, although I am curious about what you got me." Stepping away, he placed his bag on the floor and returned to my side, his eyes bright like a little kid's. Sudden, last-minute doubt struck my heart. His present wasn't fancy or anything, just a dumb box I'd been foolish enough to buy when time ran out.

As I shuffled my feet, he bumped my shoulder with his. "I was only kidding. You did not have to buy me anything."

"No, I just—." I sighed. "It's not that great of a present, okay? Don't get your hopes up."

He reached out, caressing my cheek. "I will love anything you get me."

My cheeks heated. I hoped he was right. "So, here. Happy Sonatalis."

He shook the package gently before sitting in the chair next to my bed. "Hmm. It does not rattle."

"Yeah, but be careful. You don't want to make it dizzy. And he's probably hungry."

Baldwin's mouth dropped open. "You bought me an animal?"

"Just kidding." I grinned and sat on the edge of my bed. "Just open it, Sherlock."

"As in Holmes?"

"Good for you. You remembered." Baldwin's fascination with pop culture references had caused us to binge-watch quite a few shows whenever he visited.

He finally pulled off the brown paper and ran a hand over the box. "It is beautiful."

In the light of my room, the box looked different, more decorative, with a warm honey shine. Maybe it wasn't such a bad gift.

"Look inside," I urged him.

He lifted the lid and pulled out the pen and the journal. "Thanks. Nice leather journal."

"Well, the seller said it was a treasure." Now that some time had passed, the words rang in my mind like silly hard-sell patter, designed to sucker in a desperate shopper.

Baldwin startled. "He used the word 'treasure?'"

"Yeah, I know. But I still thought you might need it. And the pen's pretty cool. If you run out of ink, you'll have to find him and get your money back, though. He promised me it would never run out."

He leaned forward, cradling the book in his hands. "What did the seller look like?"

"Well, he was an older man with a wooden leg, black and gray hair, brown hairstreak, and really odd amber eyes."

Baldwin's mouth fell open, and he sat back. "You met the Peddler."

"What?"

"The Peddler of Sonatalis. A mythical person who offers special treasures during the Sonatalis season. So what did he say this does?" He pointed to the leather-bound book.

"Um, back up. You said this guy is mythical. You know, like..." I stumbled into silence. Like centaurs, and griffins, and portals, and everything else this alternity had. Maybe I should just shut up.

"Right. Mythical. I have heard stories about him ever since my childhood. You said you had heard stories about a man named Santa. How is this different?"

"Santa doesn't really exist. Well, he did, a long time ago, but he was a saint and not a fat guy in a red suit. It's different because—stop looking at me like that."

Shaking his head, Baldwin fought a grin. "How should I look at you?"

"Like a rational person, one who knows what she's talking about."

He stood, the grin blossoming into a full-fledged smile. "Of course. A person who met the Peddler of Sonatalis." He brushed a kiss across my lips. Tingles danced across my mouth.

I fought and lost my battle against a smile. "You're impossible."

"I love the gifts, Brenna. Now your turn. Sit down and close your eyes."

Excitement swirled in my stomach, but I did as he asked.

"Keep them closed," he said.

Behind my closed lids, the light dimmed. "Did you turn out my helli lantern?"

"Just relax." He placed a heavy item in my hands. Its smooth exterior cooled my fingers, while I blindly touched depressions in the bottom of its surface. Were those holes?

His voice was soft. "Okay, open your eyes."

I did, my gaze drawn to the item I held. It was a heavy ceramic pot holding two flowering plants, lilies, I think. *Glowing* lilies. In my darkened bedroom, their petals glowed and shifted from red to orange to dark yellow. The dark centers remained a deep, glowing purple. I'd never seen anything so gorgeous.

"What are they?" I whispered. The glowing flowers created a magical space where loud sounds would shatter the moment.

Baldwin sat down next to me. "They are flame flowers. Do you like them?" His eyes were intent, his face gilded by the plant's red glow.

"I love them. But how do I take care of them?"

"They need water, sun, and some sandy soil. It is very hard to hurt them. That is why I got them for you."

"Because I'm a plant killer?"

"No, they are hardy plants."

"So it *is* because I'm a plant killer." I didn't know whether to be hurt or pleased he knew me so well.

He threaded his fingers through his dark hair. "I am not saying this well. Let me try again. This flower grows near the bottom of the Steen Mountains. In desolate, rocky areas where nothing else grows, you will find a Flame Flower blooming, its petals drinking in the sunlight so it can glow in the dark. It is resilient, stunning, and strong. Like you."

Wow. I swallowed, tears pricking my eyes. "Thank you. It's beautiful."

He nodded. "Yes, like you."

My heart swelling, I leaned forward. "Happy Sonatalis, Baldwin," I whispered before our lips met.

Part II

A week and a half later, I was back in Pennsylvania. Maybe I needed to return to Linneah and find that lying con man to get my money back. The Peddler of Sonatalis? I snorted. Right. I'd carried the journal to school, slept with it under my pillow, and left it open on my desk. It hadn't done my homework, helped me sleep better, or cleaned my room. It was a regular, boring notebook.

Pulling it from under the stack of books on my desk, I flipped through the pages. I didn't have a diary, but I'd considered starting a journal. A place to record my feelings, thoughts about the future, that kind of thing. Or maybe I could draw a picture of my Flame Flower. I'd left it in Linneah under my friend Murray's care because I didn't want it to draw attention. How would I explain a glowing flower?

I opened the notebook, the first page sticking to the cover before releasing and lying flat. My mouth fell open, and I dropped my pencil on the floor. Someone had written in my journal. But who? Dad and Grandma were pretty good about leaving my stuff alone. As I leaned closer to inspect the passage, the writing came into focus, like someone wiping off a grimy window.

There is a distance between us, although it is a living thing, taking away my peace of mind. My life slows down, gray without her. Her smile is missing, the touch of her hand. Doubt has become my constant companion. Will she return? Why would she? Her entire life is elsewhere. My heart aches at the thought. Questions circle in my head, but I cannot voice them. Our connection is special, but I fear distance may pull us apart. If only I could tell her...

Unbelievable—that seller sold me a used notebook. Why hadn't I flipped through each journal before I bought them? Hopefully, Baldwin's was in pristine condition.

I stared and read the passage again. The writing was unfamiliar. After a while, curiosity replaced my irritation. Who was the writer? How long ago had he lived? Where was he from? His words were heartfelt and poignant—the voice of a poet. Unfortunately, I'd never get answers to my questions.

Trying to rip the paper out was an exercise in futility. After a minute more, I gave up. Who cared? I'd just start my private thoughts on the next page.

So, I'm starting a journal. No promises to write in it every day, but maybe I can get my thoughts in order. I need all the help I can get! Anyway, I'm slightly annoyed because it's a used journal. Wish I'd seen that before I bought it—I could've talked the vendor down to a cheaper price.

That first entry created all sorts of questions. He must've cared for her very much. His words suggested a great love story—I hope they lived happy, full lives together. Everyone deserves a happy ending.

It was almost time for lunch, and my unwritten health paper loomed large. Too bad I couldn't take a trip through the portal. My dad would shoot me, since the deal was no trip to Linneah unless my homework was done. Writing a health paper on a Saturday—what a lousy way to spend a weekend.

Three and a half hours later, I'd word-vomited a rough draft. I closed my laptop. I hated writing so much. Keeping all my thoughts in order to support a main idea was murder.

I flipped open a fresh page of the journal and drew a rough sketch of the Flame Flower. It was a decent drawing, but a plain pencil couldn't capture its beauty. Shrugging, I turned to a new page, my thoughts needing a place to land.

I sometimes wonder what my happy ending will look like. The dreamer in me says I'll be living in Linneah, my family nearby, and Baldwin and I will be together. All good stuff. But sometimes I look at him and can't imagine why he's still interested in me. Won't he figure out at some point he can do better?

I pushed the journal away and sighed. Well, that was helpful. I felt loads better. Not.

On late Sunday afternoon, I'd typed the last paragraph of my paper when there was a knock at the door. Dad was upstairs grading papers, and Grandma Helen was gardening in the backyard. Since I was working in the kitchen on my laptop, my title was Official Salesman Eradicator. Before hurrying to the door, I hit *Save* so I didn't lose my work.

I opened the door, hoping it wasn't a salesman. Or a political campaigner.

Baldwin stood on the porch, his leather journal in his hand. Did he take that thing with him everywhere? He must really like it.

"Hey." I opened the door wider. "You've got great timing. I just finished my health paper. Of course, it probably needs revising, but I could use a break. Come on in."

He walked in and gave me a kiss on the cheek. "It is good to see you. I have an interesting story to tell you."

"Oh, I like interesting stories. You want some soda with that story?" Baldwin's new favorite drink was root beer.

He grinned. "Root beer?"

Called it. "Sure."

He settled on the couch, while I poured two root beers and grabbed a bag of chips from the cabinet. What was story time without food?

I sat next to him on the couch and crossed my legs. "So, tell me a story."

"Well, this is a true story. One I read about in my journal." He waved the leather-bound book back and forth.

My mouth gaped. "Wait—what?"

"When I opened it, there was writing on the first page."

My heart shriveled. "I'm so sorry. If I could go back to the market and—"

He grasped my hand and shook his head. "It is not a bad thing. Just listen."

Still annoyed with that sneaky Peddler, I settled back against the cushions.

"It was a story written by a young woman. Although disappointed about a recent purchase, she moved on to share her hopes and dreams, even sharing some of her fears."

Glancing at him out of the corner of my eye, I pulled a chip from the bag and popped it in my mouth. This story needed some excitement or chase scenes, maybe a dragon or two.

He shifted toward me and continued. "Then she mentioned a man she had feelings for. But she wondered why he was interested in her. She was afraid he would discover he could do better with someone else."

I froze, the chip turning to sawdust in my mouth. It had to be a coincidence. Swallowing hard, I forced a laugh. "That better not be the end."

Baldwin said nothing, his eyes steady.

As my cheeks warmed, my mind whirled. There had to be an explanation. "Wow, that's kind of a slow story. I was hoping for some intrigue. Or maybe a dragon."

Shaking his head, Baldwin leaned forward. "She did not know the truth. That man could never do better with someone else."

My voice dried up. I couldn't even look at him.

His words were soft. "There were two journals in the box, right?"

After a quick glance at his face, I looked away and bit my lip.

"It is okay, Brenna. That is why the Peddler called it a treasure."

The thrill of what the journals could do vanished under the feeling of being completely exposed. "But that—that was supposed to be private," I stammered, my eyes welling.

"So was my entry. You know how I feel as well."

A tear leaked from the corner of my eye, and I swiped it away. "The entry in my journal was from you?"

He nodded, his cheeks flushing.

Why would she return? Her entire life is elsewhere. Warmth unfurled in my chest. I couldn't resist reassuring him. "Baldwin, even if my mom wasn't the queen, I'd still come back to Linneah. After all, you're there."

Hope glittered in his eyes. He flipped open the journal and traced the words of my entry. "But Linneah is so different from Pennsylvania. And your father is here, as well as your schooling, your friends. And because your mother is the queen, you will continue to capture the notice of others. You left the Shaverim Festival early because of that attention, and—"

"Are you trying to discourage me from coming back?"

He shook his head. "No. Like I said, I cannot imagine Linneah without you." His voice dropped. "I cannot imagine my heart without you either."

Oh. My heart melted into a little puddle. "You're sweet and the most talented flirt I know."

He shook his head. "I only flirt with you."

I grinned and felt my cheeks grow warm.

He grew serious. "We do not see each other every day. So I think we need to talk more, I mean, really talk."

"Welcome to long-distance relationships."

"*Really* long-distance," he said. "But I refuse to let miscommunication cause problems. What we have is special but not because of where we come from. It is because of who we are together."

"I agree," I said and watched the last bit of hesitation melt from his face. This guy was amazing, but he didn't even see it. "And the Peddler didn't have to tell me that, although he did anyway."

"What?"

Darn it. I hadn't meant to blurt that out. "Well, uh, he kinda mentioned you and—"

"He mentioned my bravery, right?"

"No, you didn't let me finish. He mentioned the two of us. He said our special relationship is deep and true."

Baldwin raised an eyebrow. "And do you believe in the Peddler now?"

"Yeah. And I believe in us, too. You and me."

He threaded his fingers through mine, his slow smile making my heart stutter-step. "Yeah. You and me."

THE END

Anna's Island Slang

- Chasing sea glass: searching for the impossible
- Danced the drift: died
- Drift talk: nonsense, rambling
- Foam talk: empty words
- Foamed out: excellent/awesome
- Low tide behavior: sneaky & underhanded
- No drift about it: no doubt
- Reef logic: confused thinking
- Reefstars: expression of awe/wonder
- Ride the curl: travel on/keep going
- Riprider: hero
- Rogue wave: terrible situation
- Salt it down: relax; take a breath
- Sea spray: daydreaming/unfocused
- Seagull: obnoxious
- Seaweed spun: crazy
- Shell fine: good; perfect
- Shells and shimmer: exclamation
- Shimmer: magic
- Skim the blue: take off; leave
- Slick as a reef eel: agile & fast
- Stone deep: sincere; heartfelt
- Storm tossed: bad
- Surge boss: attractive guy/girl
- Tail-tied: stuck in a bad situation
- Tide called: destined
- Wave hung: crushing on a guy/girl
- Wavekeeper: friend
- Whitecapping: angry
- Wind slick: charismatic and smooth

Acknowledgements

WHILE WRITING IS A solitary activity, the journey is not. I'm so grateful to all of those who came alongside and helped me.

First of all, my never-ending thanks to my Heavenly Father. He has probably labelled me one of His most difficult children but loves me anyway. He is why I put pen to paper.

My husband, Chris. Thank you for loving me and believing in me. For letting me dream, plan, and write instead of doing the laundry. I love you more than words.

My girls, Ireland and Elleah—you are my heart and the ones who bring joy and laughter to my days. You two will set the world on fire with your gifts.

My parents. Thank you for believing in me and also raising me to believe I could do or be anything.

And to my readers. Thank you for your time. This is for you, a story about self-esteem, about worth, no matter your victories, your failings, who you are, or where you come from. My hope is you will see the unique gifts God's given to you and know He loves you and values you far more than you ever dreamed, regardless of what you've been told.

PLEASE LEAVE A REVIEW

Reviews can help other readers find good books and can create more exposure for good books by indie authors. Plus, all authors treasure reviews!

If you enjoyed this book, please consider leaving a review on Amazon, Barnes & Noble, Goodreads, or even a post on social media! A line or two is all that's needed. The information below can give you a few more tips.

Writing an Easy Book Review

Writing a book review can be hard, but it doesn't have to be.

Review Template (pick one):

Not sure what to say? Just copy, paste, and fill in the blanks! Your review can be as short or as long as you like – but every word helps this book find new readers.

Option 1: Quick + Easy

I really enjoyed [Book Title] by [Author Name]. If you like [genre/theme], you 'll love this. My favorite part was [a scene, a twist, a character]. I'd recommend it to anyone who enjoys [similar books/authors or vibes].

Option 2: Feelings First

[Title] made me feel [emotion: hooked, heartbroken, hopeful, etc.] I couldn't stop reading because [reason]. I especially loved [character/scene]. I can't wait to read more from this author.

Option 3: Vibe Reader

If you're into books that are [adjective: dark, romantic, twisty, cozy, fast-paced], this one is for you. [Book Title] gave me major [vibe: fairytale, dystopian, small town, enemies-to-lovers] energy.

Option 4: Combo Review

I loved [Book Title] by [Author]. It was a(n) [adjective] tale that left me [emotion]. I loved [scene, character, twist] and can't wait for more from this author. If you like [similar book/vibe], check out [Book Title].

Ready to leave a review? Please go to my Amazon author page (https://www.amazon.com/stores/J.-M.-Hackman/author/B01K9PJMPE), click on the book you want to review, then scroll down to leave a customer review. Thank you so much!

J.M. Hackman, the award-winning author of the Firebrand Chronicles and the Stardust Hearts series, loves thunderstorms, fuzzy socks, and thick chocolate milkshakes. Her engaging fantasy and soft science fiction stories are threaded with hope and end with a happily ever-after. While her characters are feisty and fearless, J.M. is afraid of spiders, wasps, and the crowds at post-Christmas sales. When she's not writing, she reads, crafts, watches football, and adventures with her family in the mountains of rural Pennsylvania.

Her short stories have been published in the anthologies *Crowns, Encircled, Tales of Ever After, Mythical Doorways*, and *Realmscapes*. Go to her website at www.jmhackman.com to learn more about her.